CHILDPROOF

CHILDPROOF

A Comedy Novel

MICHAEL NOONAN

PRECOGNITION

BRISBANE, **AUSTRALIA** | MONTERREY, **MEXICO**

For Raul,
who told me to do it.

CHAPTER 1 THE END

It was a Tuesday when Will and Rose decided to end it all.

They dressed for the occasion in formal, dinner-party wear (pressed navy suit for him, sequined gown for her), loaded the car with mid-afternoon snacks (chilled spring water, black sausage, olives), and put Ralph—their insecure, morbidly-aloof pug—in his day-trip basket in the back seat. They only took him because they knew he wouldn't cope without them: he panic-pissed on the carpet whenever they left him alone for more than an hour (and they had lots of carpet).

It was a two-hour drive to the "brown stump," a remote location often used for student films and murder-suicides. People (i.e., college professors) sometimes went there to commit suicide after watching too many student films, which may or may not be ironic.

Will tied three ropes to the stump, then to each of their necks through the open back door of their green, 2005-model Mercedes station wagon. If this were a movie, and you were filming from above, the whole scenario would be much easier to understand—especially if you had one of those "teenagers with a drone." *Aren't they adorable?*

When Will looped the rope around Ralph's neck, the dog yipped like he was going for a walk. A walk! *Funny little fucker.* He would definitely shit like he did on a walk, but there would be no actual walking anywhere.

It's worth noting that Rose wanted a much less dramatic final act. Pills, exhaust fumes, maybe even a gentle nudge on a subway platform (Will's suggestion). But Will had insisted on the "brown stump." He wanted their friends to notice. They *needed* to notice, to see their decapitated heads on the front page of a tabloid they would never normally read—let alone have to buy. Imagine their humiliation at the newsstand! Or having to subscribe online! This—all of this—was their fault. *Entirely. They deserved it.*

Most Youtube videos on "stump-to-car rope decapitation" suggested the combined use of a full throttle and handbrake to quickly release the required burst of speed—much like one of those hill starts you were taught as a learner-driver. Without such a sudden, rapid burst, there was a risk of slow asphyxiation—and that wasn't making anyone's front page.

Will had watched all the videos. He fixed the handbrake, nudged the throttle, looked to Rose for some final words, perhaps a hoarse-but-heartfelt "I've always loved you" through her rope-tightened neck. Instead, he got: "Hurry the fuck up." *Really?*

She had more: "Are you gonna accelerate or not?"

Will took his foot off the throttle. "I'm warming it up."

"It's ninety-five degrees out here."

"Which has nothing to do with the inner temperature of the engine," Will said. "If you don't warm it up properly, you reduce the car's life by up to twenty per cent."

"Great, that'll be a huge problem for the next owner, who-ever it is," she said. "Maybe we should leave them a note of apol-ogy: 'Sorry for decapitating ourselves in your new car, for the smashed rear window, for all the dog excrement on the back seat… oh, and we reduced the car's life by twenty per cent by not warming up the engine properly.'" Rose sighed, folded her arms.

"What's the hurry, anyway? I don't think the shops in heaven close at five," Will quipped, thinking it was a good time to be witty. Rose made it clear it wasn't.

"Who said we're going to heaven?" she quipped right back.

Will took a breath, gripped the wheel, gunned the accelerator, and released the brake. The car stalled. He had never been very good at hill starts. Rose groaned, gave him the look he'd come to know as "Are you fucking kidding me?" It was one of her most impressive looks, not as subtle as "Don't ever fucking touch me again," but more pronounced than "You disgust me."

Turning the car over again didn't help—they were out of gas. And, yeah, they were in a remote-as-fuck location that was only visited by film students and—*remember all that?* Even if another potential suicide victim turned up, it was unlikely he or she would be in any kind of mental state to give them gas or drive them to a gas station or help them out in any way whatsoever.

A Gallup poll from 2019 said people about to commit suicide were thirty-two per cent less likely to help someone in need than people who planned to keep living. Twenty-two per cent of those would say "fuck off, get away from me" if asked for help, ten per cent would say "no thanks, I'm quite busy," and five per cent would ask for money in return, even though they knew they would never be able to spend it. Most surprisingly, eighty per cent of those who said they wouldn't help someone in need would change their dying words to "Glad I didn't help that fucker in need before I died."

Rose suggested they call an Uber, even though she had never used one ("I'm not getting in a car with a creepy old man in pajamas just to save a few bucks on a taxi"). Will chuckled dryly at the suggestion. *Call an Uber?*

"First," he said. "You don't 'call' an Uber. You request one via an app. Second, what kind of Uber driver is going to let us remove the rear window of their car so we can tie ropes to our necks and kill ourselves?"

She rolled her eyes, which she did a lot, and will continue to do for as long as she's alive in this story. "I meant 'Call an Uber to drive us to a gas station,' not help us with our suicide pact," she said through tightened lips.

Will sighed, took out his phone and "requested" an Uber. An old guy in pajamas arrived in less than five minutes. He didn't want to remove his rear windscreen and help them with the ropes (Rose asked just to annoy Will) and he couldn't do a handbrake start anyway. But he agreed to take them to a gas station. They (Will) thought about stealing his car and finishing what they started—but they were not that kind of people. And the guy had little bottles of water for passengers (tip encouraged—they didn't give one).

◆   ◆   ◆

It was a thirty-minute drive to the nearest gas station—a shitty, corrugated iron roadhouse called "Crazy Jed's." Not many people ever bought gas there: it had been the location of a massacre in the seventies—presumably a direct result of their week-old hotdogs—so most of the visitors were those morbid "dark tourism" fuckwits who took smiling selfies in places where people bled out.

Will filled a gas can; Rose took a smiling selfie near a bullet-riddled sign that read "Someone literally bled out here." Before they requested an Uber to go back, Rose decided she was "peckish." Will was pissed: firstly, he despised the word "peckish" and, secondly, they'd had the perfect end-of-life meal back at the brown stump—what could possibly top black sausage and olives as a final palate cleanser? Certainly not a week-old hotdog from Crazy Jed's.

Nevertheless, Will caved, they tied Ralph to the bowser and went into the 24-hour "restaurant." There was a couple by the window sharing selfies they'd just taken ("Oh look, I took this three minutes ago from the exact same position we're sitting in right now!"), a creepy dude in a booth with a map stretched over the table (massacre sites marked), and a crew of grubby film students in berets who were probably heading the same way they were.

Rose ordered "Jed's Vindaloo Special." She said she had a craving for Indian food but she really just wanted to piss off the coroner if he decided to do an autopsy on her body. Curry did not travel well after death.

Will quietly waited for Rose to finish, refusing to order anything himself. Before he could suggest hitching a ride back with the film crew—with the promise of exclusive footage of their grisly deaths—Rose rested her plastic knife and fork, wiped the corners of her mouth.

"We're not going back," she said. "We never go back, only forward." She met Will's eyes, her pupils glistening like they did when she was about to orgasm or say something extraordinary (it was the latter this time). "I know a much better way for us to die."

CHAPTER 2 **BEGINNINGS**

Will and Rose had been blissfully happy seven years ago.

They lived in a three-story palace of brick and concrete, nestled between perfect gardens. Water cascaded from a fountain out front, the kind you'd piss in after getting drunk on expensive champagne (which they did, often).

Every Friday, and sometimes on Thursday, they'd have a dinner party on the "mezzanine" with their special clique of friends. In case you didn't know, a mezzanine is just a fancy-fucking-word for the first floor. They'd frolic and laugh and eat like pigs up there, often tumbling down stairs and continuing to laugh when they reached the landing, sometimes with bruised ribs. Bertie, their unhinged-but-cheap butler, would fill their glasses with copious amounts of alcohol in between multiple courses of unpronounceable food. You can just picture it, can't you? From the street, if you stopped to gawk after midnight, you would see their champagne-flute-holding silhouettes dancing behind silk curtains. *Oh, the privilege.*

Historians believe Neanderthal Man was the first to ever host a dinner party. Intricate paintings discovered in caves in

Peru showed men sitting around a large table-shaped rock, chewing on antelope hooves and discussing how lazy their women were. Feminists doing their PhDs have since disputed the "Lazy Women Conversation"—as it has become known in text books—because there's literally no evidence that's what they were talking about from a faded, stick-figure painting thousands of years old.

Dinner parties have continued in various forms throughout the ages, appearing in every known culture and on every continent. The Last Supper was a dinner party, the first recorded account of a guest getting smashed and betraying the host. King Arthur hosted the first dinner party at a round table, which he designed specifically to enhance the eyelines between guests during the meal and make the passing of wine goblets more efficient. Most historical accounts confirm that they too often discussed how lazy their women were.

There is no universal consensus, or a formal set of rules, as to what constitutes a "dinner party." In late October, 1972, the United Nations defined it as "a gathering of two or more people for the purpose of eating and polite conversation." This definition has been widely mocked by academics and theorists ever since, many claiming alcohol and a lack of "politeness" are the two most crucial elements of any dinner party. More recently, the International Center for Human Dignity convened in Cancun, mostly over dinner, to establish a list of principles that would ultimately define the true "dinner party experience." After intense lobbying from the alcohol and tobacco industries, which sponsored the four-day event, "offensive amounts of alcohol," "impolite conversation," "intense argument," and "mutual adultery" were all included on the list. "Smoking" was not, although "After-Dinner Weed Cookies" were, with an asterisk (the asterisk denoted "only where legal and/or for medicinal purposes.")

As children, Will and Rose had dreamed of hosting their own dinner parties. Will's parents had regular Saturday night gatherings, which often spilled out into the pool area after the meal had finished. He would watch and take notes from his bedroom window, imagining himself among them with a cigar and a glass of Clos du Bois Chardonnay. Rose, who grew up in a convent after being abandoned by her mother, secretly watched the nuns go at it every Sunday night after the last mass. It was the first time she ever saw a "Brazilian."

When Will and Rose married, they included the attending and/or hosting of "fabulous dinner parties" in their vows and, of course, in the pre-nup. It was a condition of their marital contract that "no party shall, at any time now or in the future, forbid, discourage, interfere with, or otherwise dampen the vibe when the other party proposes the attendance or hosting of a dinner party at any time of day or night, on any day of the week, notwithstanding the death or critical injury of a pet or family member."

At the peak of their life, which was six years ago, their weekly dinner party event consisted of eight people: the two of them, and three couples. The "Special Ones," as Will and Rose called them, were a perfectly-assembled group of people they'd refined, shaped, and trimmed over many years, like a really good hedge. They'd spent hundreds of man hours on that hedge: it was like the cast of their own long-running sitcom and no-one was ever going to be replaced—unless they died or were caught with child porn.

Brett and Melissa were the very first couple to be invited. Will and Rose had known them since college: they were one of those high-school-sweetheart couples who were destined to be together, forever. Prom King and Queen, Sid and Nancy in the school play. During college, they used to suck each other's faces off at every frat party they attended, which earned them the nickname "The Borg." They still carried on like horny teenagers when they went to Will and Rose's dinner parties, sometimes during dessert, which cleared the table and pleased Bertie, who often watched them through a gap in the door while he cleaned plates. Bertie may have been a convicted felon but he wasn't a pervert: he just missed his own dead wife, who had also been his high-school sweetheart (although there wasn't a high school play about Sid and Nancy back then).

After college, Brett and Melissa got married and honey-mooned in The Maldives with lots of other monogamous, sick-ly-in-love newlyweds. Two things happened there that shaped their lives forever: firstly, Melissa drank the worm in a bottle of Monte Alban and was violently ill, losing half her bodyweight in 24 hours and suffering giant worm-hallucinations for the re-mainder of the trip (and her life). Secondly, while nursing Me-lissa back to health, Brett spent an extraordinary amount of time watching the other newlyweds from their balcony. The gradual but rapid deterioration of those relationships gave him the idea for their very first business enterprise. It was called "De-Gift" and it was an online wedding gift registry which allowed people to get their gifts back if the married couple split up within a year. That's right: the toaster, the air-fryer, the expensive towels, the nested coffee tables—used or not, they would all go back to the gift-givers if things didn't work out. And, not surprisingly, they often didn't.

Brett and Melissa did most of the pickups in the first year: they were threatened with weapons twice, Brett suffered a punctured lung from an ice-pick wound (the bride/divorcee was convicted) and they both contracted a rare virus from a pet spider monkey they had to confiscate from a duplex in Wisconsin. *Yes, someone gave a spider monkey as a wedding present.*

The business thrived in its early years. They even got a call from a TV producer, who wanted to make a reality show about them and their business. He pitched it as "two unhappy fat people repossess wedding gifts from couples going through hard times." They said no.

Soon after, video of them retrieving a miniature pony in Winnipeg went viral and couples across the nation caught on—they started intentionally prolonging their broken marriages in order to keep the gifts. There was suddenly a huge uptick in people getting divorced on the day *after* their one-year anniversary.

When the business went belly-up, Brett and Melissa were still receiving thankyou cards from people whose marriages had survived because of them. One woman wrote that she'd stayed with her unemployed, drug-addicted husband just to keep a Teflon pan (he had since died, but she still had the pan).

Brett and Melissa tried and failed a number of business ventures after that, including a restaurant that only served "airplane food." It was called "The Airplane Food Restaurant" (Brett named it) and the interior was decked out like an actual plane (think "Uganda Air," not "Emirates").

Guests had to sit in seats with little to no legroom and eat from trays with plastic cutlery. *What a hoot!* Turbulence was optional in the back half of the plane, and there was an extra fee for those wanting to join the "mile-high club" after dinner (stewardess not included). It was initially popular with party groups and retirees, but ultimately shut down when a group of white guys (dressed as Islamic extremists) thought it'd be funny to stage a hijack during meal service. There were lawsuits, the plane was grounded permanently.

When Brett and Melissa attended their first dinner party at Will and Rose's house in 2007, they were deep in successful new careers: Brett worked as an online "reseller," which meant he bought cheap stuff in bulk, then sold it at inflated prices to stupid people who couldn't be bothered searching the internet properly; and Melissa was a department store detective, which suited her because she liked wandering aimlessly around department stores and gawking at people. In her first year, she reduced women's stockings theft by fifteen percent and put two octogenarians in intensive care (they had "falls").

Unfortunately—and it's worth mentioning at this point—Melissa had one of the original "snorting laughs," which she developed as a child after suffering an abusive relationship at her uncle's pig farm. No, her uncle didn't molest her—she just spent a lot of time around the piglets and they were nasty little fuckers.

For a while, probably the first six months, Will and Rose's dinner party event was just the four of them, and it was delightful (despite Melissa's laugh). A regular evening would begin with finger-food and work/life chit-chat on the balcony, continue with hors d'oeuvres and state politics at the table, kick into gear with the main course and everything-that's-wrong-with-the-world (still at the table), peak with dessert and Will's jokes (in different seats at the table), and finish with stiff drinks, dancing, and some hideous singing near the piano (and sometimes spilling back out onto the balcony). It was four-to-six hours of unabashed, unapologetic decadence.

But, like most hedonistic pursuits, cruel reality intervened.

It was an August night when Melissa announced her "cancer scare." She did it before the dessert/jokes portion of the evening, which did not please Will. He had prepared a whole new set of material, including a fantastic lymphoma gag. When she mentioned the lump in her breast, Will and Rose were immediately concerned, and briefly terrified—a dinner party with just Brett would be awkward and depressing, especially if he spent the whole time skulking over his dead wife.

Thankfully, it turned out to be just a cyst full of unhatched baby spiders (according to her Twitter feed). Rose suspected Melissa had just wanted some attention (and likes) and they were back to their regular partying within a week.

The whole incident was a wake-up call for them: they needed more guests in their dinner-party universe in case there were actual deaths (and/or facial disfigurements).

It was time to find some new friends.

CHAPTER 3 <u>THE SPECIAL ONES</u>

Rose was an excellent designer of flowcharts.

She had mastered her craft at the convent where, in her teenage years, she had created complex charts to help the newer nuns decide whether or not to take their final vows. Most got stumped at one or both of the final two boxes, "Do you fantasize about having carnal relations with convicted felons?" and "Do you often pleasure yourself while wearing your habit?" A dozen happily-married women credit her with changing their lives, a few divorcees and single mothers still send her hate mail.

Soon after the Melissa "scare," Rose and Will erected a huge flowchart in Bertie's room to begin the process of selecting an additional couple. There were ten other empty rooms in the house but they didn't want visitors or workmen to see their progress, and Bertie didn't mind: he was always too busy to spend much time in there and the exposed asbestos roof made him cough.

There were nineteen separate boxes on the first draft of Rose's "dinner party selection" flowchart (or "The Special Ones" Chart, as Will called it). It was spread across three color-coded levels: level one covered the basics, such as "Inner/Outer Beauty," "Not Sickly or Near Death," "Doesn't Eat with Mouth Open," "Advanced Hygiene." The second level dug a little deeper into character and psyche: "Wicked Sense of Humor," "Propensity for Alcohol," "Prefers Experiments on Humans Rather Than Animals." And, finally, level three, which sorted the wheat from the chaff and was more difficult to pass than the NASA entrance exam. It included "Doesn't Have a Problem with an Active Shooter in Certain Situations" and "Would Say 'Hi' to El Chapo If He Got in the Same Elevator."

Only twelve of the couples they knew advanced beyond level one, and only four made it to level three. Of those, two progressed to the end (the other two were a "no" to the active shooter question). Ned and Beth were the first of the finalists.

Will had met Ned at a business conference in early 2004. Ned was getting drunk at the hotel bar during the morning keynote (it was called "Getting High on Life, Not Substances" and it was delivered by a recovered drug addict who had made his fortune while he was on coke, and still was—there was powder on his upper lip, which was really noticeable on the massive 4K screen).

Will sat next to Ned at the bar after ten minutes of The Coke-Keynote-Guy and they hit it off immediately, starting with the icebreaker: "How fucked is that keynote?" They drank until afternoon tea.

Ned ran his own app design company, which created "stupid fucking ideas for smart phones" (his words, and the original slogan for the company). His most popular one involved sending "mini electric shocks" to the phones of people you didn't like. Will became a regular user, and once sent a shock to a sitting member of Congress (she wrote back, asked to meet). The company also designed a popular dating app for homeless people, which is credited with bringing together thousands of couples under the same (cardboard) roofs.

Ned and Beth had met at a different hotel bar, where he got her number and sent her an electric shock. They fell in love immediately—well, after she woke up in the ambulance and thought he was a paramedic (she had a thing for men in uniform). She only realized he wasn't a paramedic when her cousin choked on a vegan spring roll at their wedding reception—Ned pretended he could do the Heimlich manoeuvre, but ended up breaking two of her cousin's ribs. Nevertheless, the cousin survived (with the broken ribs and minimal brain damage) and, even though Ned had lied to her for two years and wasn't "a man in uniform," Beth realized she loved him and, more importantly, she didn't want to return the wedding gifts (especially the air-fryer). She became a socialite after they got married, which meant she basically gave up on all life purpose and learned to speak well (and not dribble) after a dozen champagnes.

They tended to overdress for parties (a cravat, really?) but they always brought fantastic wine to private events, sometimes Schnapps, which made them an ideal second couple for Will and Rose's dinner parties. Their only competition for the spot was Jack and Kathleen, or "Jackleen" as they were known to their closest friends (and some haters).

Will and Rose had met them at a fancy restaurant one time, seated at neighboring tables. Alcohol has fogged the story a little but there were some consistencies in the various accounts—namely that Jack overheard one of Will's "fetus" jokes and laughed heartily (Kathleen did not). Later, when a diverse-but-numerically-challenged waiter mixed up their meals, they struck up a conversation. Jack said he enjoyed humor about unborn babies and, before dessert was served, they had joined their tables together. They met the week after at the same place, happy the diverse/useless waiter had been fired and deported (their note in the suggestion box worked!). Soon, dining out together became a regular event.

Jack and Kathleen were a most unusual couple. If ever there were two people who were destined *not* to be together, it was them. They simply despised each other. It was adorable. Sometimes they'd be fighting before they arrived at the restaurant, they'd continue over dinner, keep going after they left. They loved to hate each other—and Will and Rose loved to watch.

They had met on one of those Mercy Ships: you know, the floating hospitals that travel to third world countries to do surgeries and medical procedures to help sick people in need. Neither Jack nor Kathleen were in the medical profession, and they had no interest in helping people whatsoever, especially diseased and infectious foreigners with no money: they'd just mistakenly boarded the wrong boat. It took them several days to realize they weren't on the "Desperate & Single Cruise" they'd booked and paid for. Kathleen later said she'd never found it so easy to hook up with "gaunt black guys" and "amputees."

The penny dropped for both of them at a costume party on night four: you had to dress up as "death and/or illness" and they were the only ones who wore actual costumes. After that, they hung out with each other for the rest of the cruise, and eventually had their first sexual encounter in the "rehabilitation pool," climaxing in the gym (they had it to themselves on most days/ nights).

Their wedding was a low-key affair, held on a fake beach in a cheap hotel. The celebrant was a former priest who had been ex-communicated by the Catholic Church for performing an exorcism during a wedding (the groom requested it). Jack and Kathleen chose him because he was a funny guy and he didn't mind them using the words "fuckstick," "cuntface," and "slutty whore-pimp" in their vows.

The reception took place on one of those party buses that travels between bars, which was actually a genius idea because they could dump guests (i.e., extended family members, mostly uncles) when they started to get drunk and/or annoying. By the final leg, it was just Jack, Will, and Rose (Kathleen was left behind at the midway point, The Pineapple Hotel, with her parents).

Their marriage began with lots of fun and frivolity. They loved playing pranks on each other: sticking funny signs to each other's backs at the mall ("Rape me, cunt!"), shaving eyebrows and pubic hair while asleep, swapping apple juice for urine. But it soon degenerated: an actual venomous snake in the shower, cutting brake cables, throwing a toaster in the bath. It reached an almost-deadly peak when Jack tried to suffocate Kathleen in a Dutch oven. No, not the heating appliance you buy in Holland. *Look it up.* She almost died from the toxic fumes, then pressed charges. The cisgender judge acquitted Jack, saying "trapping a wife under a duvet with toxic flatulent gas is a legitimate part of the marital contract." There were lots of angry tweets and protests by people who hated men and duvets but their outrage eventually faded. Jack and Kathleen were back together a week later and agreed to limit their pranks to non-life-threatening activities.

Jack was a motivational speaker. His three-day "Keep On Keeping On No Matter What" masterclass was very popular on the East Coast, even though it cost a fortune and attracted mostly-unstable people with limited social lives. Federal authorities credited him with motivating "The Eco-Friendly Killer" to commit an additional three murders, which occurred in the weeks after attending Jack's class. On the witness stand, Jack said his job was to motivate people to "do what fulfilled them and made them complete," even if that was smothering and asphyxiating teenage women with recyclable plastic bags (and planting a tree on their shallow grave). He was not charged as an accomplice and the publicity (and social media outrage) did not affect him: in fact, his courses became even more popular after that.

Kathleen never attended any of his masterclasses: she found them "repulsively uplifting." She ran a boutique corporate consulting firm that specialized in helping companies manage (read: defeat and destroy) their competitors. Sounded impressive but it was really just a front for a grubby corporate sabotage outfit: she'd send in "temp moles" to create havoc in the workplaces of her clients' competitors. "Jolene" (not her real name) was one of her best employees: she'd get a job as a temp receptionist with a competitor, start accidentally diverting calls to the wrong people, copying people on confidential emails, and initiating gossip threads wherever possible (online, and in the ladies' restroom). By the time a week was up, half the staff had resigned or been fired; the other half viciously hated each other and productivity had plummeted significantly. A job well done! Kathleen had twice received the "Woman of the Year Award" from the East Coast Women Entrepreneurs' Association. She didn't win a third time and was pissed, so she called on Jolene. The association folded soon after.

◆   ◆   ◆

Will and Rose found themselves in a deep quandary when it came to choosing between the two finalists: Jack and Kathleen, and Ned and Beth. They were both excellent choices, they had progressed through all nineteen flowchart boxes and they would add life and laughter to their weekly dinner party universe. *But who to pick?*

It was almost three in the morning when they had a breakthrough: Bertie woke up (they woke him, actually, to make them coffee) and he looked at their flowchart from his single bed, the lists of pros and cons for each couple, the printed background checks stuck to the walls. Before Will could prompt him to hurry up with the coffees, the funny little felon suggested something utterly mind-blowing:

"Why don't you just invite both couples?"

His words hovered above Will like an embossed thought bubble in 14-point Helvetica. Will and Rose shared a look: *why didn't we think of that?* Bertie, now thinking he could just keep adding thoughts at random, did exactly that: "I could bring out the really big round table, it easily fits eight people." The really big round table. *Fuck.* Bertie was on fire. They all high-fived and did chest-bumps—actually, just Will and Rose did that, Bertie went to get the celebratory coffees (finally). They spent the rest of the night drafting "invitation emails," which were sent at a stroke after midnight.

Both invitations were accepted immediately (within five minutes), which was a relief because Will and Rose had a strict ten-minute turnaround on email replies. The six invitees were now locked: Brett and Melissa, Ned and Beth, Jack and Kathleen.

Don't worry if you can't remember their names—they're all dead now anyway.

CHAPTER 4 **FOUR SIMPLE WORDS**

The view from the top of the Waterfront Plaza Hotel in Louisville was the perfect last image for a life.

Rose had made a wise suggestion: jumping to their deaths from there was significantly more dramatic than decapitation in the desert. If their bodies landed with enough force on the pavement, their spilled blood might spell out an obscure word that would have true crime obsessives debating for decades. Their friends might even think it was about them.

They took an Uber from the roadhouse (yep, the same old guy came back, and he'd replenished his water bottles and snacks), told the hotel valet they had a reservation, and went directly to the roof. No alarms went off, the rooftop door was wedged open with a brick. It was all very easy, almost like it was meant to be.

They took their positions on the ledge. Rose regretted her heels, but she refused to take them off: she wasn't dying barefoot, no fucking way, fuck that. Ralph still had enough energy to scurry back and forth on the thin strip of concrete, perhaps deciding whose leg he'd cling to on the way down. The sun began to set.

Rose finished her makeup, straightened her dress (it had dropped sequins), looked to Will for some sort of "count from three." Ralph looked too, and yipped.

"What?" Will asked, oblivious, busy studying which square of pavement he wanted to make his own.

"You wanna do the countdown or should I?" Rose asked.

He grunted, which meant "OK." He sucked in some air, puffed his chest, ready. "Ten, nine—"

"—Oh, for fuck's sake," she interrupted, "You don't need to start from ten. Three is fine."

He sighed, wet his lips, restarted: "Three, two—"

His cellphone rang at the exact moment his mouth opened to form "one." Ralph, who was easily excited and often ahead of himself, mistook the shrill ringtone for the "one" and jumped. *Yeah, he plummeted.* Will and Rose watched in confusion and horror, phone still ringing.

"It's OK, there's an awning," Will said, searching for a positive. "He'll bounce right off it." They both studied the tiny animal's deadly trajectory: he was indeed heading for the maroon awning above the hotel entrance. Maybe he would bounce off it and land on his paws, like they did in all those funny cartoons?

"It's a steel awning," Rose added, throwing cold water on Ralph's fading hopes. She was wrong: it wasn't steel at all. It was aluminum, with oak supports. Ralph's love-handles cushioned the impact, he tumbled, slid and rolled off into the arms of a frightened bellboy.

Will and Rose watched, phone still ringing, quietly relieved the little piss-machine had seemingly survived. But they'd be dead soon and he'd be all alone, and he really wouldn't cope without them. He'd probably die from the stress.

"Are you gonna answer the fucking phone or not?" Rose finally asked. Will relented, dug into his jacket pocket, hoping the final voice he'd ever hear wouldn't be someone called Iris doing a survey about dental hygiene. The caller I.D. read: "Unknown." He answered anyway.

"Hello, Will speaking."

He listened as a breeze feathered his nostril hair, which was gross. Then, unexpectedly, his mouth curled into a tiny smile. It wasn't Iris, and it had nothing to do with hygiene. Rose turned and looked at him, impatient, wondering why the call was taking so long. She knew immediately when she saw his face: it was the call they had been waiting for.

The first two years of dinner parties with "The Special Ones" were mostly flawless, spectacular events. Bertie was right: there was plenty of room for eight people at the really big round table. Sure, there were some mishaps—a few broken ribs, hair catching alight (twice), food poisoning (Bertie's fault), occasional death threats between guests, and minor flooding—but, overall, Friday nights (and sometimes Thursdays) became a staple of mindless, drunken, and life-enriching stability. Will and Rose never imagined it would end.

But then it did. Not with a bang, not suddenly, not even at half-speed. The end dragged out for an excruciating period of time, like the molasses in January (whatever that is), or the glory-hole queue at a Jesuit bar. It began with a simple, yet terrifying phrase.

Researchers studying the dinner party habits of the Innuit people in the sixties discovered there were two phrases that, if ever uttered during an evening, would result in a guest being stripped naked and drowned in icy water. They were: "No gin for me, I'm driving (my sled home)," and "We have an early start (clubbing seals)." Similar phrases, minus the sled and clubbing bits, appeared in the studies of other dinner party cultures all over the world. In western Africa, the phrase "Can you help us move?" was forbidden at gatherings of friends (you'd be stabbed with a spear if you asked it) and, in Barysh, a Russian city, you'd be lucky to escape with your life if you ever asked for "salt," "a second helping of goulash," or a "non-alcoholic vodka."

The most life-altering phrase for Will and Rose wasn't any of these. It was a hideous collection of four simple words, loaded with dread and foreboding and far-reaching consequences. These words were uttered on a stormy Friday night in November, their last dinner party before Thanksgiving.

The couples had moved beyond hors d'oeuvres and life/work chit-chat, and everyone was seated at the table, enjoying mini-dumplings and a bottle of Tuscan chardonnay, circa nineteen sixty-six. Will had prepared a new set of incest jokes to perform, Jack and Kathleen were having a violent argument, and Bertie hadn't made a single clumsy mistake all night. Everything was pretty much perfect. And then it happened.

Melissa spoke, flippant, almost in passing, blurting the words out in the course of casual conversation. It was like she was telling them about an enema she'd had or a vacation they'd booked to Haiti.

"We're having a baby."

Yep, just like that. A thousand other phrases would've been preferable that night: "Brett likes young boys," "We were raped on our way here," "We have Ebola and it's highly contagious." *Anything but the words she chose.*

An awkward silence gripped the room. Brett sat there with a smug grin, as if he'd had something to do with it. Food dribbled from Beth's half-open mouth. Jack's chewing slowed to an abrupt stop, then his teeth ground. Ned stared ahead; Kathleen quietly self-mutilated under the table. Rose almost sprayed her mouthful of wine, but bravely held it in (she knew what it cost per glass). She spoke before Will could, asked the question they all wanted to ask:

"Why?"

Melissa chuckled, perhaps thinking the question was a joke. Brett did too. Soon, everyone else started chuckling, thinking Melissa was pranking them. *Good one!* Will and Rose remembered Melissa's cancer scare and the baby spiders: another attention-seeking stunt. Relief swept across the room as the volume and intensity of the laughter grew, even Bertie joined in (although he was backed-up on plate-gathering). But then, there was a disturbing follow-up from Melissa, who suddenly couldn't shut the fuck up:

"It's due in March," she said. The laughter stopped immediately. Throats were cleared. Bertie hurried back to the kitchen, smashing a champagne flute on the way. Rose opened her mouth to ask another question, but couldn't think of one that didn't include the word "termination."

The party ended early that night, almost like there was an uncovered dead body in the middle of the room and it would be weird to continue having fun while it was there. That had actually happened once, but it's a story for another time (and they actually did keep having fun). Normally, at the end of an evening, Will and Rose would stand on the front porch and wave goodbye to their guests with wide, inebriated grins. But they let Bertie show everyone out this time, too shaken to rise from their seats.

When all the cars had left, Rose finished the nearest bottle and gradually realized the error of her ways:

"I should've put one more fucking box on that flowchart," she said.

CHAPTER 5 IT GETS WORSE

Melissa and Brett's announcement kept Rose and Will awake all night. They tossed and turned, stared at the ceiling, pulled at their silk sheets. Will woke in a sweat at 3am, clawing at the air. Rose had one of those "primal screams."

In the morning, over tar-black coffee and burnt eggs (Bertie was high again), they shared the same self-delusion: "I had a really weird nightmare last night." This went on for most of the week. Soon, they had convinced themselves that nothing had happened. Melissa's cruel words had never been spoken, they were just a figment of their imagination.

When Friday arrived, the dinner party preparations began as they normally did. Bertie chilled drinks, polished cutlery, and dressed in his livery.

Everyone arrived on time. They gorged on tapas and Romanian cognac, and conversation followed established norms: Ned explained a new app he'd designed for pedophiles (it involved an electric shock), Kathleen discussed a new retirement home she'd just destroyed from within, and Jack motivated everyone to stop talking about themselves (and talk more about him). Melissa and Brett were oddly silent. Perhaps, Will and Rose quietly hoped, their initial pregnancy test had been one of those "false positives." Maybe her gynecologist had set them straight: "you were mistaken, move on, enjoy your wonderful friends while they still respect you and don't ever put yourself in this position ever again."

Before the main course arrived, Will gently stroked Rose's exposed thigh and quietly took in their table of friends, laughing and chatting through mouthfuls of cognac. "We're gonna be OK," he thought. He squeezed her knee; she slapped his hand away.

And then reality crashed the mezzanine like a drunk soccer mom in an SUV. Like those four terrifying words, the moment was instantaneous, unpredictable, and gut-wrenching.

Later, while hunched over the toilet bowl, Will remembered it all in painful, pixelated slow-motion: he had leaned over to fill Melissa's glass and she had covered it. *Yeah, she fucking covered it.* With her chubby pink hand. He hovered over her knuckles with the bottle, confused, acted like she was kidding. She gave him a look, then made things worse by uttering the unthinkable:

"No more for me," she said.

The room froze in silence. *No more?* She'd only had three glasses. Stunned eyes descended on her like flies on a decomposing body. Will backed up, humiliated, holding the bottle like a sad little waiter who'd been told to fetch napkins. And yet, in the horror of it all, she had more to say:

"I don't want to harm the baby."

Oh fucking dear.

◆   ◆   ◆

Brett and Melissa kept turning up for another torturous month.

She reverted completely to sparkling water by the second week; Brett followed suit a week later. He wasn't even having a fucking baby! Will and Rose would take multiple trips to the kitchen during the evening to vent their frustrations, their voices often spilling through the door:

"More water! Is she having a baby camel?"

To make matters worse, Melissa started taking selfies every five minutes to keep a record of the baby's "pre-birth life." Yeah, good idea, like the kid was going to put down his joystick and crack pipe at age 12 and start checking photos from his parents' dinner parties. "Oh, wow, this is when I didn't actually have a heartbeat and my mom's friends are all doing fake smiles because they loathe her and despise me, even though I look like a shriveled worm and I'm not even a sentient being yet!" She would pose with her hand on her growing belly ("The New Cyst," as Will called it), often requiring everyone in the background to pretend to care and say something stupid (like "Hello Baby!"). No-one ever did. Will used to mouth the words "Die Evil Spirit!" each time. It was an exhausting first trimester.

As summer approached, Brett and Melissa started leaving early (so tired!), told Jack to "please stop" blowing cigar smoke in their direction, and—the final straw—made no effort whatsoever to laugh at Will's jokes, particularly ones about dying babies. Will's classic, "What's the difference between a frozen chicken and a dead baby?" didn't even raise a smirk (the answer, in case you're wondering, is "You don't cum on a frozen chicken before you eat it.") Melissa and Brett were never amused.

They didn't just kill the mood. They waterboarded it, gouged its eyes out and left it for dead on the side of a deserted road in a pool of piss and excrement. Thankfully, after Will's failed frozen chicken joke, and another one about "abortion in space," they stopped coming altogether. It was a huge relief, like that awkwardly-sick relative who eventually dies. Their unborn fetus was ruining the entire dinner party experience for everyone and they had no-one to blame but themselves. Best of all, no-one had to pose for their stupid fucking selfies anymore.

In the weeks that followed, Will and Rose grappled with whether or not to seek out (and invite) a replacement couple.

They created a chart of pros and cons, did a mock dinner party with just six chairs (and life-sized cut-outs), and even consulted a "psychic." The psychic ("Jemima"), who also happened to be delivering an Amazon order at the time, told them she had a vision of "a drug-addicted old man removing two chairs from a really big round table." She said this would be a "really positive thing for them" and left, returning an hour later because she had delivered the wrong package (somehow she didn't have a vision of that, which would've saved her thirty minutes).

Soon after, they asked Bertie to remove two seats from the table. The psychic's advice proved to be reasonably accurate: the reduced group of six was a perfect fit for the winter months. Extra elbow-space at the dinner table, fewer voices to talk over, more expensive wine for everyone. And, most importantly, Bertie now had time to smoke a full crack pipe between courses (instead of half).

Life and laughter resumed, everyone got their grooves back, and no-one ever mentioned the names Melissa, Brett, or "Unborn Fetus" again (unless it was the punchline of a cruel and/or sadistic joke). They danced, they drank, they had purpose once more. Gawking passers-by could see their joyous silhouettes again! The "Special Six" seemed impenetrable. Nothing could ever get in the way of—*oh, fuck. Really?*

Anthropologists discovered a lost tribe of cannibals in a remote tributary of the Amazon River in the fifties. Upon visiting, they encountered a kind and carefree people, none of them younger than thirty. That's right, there were no children, which explained why they were so damn happy (it certainly wasn't the human flesh they were eating because that sucked—it didn't taste like chicken at all).

After several weeks of study, during which they managed to convince their hosts not to eat them (by saying "please don't eat us" and pointing loaded weapons at them), the anthropologists realized the lack of children was the result of two things: most of the men were extraordinarily gay and, of those who weren't, their sperm count was almost non-existent (due to a rare DNA flaw). Disregarding all self-worth and every imaginable ethical boundary, the leader of the research team ("Brad") decided to help the tribe out by fucking one of the women. His journal, recovered some years later next to his rotting bones (he never made it back), detailed his twisted thought process at the time: "I may be extraordinarily horny, and these women are fucking hot and begging for it, but that has nothing to do with science and the personal sacrifice I need to make in the name of humanity and anthropology." His writings were accompanied by several complex diagrams and lots of doodles of "titties."

The lucky woman he chose (he named her "Jane") quickly became pregnant, which disturbed the elders (all gay) but excited all the fertile women (all horny). Before Jane had even entered the second trimester, at least eight others had asked Brad to fuck them too, which he did in the name of—*yeah, you guessed it*—science and humanity, *blah, blah, blah*. If you think this is a story about how a horny anthropologist named Brad revived a dying Amazonian tribe, and the power of children to bring people together, you'd be wrong. The thirteen children Brad fathered grew up, eventually slaughtered and ate their mothers and everyone else, then committed mass suicide when they realized they were either gay (*eww, gross*) or couldn't have children of their own (because of their flawed DNA). By fucking Jane, Brad had initiated a chain reaction that systematically wiped out an entire race of very happy people who liked to party, eat meat, and fuck without consequence.

In a similarly cruel way, Brett and Melissa's selfish decision to "create life" caused a ripple that would ultimately become a tsunami of misery. The true horror of what they had started didn't materialize until two weeks before Christmas.

In a (free) online therapy session some weeks after the event, Will recalled everything in chilling detail. He had returned from the kitchen with a clean glass (Bertie had missed a spot) and heard the tail end of Beth's "announcement."

At first, he thought she was talking about the matching cars she and Ned were planning to buy in the new year ("What kind of fuckwit couples buy matching cars?" he asked himself aloud as he approached). But then, as he crossed through the open doorway, he saw Rose's wine spill, pooling like blood across the crisp white tablecloth. Her face was a deathly pale. Before Will could ask, Kathleen sought the clarification he needed:

"Twins?"

CHAPTER 6 **THE FETAL POSITION**

Will wasn't sure he'd heard the word right. *Did she say "Twins?"*

His bottom lip quivered. He looked at Rose, whose face said "yeah, she fucking did." He asked anyway, out loud: "Two of them?"

Beth beamed like it was good news, as if getting two malignant brain tumors was something to celebrate.

Ned, who had designed apps to permanently quieten crying babies (no electric shock involved, but it was still a best-seller), tried to rationalize their bizarre news. "We weren't planning on it, it just happened." *Oh, please.* He would've got more respect if he'd just said: "I was jerking off while cleaning the gutters, the ladder slipped, I fell, Beth was passing, my cock accidentally lodged in her vagina and we conceived a child."

The rest of the night was a blur, the lobster tasted like cardboard, and Will worked hard to insert "evil twin" movies into as many conversations as he could. When Beth asked where they bought the shrimps, Will replied: "The seafood market on Ryde, the one that used to be a cinema."

"The seafood market on Ryde used to be a cinema?" Beth asked. *It didn't.*

"Yeah, Rose and I went there on one of our first dates. We saw 'Dead Ringers.'" Rose looked at him: *they didn't.* He continued: "That's the really fucked-up movie where Jeremy Irons plays evil twin gynecologists who mutilate women's genitals." Jack was the first to catch on, and he doubled-down.

"Those are really fucked-up brothers, almost as bad as those twin sisters in that other movie." And so it went.

When Ned and Beth finally got up to leave (not long after that), still babbling about what names they were considering ("John and Paul," "Jack and Rose," *oh, get fucked*), Rose couldn't help herself: "Sixty percent of twins are born premature," she blurted. "And twenty percent don't survive at all." The room quietened. Ned and Beth stiffened, horrified. It was pretty harsh. Rose tried to backpedal (a little): "But I'm sure you guys will beat the odds, no matter how incredibly overwhelming they are."

In the weeks that followed, an inevitable sequence of events unfolded: the covering-of-the-wine-glass, "tiredness," an eviscerated sense of humor and, finally, two more empty seats at the dinner table. Losing Melissa and Brett had better prepared Will and Rose, but the loss was still painful. They would miss Ned's expensive alcohol, the stories about his crazy apps, and Beth's, well, her, the things she did—*yeah, they'd kinda miss her too.* But they wouldn't miss either of their singing—they were both ghastly—or the way they'd occasionally hold hands for no apparent reason.

After many sleepless nights, primal screams, sweaty nightmares, and lots of staring at the ceiling and mouthing "fuck them," Will and Rose began to compose themselves and focus all their attention on those who were left: Jack and Kathleen. The stayers, the non-breeders, the only ones they could truly believe in.

They had deeper, more intelligent conversations when it was just the four of them. Jack and Kathleen seemed to hate each other more with fewer people around. They argued constantly, threw food and wine over each other, and always brought cruel and denigrating humor to the table, and beyond. A standard post-dinner conversation near the balcony would always start with a back-handed compliment:

"You know how I said your ass doesn't look huge in that dress?" Jack would say, leaning with a cigar. Kathleen would turn, dismissive, and wait for him to continue. "I lied. It looks fucking humungous. If I had to testify about it under oath, I'd call it 'bulbous.' It's a bulbous ass, your Honor." She'd sigh, probably roll her eyes while she thought of a witty comeback.

"Like your head," she'd say. They'd laugh, maybe do a little weird sex talk (usually involving a gavel and the witness stand), then start over with fresh insults. Will and Rose enjoyed every moment of it. It was the best of times.

Occasionally, after dessert, they'd all gather at the fireplace and burn the incoming mail Will and Rose had received from "the ones they'd lost." Yeah, for some reason, the exiled couples felt the need to "stay in touch." Birthdays, Christmases, any chance they could think of to send a card or letter. Emails were too easy to block or delete—they wanted Will and Rose to work harder to expunge them from their lives.

Brett and Melissa were the worst offenders. They would send inane, home-printed photos of their growing family (*yeah, they had kept breeding*) prior to every major federal holiday. They'd dress in matching costumes and/or stupid woolen sweaters, make hilarious faces or cross their eyes (Rose's pet hate), and pose as a loving, happy couple that no longer missed debauchery and drunkenness and all the wonderful things life had to offer. *Yeah, sure.* To make matters worse, they would also send "origin photos," repulsive images of each new addition to their brood.

Will and Rose weren't the only ones who received the photos: Jack and Kathleen were on the mailing list too. For some reason, the sad little couple felt the need to alert the world whenever something escaped from Melissa's womb. It was like getting colonoscopy photos from someone with rectal cancer. On the back of the photo, they'd write stupid information that benefited no-one: its name (deliberately spelled in a "unique way" just to fuck with everyone the child would encounter in life), the date of the "womb escape," and the baby's "weight in pounds," which seemed like fat-shaming (their babies were always significantly overweight).

Ned and Beth didn't send cards—instead, they wrote painfully-long letters, providing weekly updates about The Twins' increasingly dull lives: haircuts, the first day of school, meaningless achievements ("most special hurdler who came dead last"), non-life-threatening injuries that were "so cute."

"Dying would be much cuter," Rose said as the flames licked at the paper.

In the summer months, when it was too hot to start a fire, they'd shred all the mail instead and laugh heartily, making jokes about how sad and pathetic their former friends were. It became a cherished part of the evening for everyone, even Ralph, who would yip and run in circles when Bertie started a fire or wheeled out the shredder from the home office.

Jack and Kathleen were never late. In fact, they were always ten minutes early, almost to the second. So it was alarming when they hadn't arrived by the third round of drinks. It was the second Friday in February, three years since Ned and Beth's departure, and almost five since the exit of Brett and Melissa.

Bertie was becoming increasingly restless: his hors d'oeuvres were getting cold and he wanted to start smoking his pipe. Rose told Will to call Jack, perhaps thinking they'd been in a car accident while fighting. It had happened before on their way home. Will agreed and dialed.

He paced as the phone rang at the other end. Rose watched with a glass of wine, anxious. Jack picked up and they exchanged brief pleasantries, a laugh, some lighthearted banter. Before Will could ask where they were, Jack said Kathleen wasn't feeling well. She hadn't been feeling well for many days. There was a moment of uneasy silence. Will stiffened, Rose noticed. They were all fearing the worst, so Will tried to be consoling:

"Maybe it's cancer. It could be cancer!"

It wasn't cancer. It was far worse.

◆   ◆   ◆

The weeks after Jackleen's revelation were the hardest. Will and Rose had never imagined that their closest friends, the couple they trusted more than any other, would betray them. Kathleen said her "maternal instincts" had gotten the better of her, Jack said he needed a child so he could "tell it how repugnant its mother was." His excuse was actually pretty reasonable, but nothing could ease the pain.

On their final night together, Will watched Jack at the balcony, stripped of his cigar, his Schnapps and all his hedonistic dignity. In that backlit moment, he mourned and quietly said goodbye to his pitiful friend.

In the months following, Will and Rose often slept in the fetal position, curled up and quietly weeping like the unborn fetuses that had put them there.

When Fridays came, they went through the motions. They thought their own company would be enough—but it wasn't. Even the wine tasted insipid and empty. They watched the most depressing movies they could find just to dull their own pain: it was like audio-visual self-harming. Documentaries about The Holocaust, 9/11, Russian Gulags, World's Worst Disasters, movies starring Bette Midler. None of it helped. They went on long drives just to see if they could hit a deer.

"Is that one?" Rose asked as they traversed a remote road, pointing through the fogged-up windscreen.

"No, it's a cyclist," Will replied, then accelerated towards him.

Within six months of the Jackleen departure, they became so despondent and desperate for company they decided to invite Bertie for dinner, pretending he was an actual guest they'd invited. He got all dressed up, even showered, and turned up five minutes early. *So cute.* They thought he'd have some good stories, being a crack head and all. He told them he did time in the sixties for "sex trafficking," served in Korea (rice, in a Korean Restaurant), and was a pimp before there was a name for it (back then it was just "creepy man in leather who exploits hookers"). But his stories were mostly vacuous and dull with no structure or meaningful conclusion, just a whole lot of rambling. And things got weird when the oven alarm went off. He pretended he couldn't hear it and kept rambling. Eventually, he went and got the food and served them. They never did that shit again.

They soon realized they would have to settle for long, miserable, solitary lives. They ate in front of the TV (without Bertie), watched their depressing movies and some occasional "snuff" tapes (which Bertie had found for them). They even bought some of those delightful "meal cushions"—the ones old people use when they've lost the will to live. They got one for Ralph too—he destroyed it in thirty minutes, then pissed on the remaining strands of fluff. If you were watching them through the mezzanine window, you'd think their lives were done. Kaput. Over.

But then, as quickly as the mist drifted in from the west, things changed. They hit a deer. *Yes, an actual deer.* It crashed into the front grille, its body slid up the hood and shattered the windscreen. Airbags erupted, smudging Rose's lipstick. The animal had finished twitching by the time they got out of the car, its mangled antlers caught up in the wipers, which were still operational. The mist cleared to reveal its glassy eyes, which was probably what prompted Rose to say:

"We could kill them."

Will paused, confused. "All of them?"

"No, just the children." Her words cut across the cold night air like a coxless four on still water. "Then things will be like they used to be."

Will shifted his weight, played the words back in his head. It was a genius idea. He looked at her, her face half-lit by headlight. She grinned, mischievous but deadly-fucking-serious. He'd never found her so extraordinarily hot. He grinned back, they fucked in the back seat, pushed the deer off the hood and drove home.

There was hope in their lives again.

CHAPTER 7 <u>**F.U.G.T.**</u>

The deer, a caribou named "Oh!," survived the collision. She had a couple of broken ribs and some facial bruising but she was mostly fine—the whole glassy-dead-eye thing was a trick she'd learned from her mom ("Rain"), who was a direct descendant of the actual "Bambi" and didn't like humans much.

After Will and Rose had driven off, she dusted herself off and headed home. Her husband John, an elk with abandonment issues, asked where she'd been and why there was a windscreen wiper tangled in her antlers. She said a strange couple had run into her with their 2005-model Mercedes, seemingly on purpose. She didn't get a license plate.

"I fucking know those fuckers," he said, nostrils flaring. "They tried to hit me and the kids last week." They had two fawns, but called them "kids." John asked Oh! if the strange couple had said anything after running into her. Oh! said they were talking about killing all of their friends' children so they could have dinner parties again.

"That makes a lot of sense," he said, briefly turning to look at their fawns, who had started to become very annoying since their hooves had grown. Oh! noticed, so he quickly shifted topic: "Want some lichen juice? I'm going to make a batch."

◆   ◆   ◆

On the way home, struggling to see over inflated airbags, Will and Rose discussed the beginnings of their plan. They weren't the kind of people who got their hands dirty and, if the incident with the deer was any indication, neither of them could stand the sight of blood and/or death. They needed to hire someone do it.

As it turned out, it wasn't that easy to get someone to kill a bunch of children. Priests, politicians, entertainers, UN workers—easy. Children and babies—surprisingly difficult. Which was odd because so many people despised them and wanted them dead, especially at restaurants and on long-haul flights. They said it out loud, just never wanted to follow through. There was no app, no Facebook group, not even a thread on the Dark Web. Bertie didn't have a single contact, and he was a convicted felon. Not even Tony would do it, and Tony never turned down a kill.

Tony, you ask? Who the fuck was Tony? Well, to know who Tony was and why he mattered, you need to know what Will did for a living, the reason for Will and Rose's wealth. Ponzi schemes? Hedge funds? Cryptocurrency? Nope, none of those. Two words: Chicken. Nuggets. That's right, Will made chicken nuggets. Not just any chicken nuggets—Gold Gourmet Nuggets, the best in the south-west.

To understand what made them the best requires an understanding of how nuggets are "normally" made. If you're unemployed and/or have a spare week or two, get a job at a chicken processing plant. It's repulsive and the stench will stay with you for years, but you'll learn something, you might meet an attractive single parent, and you'll probably never eat a "normal" chicken nugget ever again.

◆   ◆   ◆

The process was relatively simple, as described in the official manual of The American Association of Chicken Nugget Manufacturers (est. 1814): first, whole chickens arrived on big trucks, driven by "rednecks and/or lesbians in flannel, with poor diets." The chickens were dead, of course, plucked and all that, with no heads. They were loaded onto the first of many conveyer belts, "The Vulva Velcome," which was originally named by a Swedish lesbian trucker and was the most welcoming of all the conveyer belts. It even had a "Velcome/Welcome!" sign over the little door where the carcasses passed through, after which they were immediately stroked by thin strips of plastic.

Once inside, the chickens were "deboned," a process which stripped them of all their bones, including the spine. According to the manual, the human equivalent of this process was "when a man attends a baby shower or lets a woman drive him around in her car." Yes, this was actually written in the manual, accompanied by photos of a man at a baby shower and a woman driving a (different) man around in a car.

After "deboning," the chicken carcass was just a flimsy, unstructured mess of flesh, wobbling about like jelly. It traveled along another conveyer belt, "The Humiliation Pass," where process workers shouted personal insults at it (the usual stuff, "I feather-fucked your mother last night," "suck my dick, rooster faggot"). It was thought that this pass weakened and tenderized the chicken flesh, although there was no known scientific evidence to back that up. Some processing plants have reported that this step is fundamental to the workers' health and wellbeing and has reduced after-work bar fights by more than thirty percent.

The individual identity of each humiliated chicken came to an end at the next conveyer belt, unofficially called the "We're All In This Together" pass. As the title implied, all the flesh got mixed together and dropped into a huge vat, where lots of other additional "secret shit" was added (definitely not herbs or spices). Eighties music was played on loud speakers, usually a track by Bucks Fizz or Rick Astley, while the spinning vat blades gathered speed and intensity. When it was over, all that remained was a gooey "chicken" paste, which spewed out in the shape of nuggets (or stupid little smiling faces, if desired) on the penultimate conveyer belt, or "The Rebirth Tract." The fleshless blobs were coated in breadcrumbs, fried and packaged, and returned to a different set of trucks driven by illegal immigrants and divorced dads who used to work in coalmines.

The secret to Gold Gourmet Nuggets' success was the company's complete disregard for everything in the manual. OK, not everything—they kept the illegal immigrant truckers, the eighties music, and the part where everyone shouted insults (it was too much fun)—but the rest was completely reinvented, thanks largely to its founder and Will's great grandfather, Cecil R. Calhoun, the third (or second, if you don't count his bastard grandfather, who was one of the first people to ever be canceled after sniffing a Native American woman's neck).

As a young boy on the frontier, Cecil was repulsed by the quality of nuggets his dad would bring home from The Saloon (in those days you could get takeaway frozen goods from The Saloon, as well as tampons and disposable razors).

One day he complained to his mother about the nuggets. She said: "Shut the fuck up, there's a famine, your father's recovering from an infected arrow wound and your sister has polio." So he stayed silent for a few months after that, knowing one day he would change the face of nugget manufacturing forever. When his sister finally stopped whining about the polio (she died) and he got his mother's full attention again, he asked her to forgo his Christmas present for a chicken, a live one that he could "experiment on." She wasn't actually planning on buying him a Christmas present (they were dirt poor and she had to pay for his sister's funeral) but he scared her a lot so she whored herself out to a nearby chicken farmer, who gave her one of his deformed hens in return for a hand-job behind the barn.

She presented Cecil with the odd-looking chicken (it had a huge goiter on its neck) on the day before Christmas, telling him to "wear a condom," which had now become readily available at The Saloon. He was confused by her advice: *why would he need a condom to redesign how nuggets were made?* He grappled with her words as a young adult in therapy and eventually asked her about it on her deathbed. "When you said you wanted to experiment on a chicken, I thought you wanted to fuck it," she replied, clinging to life. "You were a very horny teenager and you also scared me a lot."

After she died, Cecil returned to his work, troubled his mother had thought he was engaging in bestiality for most of his teenage years (and that he scared her). The original deformed chicken ("Dolores") had died by that point, but Cecil had successfully bred her offspring and he had twenty chicks to work with, all carrying the same deformity as their mother: a large goiter on their necks. That goiter changed everything.

The littlest of the chicks, "Lord Byrom," had a significantly larger goiter than his siblings. It was so big that it hampered his breathing, made eating difficult and caused him to make a very hoarse and irritating "chirping" sound at night. Cecil mentioned this to his friend Dalziel, a petty thief who had once performed a tracheotomy on a horse (the horse had choked on a plastic carrot). Dalziel dreamed of becoming a veterinarian and he was equally bothered by the quality of chicken nuggets in the west— so he agreed to help Cecil separate goiter and chick, as long as he could write a scientific paper about it afterwards.

The removal was swift and bloody, but the result was unexpected: instead of the goiter containing disgusting pus and goo, its interior was filled with tender, white flesh. Cecil seasoned it with salt and pepper, fried it in grapeseed oil and—much to Dalziel's complete horror—ate it with a side of ranch sauce. It was, as Cecil later typed on his Apple II, a "savory delight for the ages."

In the months that followed, Cecil and Dalziel removed the goiters of the remaining nineteen chicks and ate them (they did six in one day and put them in a small cardboard box before eating them, which was widely credited as being the world's first-known "six-pack of nuggets"). Best of all, once the goiters were removed, the chickens quickly overcame the trauma of their surgery and grew their deformities back within months—an endless source of tender nuggets and no-one had to die!

But Cecil was competent enough at economics to know that a few "goiter-nuggets" from nineteen chicks would never be enough to sustain a business and change the industry. He needed a way to add more goiters to the existing chicks and create goiters in healthy chicks who didn't already have them. His plan became unofficially known as "F.U.G.T." (or "The Fucked-Up Goiter Theorem").

The major breakthrough came during a heavy winter at the turn of the century: Cecil injected an unhatched chicken egg with a complex synthetic hormone and—*voila!*—the chick emerged with a goiter-covered body: as many as twenty perfectly-shaped nuggets attached to its body, like oversized pecs on a skinny man in the gym.

The rest is history: Cecil and Dalziel formed a nugget manufacturing company and became overnight millionaires. They were even on the cover of "Laid" magazine (the chicken/egg publication, not the porn one). Their company became the number one manufacturer of nuggets in the country and they both lived happily until their deaths in the twenties—well, actually, Dalziel died a little earlier and he wasn't that happy: he was fired from the company for wearing blackface at the annual "Pimps & Hookers Ball" and his reputation never recovered, which led to his suicide on the day before Gold Gourmet Nuggets manufactured its one-billionth nugget. But his contribution was immortalized with a bronze plaque on the conveyor belt in Factory A (although it was demolished in the seventies to make way for an onsite Starbucks).

Before his death, Cecil passed the company—and the secret of the F.U.G.T. hormone—to his son Randolph (Will's grandfather), who improved the hormone injection process and briefly introduced "chicken tenders," which were very unpopular with both chickens ("too heavy on our bodies") and consumers ("too dry"). They were discontinued after one year.

Randolph died in the eighties—he choked on a turkey bone at Thanksgiving, which was ironic because he hated family gatherings—and Will, his favorite grandson, was anointed his successor, much to the horror and disappointment of Will's alcoholic father, who had already ordered a gold-embossed nameplate for his desk. *But more about that fucker later.*

Will made two significant improvements to the F.U.G.T. process: first, he added a new DNA strand to the hormone, which caused the goiters to "self-crumb" as they grew. This saved millions in breadcrumb costs and relieved hundreds of workers of their low-paying jobs, including Will's father (who was V.P. of Breadcrumbs).

Secondly, and most importantly, he added a crucial step to the process: the "Oil Massage Bath." Chickens were treated to an hour-long bath in a tray of warm oil and sesame seeds just before surgery, which made the goiters/nuggets crispier on the outside and more tender on the inside. This new approach was the envy of the nugget world. Demand skyrocketed; Michelin star chefs made orders. Even the Animal Welfare Association awarded the company a five-star rating, saying the baths gave the birds "a sense of comfort and self-esteem that's sadly lacking in most manufacturing sectors."

As you'd expect, talentless competitors noticed Will's success and tried to copy what he'd done: "Nanna's Nuggets" (not a Nanna at all, a Nigerian immigrant named Phil), "All-Natural Homemade Nuggets" (made by a crackhead who left home when she was five, then returned at age ten to burn her parents' house down), and "Tasty Nuggets!" (which went bankrupt when its mascot/co-owner was arrested for distributing pigeon pornography). Some of the competitors survived longer than others, and several of them inflicted significant damage on Gold Gourmet Nuggets' market share. This did not please Will.

Which brings us to Tony, *finally*.

CHAPTER 8 TONY

Anthony Gerald Calhoun ("Tony") was Will's younger brother.

He wasn't the black sheep of the family, not at all—he was the matted bits of shit-covered wool that hang from the black sheep's rear end (or "dag," as it's called in countries where they have lots of sheep, and shit).

Tony's troubles began in the womb with a "nuchal cord," which is when the umbilical cord wraps around the unborn fetus' neck. Doctors said it was self-inflicted (he wrapped it around his own neck) and he was "self-harming to get attention." As a toddler, Tony's parents thought it was funny when he would pull the wings off flies and arrange them on the dinner table to form words from his growing vocabulary: "DIE!," "PAIN," "MUTILI-ATION." They'd chuckle and pat his little head and say, "You're a funny one, Tony." But they stopped laughing when he brought in his first pigeon.

He survived an exorcism at his fourth birthday party (his uncle's idea), was banned from most playdates and social gatherings, and the childcare center built a special room to house him in: they called it "Cell Block T" as a joke, although it was actually made of steel bars and there was a toilet next to a concrete bed.

He threatened his way through high school (lots of A's), was once featured on an episode of "World's Most Troubled Teens," and eventually accepted a job at the chicken nugget factory, mostly because his grandfather (Randolph)—one of the only people he truly loved—told him he could pull the wings off as many birds as he wanted and get paid. For a while, Tony worked on "The Humiliation Pass," where his insults caused the deaths of at least a dozen chickens (and his supervisor).

It was there he met Trudy, the love of his life and future mother of his children. She was belittling an overweight hen ("fuck you, fat motherfucking cunt") when she caught Tony's eye: they immediately connected, fell in love, and got married on a sinking trawler. It was a pretty cool wedding, actually: their vows were a collection of insults from the factory ("I'll stay with you forever, you repugnant rooster cocksucker") and, when it was over and they kissed, the boat went under and all the guests had to swim to the nearest shore, where beer, wine, and chicken nuggets (of course) awaited. Sadly, they forgot to check if the celebrant could swim: he could not, and drowned, but they did a special toast to him during the speeches.

Will and Tony had a special bond. Sure, they had the usual brotherly issues—knife-fights, death threats, multiple hospitalizations—but they shared a deep, mutual respect for one other. When Will took over Gold Gourmet Nuggets, he saw potential for Tony beyond hurling insults at hens. He initially promoted him to "Head Euthanasia Consultant"—in short, he killed chickens who weren't coping with life (or growing enough nuggets on their bodies)—and it was a perfect fit. But Will knew his erratic, violent brother had more to offer the company.

It was during their weekly firing-range lunch that the idea first took hold. Will was complaining about a new competitor— "Smiley-Face Nuggets," run by a sadistic former potato farmer who had never smiled once—and Tony offered a light-hearted but deadly-serious suggestion: "Why don't I just euthanize the fucker?" he quipped.

Will paused, put down his AR-17 and turkey burger, and met Tony's eyes. "That would definitely put a smile on my face," he replied. The next moment of silence between them spoke volumes: within twenty-four hours, Smiley-Face Noel had "accidentally" choked on twelve of his own nuggets.

In his report, the coroner noted that it was "very odd that a man would try to eat so many nuggets at once," and "it was most likely a suicide because he was a really glum fuck who never smiled once." He only included that last line after Tony visited his office.

Before long, Will knew Tony could do what needed to be done to keep the competition at bay—or, in the bay, if that was required. He gave him a new title (V.P. of Competition Strategies), a corner office that he never used and all the resources he needed to keep Gold Gourmet Nuggets on top.

Tony snuffed out lots of budding entrepreneurs who dreamed of nugget market share: two college grads who thought inserting cheese into the goiter would make them millions, a failed popcorn czar who believed smaller was better, and a transgender housewife who hoped "oven-baked" nuggets would get him/her rich (instead of inside an industrial oven, which is where he/she ended up).

But it was "Frank the Chicken King" who proved to be Tony's toughest, and most rewarding, hit. And, for reasons we'll explain later, it was also the one that cost Tony his hair, his left testicle, and the use of his right arm.

Will had first become aware of Frank's "grand nugget plan" at a boneless chicken conference in the Midwest. The greasy fucker had cornered the market on legs and wings and jokingly said he was considering a foray into Will's territory.

"How hard could it be?" he said from the other end of the bar, nursing a mimosa. "I could make them from all the assholes and entrails I already throw out and they'd still taste better than yours." Will laughed him off; he knew Frank didn't stand a chance (and quietly imagined Tony drowning him in a vat of chicken entrails).

Nothing happened for several months after that. Will suspected Frank had lost his nerve, probably realized that "assholes and entrails" tasted as awful as they sounded and weren't going to cut it in the major leagues of nugget cuisine. But then, almost a year later, Will saw his smug advertisement on a passing bus— Frank's bulbous head with a shit-eating grin. "All New!" it read, stroked and embossed. "Frank's Golden Nuggets!" Will seethed, crushed a busker's guitar with his boot, and immediately called Tony.

"The Frank problem has officially become a major problem," Will said.

Tony paused, finished a mouthful, and replied:

"Can't wait to fix it."

Even though they had adjoining offices at the factory, Will and Tony usually met to plan a hit under the Hooper Bridge, where Will would give Tony unmarked bills (his regular pay) and the details of "the job." It was all very noir. Tony would often try to be witty about how he was going to do it, usually with some kind of chicken-related reference: "battered or flame-grilled?" or "seared and cut into eights?" On this particular occasion, Will was unusually blunt:

"Just make sure he doesn't come back this time," he said. Frank had a way of re-emerging whenever it seemed he was done: he'd started his legs and wings empire from nothing, re-covered from bankruptcy twice. He was a slippery little toad who never quit.

Tony may have been erratic, unpredictable, and violent, but he was also very meticulous when it came to planning his kills. He studied Frank's daily routine, tracked his journey to and from home, and obtained floor plans and maps of all the locations he visited regularly. He noted where cameras and exits were located, timed distances, and thought deeply about when, where, and how he could make it happen. Trudy visited his basement lair during the planning phase. She had an eye for detail and would often see possibilities that Tony had missed.

"There's a blind spot there," she said, pointing to a blueprint of Frank's factory headquarters. "When he leaves the lift and crosses behind the pylon to get to his car. Neither camera has the angle."

Tony looked, delighted. *She was always right.*

"You're right," he said. "It's the perfect place to snatch him up."

"Or just put a bullet in his head." Trudy preferred quick, efficient kills. But this one was different for Tony. He stroked his stubbly chin, which was what he did when the right (creative) side of his brain kicked in.

"No, I want to take my time with him."

He followed Trudy's advice and grabbed Frank on the way to his car, then drove him to an abandoned chicken factory on the outskirts of the city. It had previously belonged to the "Nanna's Nuggets" guy; in fact, he was buried under the warehouse floor (with his wife and two children).

Tony had constructed a huge rotary over a firepit, large enough to hold a person. He coated Frank in sesame seed oil and Italian herbs, fired up the Peruvian charcoal and called Will to give him an update. Will never asked him to call before a hit, in fact he expressly said not to call "before, during, or after any illegal activity." But this was a very special job for both of them and Will appreciated the gesture. Besides, they both had a generous supply of burner phones.

"Is he shitting himself?" Will asked. Frank pulled against his constraints, screaming muffled profanities through his gag.

"Not yet," Tony said. "But he will."

"Tell him I said 'Hi.'" Will hung up, Tony turned to Frank.

"Your second-favorite son said 'Hi.'"

Yeah, you read that right. Frank The Chicken King was their dad. A very shitty dad too.

Tony set the rotary to its slowest (and most painful) setting, which meant Frank would probably roast for most of the evening. It was an industrial area so no-one would hear the screams.

When it was over, Tony texted Will: "It's done. He didn't say 'Hi' back."

Rather than bury Frank's crisped body next to the "Nanna" guy and his family, Will instructed Tony to dump it on the side of an inner-city street. It was the best way of making a clear and unequivocal statement to the world: "Fuck with Gold Gourmet Nuggets and this is what you get, even if you're family." It worked. All the newspapers ran stories, and there were no serious competitors after that.

Two days after they'd hit the deer, Will arranged to meet Tony at the bridge. He texted that it was "an urgent, personal matter."

Tony arrived on time, got off his motorbike, and flipped the visor on his helmet.

"What's so urgent?"

"I need you to kill some children," Will said.

"How many?"

"Seven," Will replied, "But there's a ten-month old so it's really only six-and-a-bit." *Yes, seven.* That was how many had grown between the three couples. *Shocking, right?*

Tony shifted his weight, uncomfortable. He never shifted his weight, and he was rarely uncomfortable (only near buffets). After a tense breath, he explained:

"Trudy would bust my balls if I did it. She won't let me kill kids or European polecats." Don't Google it, it's a type of ferret: vicious, grotesque, and disturbingly antisocial. No-one likes them. If all the animals in the jungle had a WhatsApp group, they wouldn't include the polecats. Even the World Association for Endangered Animals wanted them wiped off the face of the earth. They once had extra money in their budget so they ran a campaign featuring the polecat, with the tagline: "Endanger The Thing. Please."

Despite the overwhelming loathing of their existence, Trudy was very protective of the angry little fuckers. Perhaps it was her troubled upbringing or "that time she got lost in the forest." The reason didn't matter—whatever Trudy demanded, Tony obeyed. She took very unusual steps to keep him in line: when he forgot to buy milk once (OK, maybe twice), she had "GET MILK" tattooed on the back of his right hand so he'd never forget again. He never did; in fact, they started to throw out a shitload of milk because Tony would see the tattoo when he was drunk and buy some just in case. He once got drunk on tequila with a weapons supplier named Wayne Milk. It didn't end well.

In recent years, Trudy had forced him to add another tattoo ("+FLOWERS") to his left hand. At the same time, she got "NOT HERE, FUCK OFF" above her own buttocks.

Despite Trudy's "no kids/polecats rule," Will tried desperately to convince Tony to take the job. He said the deaths of these particular children would help Rose "get her smile back." It wasn't enough. And it was the first time Tony had ever said no to him. But he didn't leave Will hanging: he said he knew a guy who might be able to help. New to the area, deeply psychotic, and willing to kill anything with a pulse, Tony said.

"They call him 'The Mincer.'" Will was giddy with excitement, but he worked hard not to show it. Tony got back on his bike and spoke through his darkened visor: "I'll reach out and get him to call you." But Will couldn't hear a word. Tony flipped up the visor, irritated, decided to edit what he'd just said into something much more ominous and cool.

"Expect a call."

CHAPTER 9 __THE CALL__

The call hadn't come by the fall. Or winter.

Will had given Tony a number from one of his "exclusive" burner phones so he'd know—if and when it rang—it would be "The Mincer" calling. He kept it with him at all times, checked it constantly. He'd often ask Rose to call the number to make sure it was working—it would ring, he'd get excited, then remember it was Rose. This happened every other day.

When pressed, Tony assured Will he had passed his message on. "But he's not a normal person," Tony added. "He's extraordinarily unstable and may get sadistic satisfaction out of not returning your call for some time."

Will and Rose slipped back into a deep depression, even deeper than their "pre-deer" phase. They exhausted their supply of Bette Midler movies, rewatching them so many times they could quote lines (and imitate screams) from them, which they sometimes did in food courts (*yeah, they were so depressed they were going to food courts*).

Before long, they had lost all purpose. Their will to live weakened. They considered taking a Masterclass on "Killing Minors" (there was one, according to Tony) but Rose resisted. She said, "I'll leave the trash on the curb, but I'm not putting it in the truck." This confused Will, so he asked what she meant.

"It means I'll batter the fish but I'm not frying it," she replied. *Nup, still confused.* "I'll pay for someone to kill the fucking children but I'm not doing it myself!" she yelled, loud enough for everyone in the food court to hear. OK, he understood. And agreed. They waited until the spring, clinging to hope.

The burner phone rang on the Friday before Memorial Day. Will leapt out of the pool, almost flattened Ralph to get to it. His greeting was breathless and desperate, but still professional: "Will Calhoun speaking." Nearby, Rose had run from the shower. She dripped on the tiles, waiting, listening as Will listened. It was a fucking robocall. Asking Will's opinion about fucking robocalls.

"How the fuck did you get this number?" Will asked, expecting the robot to reply. *Strangely, it did.*

"I'm a robot, I call a million random phone numbers a day. Why the fuck would I skip yours, shit-for-brains?"

The conversation went back and forth for several minutes, Will threatened the robot's life, the robot said his sister was a drone and could drop shit all over his car if he asked her. He also said she could torment his "pissy little dog" by flying over it with a bag of thigh bones. Will hung up: *how did the robot know he had a dog?* He stayed awake most of the night thinking about this, which was good because it distracted him from obsessing about the call they were waiting for.

The following day was significant for a number of reasons. Firstly, a drone dropped human excrement all over Will's car. Secondly, and most importantly, the "psychic" arrived to deliver another package from Amazon: Will had ordered a "torture animation" DVD (Bertie's idea). Before she left, Rose asked her for a quick "reading." She paused, tucked the cash in her bra, and looked off like a higher power was whispering in her ear (it was actually her supervisor, telling her to get to the next fucking job).

"That Mincer guy's never going to call," she told Rose, hands on hips, matter-of-fact. "And you'll never have another dinner party again." Rose broke down after she left, Will stuck his head in ice-cold water, something he'd seen boxers do after losing the fight of their lives. And they had just lost that fight.

They packed the car the next day (after Bertie had cleaned off all the shit) and drove to the brown stump. You probably remember what followed. *If not, stop checking your smartphone, go back, and pay-the-fuck attention.*

◆   ◆   ◆

An obese pigeon landed near Will's shoe as he listened to The Mincer's words. The rooftop was a significant part of the pigeon's territory (he had three rooftops and a third of the east boardwalk) and he wasn't pleased. Having Will and Rose on the ledge was the equivalent of two random hedgehogs turning up to your house and standing on the balcony for an hour (and then yapping on a smartphone in hedgehog language, which is apparently quite aggressive).

Nevertheless, the pigeon ("Pablo") couldn't care less: he pecked Will's shoe a few times (pigeon code for "you're a cunt, fuck off soon"), then focused all his attention below, where Ralph was being placed on a tiny gurney. He'd broken both legs, which was either the result of hitting the aluminum awning or landing in the arms of the white-rage-filled bellboy.

The bellboy, Tyrus, later tweeted an apology, saying his privilege had enabled him to go to the gym, which had inevitably strengthened his forearms to an unconsciously-deadly level. The hotel fired him and he eventually became homeless, spending most of his days in the alleyway across from the hotel, where he would drink cask wine, doodle chalk drawings of Ralph on the sidewalk, and curse the awning that had put him there.

"The Mincer" had a weird lisp and he tended to ramble, but Will didn't care. He was just happy he'd finally called. Rose looked on, trying to listen in, but the traffic noise from below, and the shrill Animal Ambulance siren, were irritatingly loud.

Finally, she heard Will ask:

"So, you'll do it?"

She didn't need to hear The Mincer's answer: it was clear from Will's face, and his lame fist-pump, that he'd said "fuck yes." Will listened as The Mincer gave instructions, then they got down from the ledge, dusted themselves off, and took the lift to the underground carpark. Pablo (the pigeon) did a "fuck-off" dance after they were gone, then left to see if there were any other fuckwits on his two other rooftops.

On the way home, Will and Rose held hands, which rarely happened. They seemed reasonably happy to be alive again. Will even swerved to miss a deer. *They were better people already.*

◆   ◆   ◆

The Piña Colada Bar was not a bar Will would normally frequent. In fact, he wouldn't be caught dead there in an apocalyptic hail storm (or even in light rain).

It was on the outskirts of the inner-city, the kind of place where valets would take your keys, go rob your house, and get back before your second round of drinks had been served.

It was founded by the bastard grandson of Roberto Cofresi, the Puerto Rican pirate who invented the "Piña Colada" in the 1800s. In addition to creating the famous rum-pineapple-and-coconut cocktail, Cofresi also popularized the "eyepatch look," even though he had two perfectly-functioning eyes (he just thought it looked "cool").

In the early days of The Piña Colada Bar, guests were required to wear eyepatches at all times and could only remove them while eating or drinking. Often there were violent fights when careless people let their eyepatches slip below their eyebrows. In the nineties, a Senator from Arkansas who refused to wear one was attacked by a mob of middle-aged women in track pants. He lost the vision in one eye.

The bar became popular with lacrosse mascots in the early 2000s: there was a costume factory nearby so all the mascots (mostly deranged and insecure people) would come there after a "fitting," often wearing their outfits. It got ugly one time between a huge pink donkey with a pick-axe and a cassowary with a bow-and-arrow. Witnesses said the cassowary refused to wear two eyepatches, which had become the "new normal."

◆   ◆   ◆

Will had been so excited to hear from The Mincer that he had allowed him to dictate the specifics of their meeting: "The Piña Colada Bar, 7pm Thursday, come alone."

When he approached the location in his car, he noticed the neighborhood was gradually deteriorating with each passing block. "Fuck me," he said aloud, which prompted his voice-activated assistant to play Sting.

He shut the music off and pressed on, then texted Rose: "If I don't make it home alive, finish the book." He wasn't writing a book, he just liked to fuck with her. He quietly chuckled at the idea of her leaving his wake early to go search for an imaginary book he'd never even started. She'd probably be going through his shit for days, wondering what secrets he'd revealed about her.

Will arrived early at the bar. The valet took his keys, asked where he lived (which he thought was odd), then gave him a double eyepatch to wear inside. He did exactly what The Mincer had instructed him to do: order a large Piña Colada, remove the cocktail umbrella, and sit on the south-west corner of the bar. He waited.

They played that hideous "Piña Colada Song" on a loop, probably for all the adulterous men who'd come there to cheat on their wives, only to discover their wives were cheating on them too. *How sweet!* They occasionally interrupted the loop to play the grunge/electronica sequel to that song, which picked up when the married couple got home, realized they were both intending to fuck other people and engaged in a violent knife-fight that caused both their deaths. It was actually a pretty uplifting song because all their friends ended up drinking Piña Coladas at their double-wake, which was held outside, at midnight, in the rain.

Will had just ordered a second round of drinks when Bertie called. He said some weird guy in a valet's uniform had entered the house with a key and walked out with the TV. Will shrugged, thought Bertie was probably high and/or hallucinating, and asked him to put Rose on the phone.

She'd gone out, Bertie said, something about "Ralph waking up from surgery." *Fuck, the little shit-machine had actually survived.*

CHAPTER 10 **THE MINCER**

The Mincer arrived about ten minutes after the hour. He stood behind Will at first, darkened by shadow, and began the scripted conversation they'd agreed to have: "That's a big Piña Colada you have there," he said. *Worst acting ever.*

Will half-turned to reply—but The Mincer raised his palm and spoke in a whisper: "Don't turn, just say the line." Will shifted in his seat, and delivered the line as required:

"It's got extra Piña. Like in the movie." *The movie? What movie?* Nearby, the barman, a bald, tattooed guy who'd overheard his fair share of moronic conversations, put this one in his top five. He looked over like they were fucking idiots, set aside two unpolished glasses for their next round.

With that, The Mincer dropped the stupid roleplay and squeezed into the stool next to Will. His appearance did not match his voice: he was a short, bearded guy with big round eyes and a manbun-gone-wrong. He was wearing overalls and galoshes, mud-stained.

"Sorry I'm late," he quipped, "I had a job in The Glades. It got real messy."

The Glades? They weren't anywhere near Florida. Will thought about asking, decided not to. The Mincer offered his knuckles for a fist bump, Will obliged, they kinda missed. It was awkward all around.

"Anyway, you can call me Zack from now on," he said, repositioning himself on the stool cushion. "That's what my friends and clients call me. The Mincer is really just for dying victims and people in the service industry." He glanced briefly towards the barman, who was still listening. "The Piña Colada Song" started a new rotation.

Zack heard it, delighted. "Oh, I love this song," he said. "What a coincidence that it's playing here?"

He was actually serious. Will couldn't let it pass.

"They play it on a loop," he said.

"Really? Once is a coincidence, on a loop is fucking cosmic." Will sighed, discreetly checked his watch. Maybe this was a really bad idea, he thought. A valet interrupted, double-checking Zack's home address: "was it 1210 or 1211?" It was 1210. He left.

Zack grabbed the drinks menu, which was unusually sticky, shaped like a cocktail glass, and featured eighteen different versions of Piña Coladas (regular, light, extra light, strong, without piña, extra piña, toxic piña, and fuck-you piña, which had an asterisk that denoted "may kill you"). He ran his eyes over the choices, chuckled as he quietly mouthed "fuck-you piña," then made an odd clicking sound with his tongue, which he did whenever he was grappling with a decision (or suffering reflux).

It was a habit that had irritated every single person he'd ever met in his life, including the midwife who delivered him. Her first words to his mother were: "He's going to be really fucking annoying, I can switch him if you want." Zack's mother was still high on morphine (it was a caesarean birth and she got breast implants done at the same time—her husband's idea).

She sat up, replied: "Sure, who are you again?" Unfortunately, the midwife was not very bright and she switched Zack with conjoined Samoan twins. The babies were switched back the next day, everyone laughed and called it a "funny mix-up" (except the Samoan father, who was later acquitted of "involuntary manslaughter").

Zack's mother never mentioned the attempted switch to him, but whenever she got really drunk (all the "T" days), she'd say: "If only that stupid cunt midwife hadn't switched you with a Samoan, I'd be much better off right now!" Zack never understood what she was talking about, but presumed she was confusing him with his half-brother Hal, who was actually half-Samoan (yeah, his mom ended up fucking the Samoan father after his trial—he was single by then).

Zack's tongue-click proved to be a burden in most day-to-day situations of his life: he was bullied in the church confessional, laughed at during funerals, and shooshed in adult cinemas (by people exchanging hand jobs in adjacent seats). A staff member at Best Buy was so annoyed by the sound that she stopped serving him (he was buying a blow-dryer), quit her job, and drove her moped into oncoming traffic. Her digital suicide note mentioned her terminal cancer, the mother she hated, and "that fucking clicking sound this tosser customer made today at work."

Will noticed the sound but he didn't let it bother him: he had more important issues to deal with and he knew Rose would be pissed if he didn't get these kills to happen.

Zack finally made his decision and nudged the menu aside. "Right, let me get one of these toxic piñas and we can talk about killing these fucking kids!" His voice traveled. A businessman, wet from the rain and waiting for his cheating wife, looked over. Zack summoned the barman with a weird hand gesture: *it wasn't appreciated.*

They moved to a booth with cardboard palm trees to discuss the finer details. Zack dug scrunched-up notes from his grubby pocket, spilling lint creatures who'd committed suicide (probably because of the clicking). He found the paper he was looking for, straightened it out on the table, and struggled to read his own handwriting.

"Right, here we go," he said. "Tony told me you want 'six-and-a-bit' children killed. Is there an amputee?"

"No, it's a baby. Ten months' old," Will replied.

Zack paused, surprised. It wasn't a pause that Will enjoyed. Did he have problem with assassinating an infant? Was Tony mistaken when he said this guy would kill anything with a pulse? Were they going to have to start over and find someone else? *Fuck, why so many questions?* Will feared the worst, finished his drink.

Finally, Zack spoke: "Oh, right. I was kinda hoping it was an amputee. I haven't done one of those. But a ten-month-old works too." *Phew.* They ordered more drinks.

Before they got too hammered, Will pulled out a dossier that he and Rose had been preparing for a week: it was a glossy, spiral-bound document with photos of the victims, addresses, maps, possible kill locations, and lots of clip art of deadly weapons. They even listed preferred "ways of killing." For example, Rose really wanted The Twins to die in the most painful way possible, maybe with "a garotte." So, there were several Google images of various "garottes," as well as detailed drawings of red-headed twins being strangled with them (Rose was very good at drawing).

The document was titled "The Kill Dossier" (Will suggested "Death Dossier" but Rose hated alliteration absolutely) and it was printed in color on special, off-white paper from The Netherlands. The guy at Kinko's thumbed through it as he made three copies (one each for Will and Rose, one for Zack), quietly chuckling to himself through teeth he hadn't brushed. He thought it was a screenplay Will had written, because that was ninety percent of his copying work (they were located next to a Starbucks). When he handed over the copies, the Kinko's guy said, "Good luck getting that shit made, the formatting's all over the place." If he'd had time (and it wouldn't have ruined the spiral binding), Will would have added an extra page with the guy's smug little headshot, the address of the Kinko's store and two suggested ways of killing: "drown in toner," or "impale on spiral binding machine."

Zack's expression hardened when Will put "The Kill Dossier" on the table in front of him. "Rose and I thought this might help," Will said, nudging it a little. Zack pretended he couldn't see it, slid it back to Will like it was coated in baby scorpions.

"Not yet," he said. "We'll do all that later."

Oh, right. Will was new to this: he blushed a little, took the document back like an overeager waiter who had presented the check before the main course. "Sorry," he said. "I wasn't sure how all this worked."

"It's OK, relax," Zack replied. "Tonight's just a meet-and-greet for everyone." Will relaxed momentarily, then replayed Zack's words in his head. *Everyone?*

"Is someone else coming?" he asked. Before he could respond, a wiry, shaggy-haired creature disguised as a homeless man arrived. This was Gareth. He hovered at Will's shoulder, cleared his throat, delivered the line he'd been practicing in the Uber:

"That's a big Piña Colada you have there," he said, eyes drifting to Will. An untrained monkey with dyslexia could have acted better. Will turned, Zack eyeballed him.

"I've already done the line, Gareth. We've done the whole scene. I'm sitting right here," he said. Gareth realized, squinted at Zack like he didn't recognize him.

"Oh, sorry. I didn't recognize you. Did you get a perm?"

Zack sighed, annoyed he'd mentioned it. It was the worst perm he'd ever had (he got it in Florida and the hairdresser had "forgotten her glasses"), which was why he'd tried to disguise it in a manbun. "No," Zack replied, "And you're late." He made room for Gareth on his side of the booth. "Sit down, the meeting's already started."

Gareth sat, Zack did the introductions: "Will, Gareth. Gareth, Will." They fist-bumped, even more awkwardly than the earlier one. Gareth's knuckles were greasier than his hair and he had bits of rice in his anemic goatee.

Will looked him over, disturbed and confused in equal measure. "Tony didn't mention anything about a partner," he said.

Zack chuckled heartily. "We're not partners," he replied.

"We're not?" Gareth seemed genuinely surprised.

"No. You're the intern, remember?"

"I was the intern last semester. I thought I was a full partner now?"

"Do you know any functioning business where someone goes from intern to full partner in one semester?" Gareth tried to think of an example. "Some internships last for five years."

"Five years?!"

Zack exhaled, made a face at Will. "Kids these days, they want everything right now."

Will was still confused. "He's an intern?"

Gareth and Zack replied at the same time: "No/Yes." Zack turned to Gareth, said "shut the fuck up" with his eyes. Gareth quietened, sulked.

"Yes, he's the intern," Zack reiterated, immediately noticing Will's concern. "But don't worry, he doesn't do any of the actual killing. That's not allowed."

Gareth interrupted, with attitude: "They don't give extra credit for killing anyway."

"You get credit from the university?" Will asked him, incredulous.

"It's a community college," Gareth replied. "And, yes, I get credit for two courses: Small Business Strategies and Farm Management."

"Farm Management?"

"We did a job with a horse once," Gareth said, dismissive, picking up the drinks menu.

Will looked at Zack, hoping for clarification. "You kill animals too?" he asked.

"Not usually, no," Zack replied. "The kill target was riding a horse at the time. And I got distracted."

"He missed," Gareth added. "Point blank range."

"Because you were yapping on about your femoral artery."

"Which was punctured."

"Yeah, sure it was." Zack widened his eyes at Will, suddenly distracted by his own ringing phone. The interruption was a relief for everyone, including the barman and the Businessman Waiting For His Cheating Wife, who'd both been listening the entire time and were exhausted.

Zack checked the caller I.D, answered through gritted teeth: "What is it, Mom?"

A shrill, indistinct voice spilled. It was like the sound of glass being crushed on top of a dying raccoon. Will waited, becoming impatient and thinking about what he was going to tell Rose about these fucking morons. Gareth gestured to the barman to come serve him: he was ignored.

"No, Mom," Zack continued, lowering his voice. "You're seeing things again. Did you take your medication?" The call went back and forth for several minutes. Zack kept telling her to take her pills and eventually hung up with a very quiet, "No, I'm with people and I'm not saying it. No! I'm never fucking saying it again! Bye". He sighed. "Fuck me, that woman."

Will sighed too, ready to get back to business—but Zack felt the need to explain the call they'd all just sat through. "The woman's got low-level dementia," he said, referring to his phone like it was his actual mother. "She thinks there's a guy in a valet's uniform stealing shit from our house."

"You still live with your mom?" Will asked, not even registering the bit about the valet stealing shit.

"I'm in between houses," Zack quipped. *He wasn't.* Gareth knew this, and grinned.

The "meet-and-greet" ended soon after that. Gareth used a fake I.D. to try to order a "fuck-you piña," the barman phoned the police, and they all went their separate ways very quickly (after leaving a pretty woeful tip).

Once they'd gone, the businessman's cheating wife arrived, realized he had been planning to cheat on her, and stabbed him in his femoral artery with a salad fork. Luckily, the police were already there (looking for Gareth) and she was put in handcuffs while he bled out (a double eyepatch is not an effective tourniquet) and the "Piña Colada Song" kept playing on its loop. The barman polished glasses the whole time and thought about his cat, "Nemesis," who had been developing an unusual relationship with a marmot. After hearing Zack talk about shooting the horse, he decided he was going to do the same thing to the marmot when his shift finished.

Will had a lot on his mind as he drove home. He thought it was weird the valet was wearing his "Weekend Rolex," but he didn't dwell on it: it was a thirty-five minute trip and he had to come up with something positive to tell Rose. She'd be livid if she knew they were about to put their trust in two extraordinarily incompetent people.

CHAPTER 11 **THE PLAN BEGINS**

Rose called Will as he exited the highway.

She asked how the meeting had gone. "It was great," he said. "They're both highly unstable." She took that as a positive. Will's car weaved through mist.

"They?" she asked.

"There are two of them," he replied. "They're partners."

"Gay assassins, really? Fucking diversity."

"No," he reassured her. "Business partners, not life partners."

"Oh, thank fuck. And they're OK about killing a ten-month-old baby?"

"They can't wait."

Rose smiled, delighted. She was about to ask about the dossier (and whether they liked her drawings and the "garotte" idea) when the shrill alarm of a heart monitor interrupted.

Behind her, a Native American veterinarian and his transgender nurse (who had been listening to the entire conversation, including the "fucking diversity" bit) were performing C.P.R. on Ralph. It wasn't going well. Will heard the commotion.

"Where are you and what's going on?" he asked. She turned: a second nurse, who identified as "Himalayan" but was clearly white and had never been up a mountain ever, arrived with a miniature crash cart designed specifically for small-to-medium dogs.

"I'm at the animal hospital with Ralph," she said. "He woke up from the first surgery but there were complications after the second, when they tried to attach the little wheels to his back half."

Will hated those little wheels: he knew they'd leave trail marks all over the carpet and would make a really annoying screeching sound whenever Ralph entered or left the room. His aunt Methyl, who had died alone on the toilet, had a Pomeranian Shih Tzu "with wheels." At her funeral, which the dog was banned from attending (the funeral home had just re-carpeted), her ex-husband blamed the wheels for the disintegration of their marriage and his decision "to fuck his bowling partner's wife on multiple occasions" (the actual quote from his eulogy).

"They should forget the wheels," Will said, heart monitor increasing in intensity (which was bad for Ralph, but promising for Will). "It'll better for everybody if he just drags his body around on the floor—it'll probably save time for Bertie when he's vacuuming."

"It's too late," Rose replied. "They've already fused the axle to his spine. He's like Robocop now." The veterinarian charged the defibrillator pads and placed them on Ralph's tiny chest. "Clear!" he shouted.

Will asked Rose what was happening.

"They're trying to resuscitate him, I should go," she said, about to hang up.

"Tell them not to resuscitate!" Will shouted down the phone. "D.N.R!" But she was gone.

Soon after Will got home and realized the TV was missing (and his Rolex), Rose called again with an update. The news was bleak: Ralph had pulled through and the wheels were functioning (and already making "a really-fucking-annoying-screeching-sound" even while he was unconscious). She said "Dr. Apache" (his real name was Dr. Rogers, as printed on his badge) called the dog's survival from the fall "a miracle" and his recovery from two surgeries "a second miracle."

Will sat on the balcony while he waited for Bertie to make him a Piña Colada (he had suddenly developed a craving for them). He looked off, pensive, quietly reflecting on the night's events. "Fucker used up two miracles," he thought to himself.

◆   ◆   ◆

Over breakfast the next morning, Will gave Rose more details about the meet-and-greet with Zack and Gareth. She was pissed they hadn't looked at the dossier.

"Do you know how long it took me to draw those creepy little twins?" she said.

"They're going to look at it next time," Will reassured her. "Last night was just about getting to know each other. Childhood anecdotes, teenage struggles, hopes and fears."

Rose rested her knife and fork, perplexed.

"Hopes and fears? Getting to know each other? Doesn't this whole 'hiring-a-hitman thing' work better if no-one knows anything about anyone? You know, like 'anonymity'?" Will thought about it. Bertie arrived with fresh coffee.

"Bertie," Will asked before he left. "Have you ever met an assassin that did a 'meet-and-greet' with his client before the hit?"

Bertie didn't need long to think about it.

"No, never," he replied. "Most assassins use fake names and never show their faces." He left, and Rose gave Will a look that complemented her words:

"See?"

Will sighed, sipped his latte. "Well, this isn't a normal hit." They both sat quietly for a moment. Rose wondered what "hopes and fears" he'd shared with the assassins, Will thought about printing a Piña Colada recipe for Bertie (the one he'd made the night before was ghastly).

"Anyway, what's the next step? A Zoom call to discuss pet names and hobbies?" Rose asked.

Will chose to ignore the sarcasm. "Another meeting to discuss the details, maybe look at the dossier. Zack said you can come this time."

She feigned excitement. "Oh wow, he said I can come!? Where's the meeting?"

"A tapas bar in the city. He said they do great tapas and you don't have to wear eyepatches." *Eyepatches?* She didn't need to ask.

"Great idea. Let's all meet up and get captured having tapas on the two-thousand CCTV cameras in the city." She eyeballed him, realized his stupidity still surprised her. "Tell him we'll meet in a secret location."

"With tapas?"

"Not unless they serve tapas in the woods or in a dark underground carpark."

Will paused, wondered if there were any tapas places in underground carparks. Probably not, he decided. He dug out one of his burner phones, punched keys.

"OK, I'll text him," he said, speaking as he typed the words: "Hi. It's Will. Your client. From last night. You know, the guy with the irrational fear of walk-in robes."

Rose looked at him, incredulous. He continued: "Rose said she'd prefer to meet somewhere dark, possibly underground. Don't worry if there are no tapas." He hit send. Rose shoveled scrambled eggs into her mouth, chewed slowly, imagined this ending soon. A message chimed on Will's phone. He read it aloud:

"Hey Will, I remember you. I know just the place. No tapas but it's dark and underground. Maybe you could bring a plate? I'll send co-ordinates."

"A plate?" Rose asked through a mouthful.

"We should get Bertie to do those pigs-in-blankets." He turned and called through the doorway. "Bertie!"

"We're not taking a fucking plate." She looked at his phone. "Tell him 'no plate.' And ask him how long this whole job is going to take. I'm already exhausted."

Will obliged, and typed, "Hey Zack, it's Will again."

"OK, just type it without reading it aloud."

He closed his mouth, exaggerated, typed a little—then started silently mouthing the rest. He hit send, Zack replied almost immediately.

"He said it'll take two weeks." Rose's mood shifted immediately (in a positive way). *All seven? In just two weeks?*

"Are you fucking kidding?" she asked, then rephrased: "Is he fucking kidding?" Will started typing that. "Don't type that."

"I don't think he's kidding," Will said. "He's not very funny. And there are two of them so I guess they can get it done faster."

"If they get it done in two weeks, we could have a dinner party on the nineteenth," Rose said, buzzing. Her Filofax was open on the table before Will could say "pass Bertie's crack pipe." She turned pages, suddenly busy. It was a magnificently-organized Filofax: color-coded tabs, perfectly-arranged post-it notes, underlining, highlighting, and circling that was both clear and consistent.

A guy in a stationary store once saw it (she'd opened it briefly to check how many highlighters she needed) and he introduced himself: he was a sales rep for the company that made the Filofax and he wanted to take photos of her work to use in advertisements. She was flattered, he was quite hot, so she let him take a few snaps of some of her "best pages."

It was only when she got back to her car that she realized what he'd photographed: the week of the sixteenth, which is when they'd hit the deer and come up with the plan to kill the children. See, it wasn't just a "planning" diary—Rose would also tick and circle items once they'd been achieved, and add notes and thoughts afterwards ("fuck that," "crushed that shit," "never again"). It was a record of everything—and the hot sales rep now had pages with lots of incriminating shit that would certainly not be suitable on a billboard: post-it notes with "KILL THE CHILDREN?" and "FUCK YES!," a to-do list featuring "ASK BERTIE ABOUT ASSASSINS," "BUY BATTERIES FOR VIBRATOR," "THINK OF WAYS OF KILLING," and "DOWN-LOAD GAROTTE PHOTOS."

Mildly panicked, Rose went back into the store to find the rep—but he'd gone. She figured he'd probably have travelled to the nearest place that sold Filofaxes, so that's where she headed. Sure enough, he was there, asking another attractive married woman to take photos of her Filofax. *Ah, she thought.* This fucker's got a modus operandi and it's got nothing to do with advertising. She waited until he left the store, followed him to his car and approached the window before he had time to key the ignition. He smiled when he saw her, thought she wanted to give him a hand job and let her in the passenger seat.

He almost pissed himself when she said she was going to accuse him of "forced anal rape" if he didn't give his phone to her. He handed it over, she deleted her incriminating pages, then found a whole trove of explicit torture porn—yep, he'd been stalking and raping all the women whose Filofaxes he'd photographed. She forwarded them anonymously to Filofax headquarters, got a lifetime supply of Filofaxes (sent to an anonymous P.O. box), and "The Filofax Rapist" was arrested two weeks later. He got life without parole and was later quoted as saying he "rued the day he met the woman with perfect underlining."

"The Woman With Perfect Underlining Project" was formed soon after and became a significant lobbying group for women's rights, eventually petitioning Congress to "ban men from stationery stores everywhere." As a result, thanks largely to Rose, a man now has to get a woman to go buy staples for him.

"The nineteenth might be a bit soon for a dinner party," Will said. He didn't want to burst Rose's bubble but he knew her timeline was a little ambitious. "They'll need time to grieve. The last thing we want is a table full of people moaning about their deceased children." It was the most sensible thing he'd said all morning. She quietly agreed and flicked a page to the week after.

"The twenty-sixth then?" she asked. Will shrugged, which meant "I guess so." She blocked out the date, already thinking about appetizers.

They now had a firm deadline.

CHAPTER 12 ROSE AND THE NUNS

Will received the address co-ordinates for the meeting by text message the next day.

He also received a map to the location in the mail, folded neatly inside a nondescript envelope addressed to "Mr. Will." The letter inside was constructed out of magazine cut-outs, kinda like a ransom demand—only less professional.

It read: "137 SyCAmoRE DrIvE, WeSt BucKTon." For some reason, Zack also decided to include his business card ("ASSAS-SIN-AT-LARGE, INC.") and a handwritten note ("Can't wait to start killing those fucking kids! See you guys soon, Zack (& Gareth)"), all of which defeated the purpose of all the anonymity (and the multiple burner phones they'd been using).

Will went looking for Rose to tell her he'd received the meeting co-ordinates. On his way upstairs, he stopped dead in his tracks, distracted by a mess of muddy, overlapping circles on the living room carpet. *Ralph!* The little fucker had returned from the animal hospital the day before and he'd already made his presence felt (even though the veterinarian said he'd probably "lie low" for a few weeks. *Yeah, right*). Rose entered to find Will on his knees, studying the damage at close range.

"What are you doing?" she asked.

"I told you those wheels were going to ruin our lives," Will said. The mud had already settled in. "What part of 'Do Not Resuscitate' is hard to understand?"

Rose sighed, didn't seemed to care. The door swung open a crack and Ralph hurried in—yeah, he was now hurrying on those fucking wheels, like one of those piss-angry old people who suddenly get a motorized wheelchair and think all pedestrian traffic must part for them. Ralph's wheels got caught in the closing door, which served him right. Will didn't help, neither did Rose.

"I'm sure Bertie can get the stains out," Rose said, standing over Will.

"How did he make all these circles?" There were at least ten. She looked at them, trying to work it out. Ralph continued to struggle at the door, wheels spinning.

"He must have been chasing his tail," she suggested.

"I thought his back half was paralyzed. How does he even know he has a tail?"

Rose sighed, made a face that said "Do I Have To Explain This Again?"

Will looked up at her, replied with a face that said "Please Fucking Do."

She shifted her weight, hands on hips. "The psychologist said he might get phantom pain, remember?" she said. Will didn't remember.

"When did we hire a psychologist?"

"She's part of his Wellness Team," she replied, with an actual straight face.

"He has a Wellness Team?" Will stood up, exasperated.

Rose glanced at the letter he was holding. "Anyway, what's that and why were you calling for me?" she asked, eager to shift topic.

"It's the co-ordinates for the meeting," Will said. "With the assassins."

"They sent it by physical mail? What kind of morons are these people?" She reached for the letter but Will held it back, reluctant to let her see it.

"It's just a series of numbers," he said. "Did you ask Bertie about the pigs-in-blankets?"

She groaned and stormed off, stepped over Ralph on her way out. Her voice trailed: "We're not taking a plate." Ralph yipped, Will looked at him.

"If you'd just died like everyone else who falls twenty stories from a rooftop, you wouldn't be in that position." Will went to his office to Google "removing mud stains" and "how to fire a wellness team." No-one came to free Ralph until just before dinner that night (Bertie did it, but only because he needed to get the drinks cart through).

There was a reason Will didn't want Rose to see the letter from Zack. Yes, the punctuation and general formatting would've horrified her, but it was the "magazine cut-out letters" that concerned him. Rose would likely be traumatized if she saw them; at the very least, she'd probably toss and turn all night, pulling at the silk sheets and completely ruining Will's sleep.

Growing up in the convent, Rose was sheltered from much of the outside world and all its crudeness. But a time came—just before her thirteenth birthday, in fact—when it was necessary for her to understand more about the workings of nature and, specifically, her own body. Mother Superior, who watched a lot of fetish porn before she took her vows, realized someone needed to give her "the talk."

She invited Mother Inferior to discuss the matter over tea and a cheesecake shaped like a vagina (which was just a coincidence, even though the convent's sous chef was a registered sex offender). Mother Inferior was not her real title, it was just a nickname everyone used because she had "very small tits," which all the nuns laughed at when they went on their annual cruise to The Bahamas (the convent was loaded).

"Someone needs to give Rose 'the talk,'" Mother Superior said between mouthfuls of vagina-cake. "Otherwise we're gonna have a 'Carrie' moment in the showers." Mother Inferior had never seen the movie "Carrie," so Mother Superior quickly acted out the scene she was referring to, although her acting was very poor and Mother Inferior still didn't get it. Eventually, Mother Superior gave up, put her habit back on, and downloaded an illegal copy for her to watch later. "Forget the 'Carrie' reference," she said, losing patience. "Have you seen 'Deep Throat?'" Thankfully, she had—all the nuns had watched it during one of their Friday movie nights (it was a double-bill with "The Sound of Music")—so they were finally on the same page. *Fuck!*

By the time they'd finished the cake, Mother Inferior had agreed to find someone to give "the talk" to Rose. She went to the usual sluts but no-one wanted to do it. One of the newbies, Sister Celeste, told her there was a company that kidnapped children, gave them "the talk," then returned them to their parents a few days later. It was the perfect solution.

Mother Inferior called them up and chose a plan ("regular talk," "intense talk with live, third-party demonstration," or "life-changing talk where you also find out you were adopted"). She picked the regular one and organized for Rose (her "daughter") to be "collected" the following day.

Mother Inferior and Sister Celeste left Rose at the agreed collection point (a street corner), told her an Uber was coming to take her to a Justin Bieber concert, then went back to the convent and smoked weed while they watched from one of the bell-towers. Sure enough, a white van arrived and whisked her away. It was all very dramatic—the "kidnappers" even wore balaclavas and covered her in a hessian sack to make it all seem real.

Mother Inferior and Sister Celeste did massive high-fives, got smashed on sacramental vodka and waited for Rose to be returned home.

The ransom note arrived early the next day. Letters cut from magazines formed the words "wE hAve THe LittLE biatch. PaY $50 GrAnD oR shE DyEs." Mother Inferior shared it with Sister Celeste at breakfast: they had a good laugh, then agreed the company took its job very seriously (and would definitely recommend it to others, despite the poor spelling). "I bet she's learning a shitload about female genitalia," Sister Celeste said, her voice traveling a little too far.

A human finger arrived the next day. It was the tip of a pinky, wrapped in plastic and accompanied by another note: "MooRe tO cOmE IF yU doNt PaY." Mother Inferior chuckled at first, thinking the severed finger was plastic, but then got pissed when drops of blood spilled on the white part of her habit, which was really fucking hard to clean. She called the company to tell them not to send any more packages containing fake blood, and also thought she'd check on Rose's progress. The manager was confused: he said they had arrived to collect Rose at the agreed location but she wasn't there. He'd sent an email to reschedule, but it had gone to Mother Inferior's spam folder (marked as "extreme phishing").

Rose was being held in a two-bedroom house by Rick and Samantha Walsh, a married couple from Connecticut who had met and fallen in love at high school. They desperately wanted to have children as soon as they were married but couldn't get pregnant: doctors said Samantha's eggs had "Tommy Lee Jones Syndrome," which made them extremely antisocial and disinterested, especially around other eggs and sperm. Frustrated and eager to have a child in their lives, they decided to adopt. They found a Yelp-recommended adoption agency on the internet that had lots of "Nigerian children" who needed loving parents with money. They signed up, paid the cash (in unmarked bills), passed all the selection interviews and, finally, waited at the dock for little "Chinara" to arrive.

But it was a scam: instead of a cute four-year-old girl, Chinara was actually an eighty-year-old white man from Nantucket who'd changed his name from "Theodore" and had just been on a cruise to the Virgin Islands. The agency denied culpability, said Theodore identified as a "cute little Nigerian girl" and threatened to call them racist and transphobic on Twitter for not wanting to take him home. Fearing condemnation from a handful of unemployed social justice warriors they were never likely to meet, they ditched the child seat they'd bought for their car and made room for Chinara/Theodore (and her five suitcases) in their lives.

For a while, they convinced themselves that she was indeed "cute and funny." She slept for most of the day, dribbled when she ate, and fell over a lot, which they filmed on their smartphones and posted to social media. She ran away on an Amtrak train when she was 82, stealing most of their savings and Samantha's vinyl collection. They were devastated. When they posted the news on social media, they were blamed for being "bad parents" and permanently suspended from Facebook.

They were on their way to the brown stump when they saw Rose, alone on a street corner. They stopped to ask her if she was lost: no, she told them, she was "waiting to be kidnapped." She explained that she lived in the convent with a bunch of nuns and they had arranged for her to be taken by strangers because they were too "piss-weak to explain how her pussy worked." Rose had hacked Mother Inferior's emails—the whole "we got you a ticket to see Justin Bieber" thing didn't sit right. She followed Bieber on TikTok and knew he was on a private island trying to overcome his childhood fear of being left alone on an island.

Horrified, and thinking they might be able to do a final good deed before their suicides, Rick and Samantha offered to take her to the police to make a report. But Rose had a better idea, and she could see the nuns smoking weed and watching her from the belltower. "Do you guys have balaclavas and a hessian sack in your van?" she asked. Surprisingly, they did. The plan was afoot.

The magazine cut-outs were Rose's idea, messy and deliberately misspelled to make the nuns think they were dealing with "unhinged people who had no regard for human life or the English language" (which one of the nuns had whispered during a Friday night screening of "Ransom"). They sent five letters in all, each one more threatening than the last. Samantha had a contact at the morgue, who provided the pinkie and a few extra body parts.

Realizing that Rose had actually been kidnapped "for real," Mother Inferior and Sister Celeste went to Mother Superior to explain what they'd done. She was pissed and wanted to tell them they were "stupid cunts," but she had just started a self-imposed vow of silence after calling the bishop a "cocksucker in velvet" (during Mass). So she took them to her chambers to express her thoughts on a whiteboard. She wrote: "Stupid cunts!" followed by "We don't negotiate with kidnappers."

Rose initially felt rejected and worthless when the nuns refused to pay her ransom, but her new life with Rick and Samantha showed promise. They played frisbee, cooked meals, and trapped small animals in cages for no reason. Finally, it seemed, Rose had found the parents she'd always dreamed of.

But Rick and Samantha were deeply unhappy. Rose really annoyed them and they still missed Chinara, even though she was now 85 and would often send them taunting naked photos of herself holding a different vinyl record each time: "The Nylon Curtain," "Pet Sounds," "Off The Wall." They weren't bothered by the nudity or her smug grin; they were just happy to see her wrinkly, pock-marked face again.

Desperate for Rose to leave, they wrote her a letter out of magazine cut-outs ("rOsE, pLeAsE LeEvE!) but she thought they were kidding around and wrote back ("I FuCKing LoVe U gUys. FrisBeE tOdAY?") Too weak to tell her directly, they eventually decided to have her "collected." It was the same guy who was supposed to kidnap her the first time, which may or may not have been ironic. The guy explained to her that Rick and Samantha thought she was "really annoying" and didn't want her "hanging around anymore." He dropped her back at the convent, where Mother Inferior pretended like nothing had happened, even though she'd been gone for six weeks.

"How was the Justin Bieber concert?" she asked.

Will decided to burn Zack's letter, just in case Rose stumbled across it. He put it in the fireplace—with the most recent batch of photos and family updates from their former friends—and set it alight.

Bertie entered from the kitchen as the flames thickened. He had an urgency about him that only ever happened when he misplaced illegal substances. "They're on their way back," he said.

Will turned, serious. "Oh, fuck."

CHAPTER 13 **THE STANTONS**

There's a minor detail that requires some clarification at this point.

It's about Will and Rose's house. You know, with the mezzanine and the perfect garden and the fountain out front that you could piss in. The thing is, it wasn't actually *their* house. Neither was the country manor. *Did we mention the country manor?* It was a fantastic manor (as far as manors go), and Will and Rose used it all the time for vacations, but it wasn't theirs either. Both properties belonged to The Stantons, two rich, pompous assholes who deserved to die.

Will and Rose had first seen the "mezzanine" house online and knew immediately it was the place they wanted to spend the rest of their lives. They went to the open house and visited four times after that, making love twice in the upstairs wardrobe (to check floorboards/acoustics).

The realtor liked them—they'd let him watch them make love both times—and he said the owner really liked them too (he'd watched the realtor's video of them making love). So, it seemed like everything was in place as auction day approached.

The realtor told Will and Rose what price they'd need to bid, assured them there were no other serious buyers and said he would reserve the perfect spot for them on the front lawn (next to the fountain). They organized two pre-approved loans, practiced bidding at their own "mock auction" in their apartment, and even bought new clothes for the occasion.

When auction day arrived, they left home early, hoping to double-check everything with the realtor and maybe sneak in an upstairs quickie before the bidding started (the realtor's idea). But the gates were locked and no-one was there. Rose noticed the "SOLD" sash first, pasted across the "FOR SALE" sign on the front gate. *Sold? Sold?!!!* Did they get the day of the auction wrong? Panicked, they called the realtor—but his phone went to voicemail.

As they drove home, he sent them a text message and confessed everything. He wasn't actually a realtor: he was an assistant to a scientist who grew human lips on pigs and was on his way home for lunch when he'd seen the open house. He was peckish (he'd been around pigs all day) and thought there might be snacks so he went inside and pretended to be a potential buyer, even though he had no intention of buying it (he lived with his parents and still had a huge student debt to pay).

When he passed the master bedroom and saw Will and Rose making love in the wardrobe, he thought he'd stay to watch while he finished his spring roll and mini-fig salad. Rose saw him standing there, he panicked and said he was the realtor, she replied: "OK, you can keep watching us fuck if you help us get the house."

After that, they sucked up to him like no-one had ever sucked up to him before, and even offered to let him watch them fuck again if he would put in a good word with the owner. So he kept up the ruse, broke into the house before they arrived for their "private visits" and googled common realtor terminology so he sounded like he knew what he was talking about. He made up a fake day for the auction, unaware the actual realtor, a sixty-year-old woman named Betty, was in final negotiations with The Stantons, a hideously-wealthy couple who were looking for a tenth home. The fake realtor apologized to Will and Rose, said he would destroy the video (he didn't, it went viral), and promised them a significant discount if they ever wanted lip transplants and/or pork trotters.

Will was devastated, Rose was pissed. Their world collapsed a little more that day.

◆   ◆   ◆

Despite their enormous wealth and penchant for purchasing multiple homes, Arthur and Gertrude Stanton were extraordinarily frugal people.

They never tipped waiters more than five percent, waited for change from taxi drivers (even when it was a nickel), and aborted their first child at twenty-two weeks when the average cost of raising a child rose by 1.2 per cent (Arthur kept a spreadsheet). If they were ever forced to give money to a homeless person or a busker, usually to impress their rich friends, they would go back later for change and a receipt. Gertrude would sometimes return dresses after wearing them once (she'd reattach the tags), they wouldn't dine out unless they had a two-for-one coupon and they'd often claim their bottle of wine "had spoiled" (and request another) after drinking two-thirds of it. When they stayed in hotels, they would always steal the extra soaps and shampoos, drink all the clear liquor in the mini-bar and replace it with water, and order food in the restaurant using a fake room number.

They had made the majority of their fortune from a hugely-successful line of "deathbed toys," the most popular of which was "Clutch! The Bear." It was a stuffed brown bear with a soothing voice and an adorable red vest and bowtie, designed to give comfort to dying people (*yeah, on their deathbeds*). So, for example, if your father only had a day to live and you couldn't be there (because you were on a beach in Florida or you just didn't like hospitals, or him), you could open the app and send him a "Clutch! The Bear" with a personalized spoken message, something like "Peace, Dad," "Sorry I Can't Be There," or "Walk Towards The Light, It's Not A Train, You'll Be Fine." The bear was machine-washable, tear-resistant (as in, resistant to people crying on it) and re-usable (because lots of people will die in your life and you don't always want to be there). You could pick from a variety of celebrity voices, including Helen Mirren, Keanu Reeves, and Kevin Spacey (only on pre-2018 models), or you could upload a message in your own voice (from Florida or anywhere else).

The brand faced a major scare in 2017 when a group of teenagers hacked into the voice-boxes of more than three-hundred bears (en route to dying people/deathbeds), leaving a variety of cruel messages, including "Die, Old Cunt, Die!," "Rot In Hell, You Sick Motherfucker," and "Thank God You're Almost Gone, You Miserable Piece-Of-Shit." Surprisingly, the publicity worked in the company's favor—people thought the hacked messages were hilarious, they trended for weeks and the teenage hackers were eventually hired to run a "darkly comic" version of the bear, which became its top-selling product of the year.

The company went from strength to strength after that, releasing a "terminal diagnosis" spinoff bear, its most popular version ever, in time for Christmas of 2019. It had revolutionary "dribble-resistant" material and was designed primarily for doctors and medical practitioners, who could finally avoid having to tell patients they were going to die. Instead, they could just give them a bear with a pre-programmed message and send them on their way ("You've Got Two Weeks, Earl!," "Stop Praying, Dolores, There's Really No Point," and "At Least You'll Never Have To Go To The Dentist Ever Again, Herbert.")

◆   ◆   ◆

Will and Rose returned to the house the next day to throw rocks at it and piss against the gate.

They burnt a small effigy of the fake realtor, then pissed on that too. On the way back to their car, they noticed a "FOR SALE" sign on the property across the road. It certainly wasn't their dream home—it was a piece-of-shit-two-story-shack that defied demolition—but it had potential to be "less shit" (the "FOR SALE" sign actually included the line "Has potential to be less shit!")

They called the realtor, checked he was actually a realtor, and said they were interested in the house. He laughed, hung up, they called back, he asked them if they were kidding (twice), they said no (they weren't kidding, and please stop hanging up), then he drove to meet them immediately. The interior of the house somehow made the exterior look significantly more attractive. There was no running water or electricity and it didn't have traditional "floors," just some loose planks arranged haphazardly to fill holes. The realtor said seven people had been violently shot dead there, which had actually improved the odor and added some texture to the walls.

Will and Rose went back to their apartment and made a flowchart. By morning, they had a plan: they would "reimagine" the house completely, transform it into their dream home and make The Stantons jealous-as-fuck whenever they opened their front door and looked east.

But the "reimagining" was going to take more money than they had, or were ever going to have. The chicken nugget market was in a severe downturn and it didn't matter how many competitors Tony eliminated. Customers wanted diversity in their nibbles and were turning to other finger foods in droves: dumplings, vegan rolls, mini quiches, fish sticks. *Really, fish sticks?*

After two years opposite The Stantons, they had made little progress with their renovations. Will designed and built a deck, which collapsed, and Rose started a garden, mistakenly planting one of those flowers (a "titan arum") that smelled like rotting human flesh. On Fridays, they would drink wine on the broken deck, breathe in the decomposing air and look at The Stantons' mezzanine, the fountain, the pristine gardens, dreaming of a day when things might change.

The Stantons were rarely home. They went to one of their three villas in Europe in the winter, their country manor in the spring, and one or two of their other seven houses on the west coast in the summer and fall. Will and Rose thought about sneaking in one time, perhaps visiting the upstairs wardrobe, but didn't. They probably had cameras, they thought, and they really didn't want another "viral moment."

It was just after Easter in 2014 when things changed. Will had started teaching Ralph how to cross the road to The Stantons' house so he could leave "piss and shit" gifts on their lawn. The little guy learnt well and would save a full load for the journey, sometimes stopping on the way back to dig a hole or tear leaves from plants.

There was an electrical storm one night and Ralph took shelter on The Stantons' porch after crossing in front of an eighteen-wheeler and doing a massive shit in the fountain. Will didn't notice he was gone until there was a knock at the door: it was Bertie, with Ralph in his arms, soaked. Will invited him inside and offered him cheap cognac as a gesture of thanks.

They got drunk, talked about chicken nuggets for two hours, and bitched about The Stantons until sunrise. Bertie loathed them as much Will and Rose did: they paid below minimum wage, made him sleep in an asbestos-riddled room and wouldn't let him smoke his crack pipe during work hours. Will told him if they lived there, he could smoke crack or shoot heroin before, during, and after meal service. Bertie was impressed: Will was the kind of boss he'd always dreamed of having—and Rose seemed pretty cool too.

Before Bertie left that night, they had made a deal, an after-midnight promise that wouldn't be broken by any dawn. He'd tell Will and Rose when The Stantons were out of town and they'd come visit, pretend it was theirs for a while, perhaps invite friends for dinner parties. In return, Bertie would get a thin wad of cash, the freedom to get drug-fucked whenever he wanted to, and a lifetime supply of the best nuggets in the south-west.

Will and Rose spent at least ten months of the year there. Bertie eventually gave them the keys for the country manor too, which was double the size, had two fountains and was only an hour outside the city. Everything was just as they had dreamed— until The Stantons came home. Whenever it happened, it was like a big fat ice-bucket challenge full of shit being dumped on their heads.

◆   ◆   ◆

Bertie was still scrubbing Ralph's wheel marks from the carpet when Will and Rose scurried out the front door with their suitcases. Ralph followed, wheels squeaking. They exchanged brief goodbyes, Will left Bertie his cash and they told him to call them as soon as The Stantons left again. They hoped it wouldn't be long.

Their shitty two-bedroom house awaited them. It'd been a few months since they'd been there: mold, grass, and dust had multiplied, weeds had birthed new generations. No-one was happy to be home. Ralph yipped and pissed on the front doorstep. Rose thought about doing the same. They ate cold hot-pockets and drank expired cask wine for dinner. Ralph hated cask wine but the water had been shut off so it was wine or nothing. From the balcony, they watched The Stantons arrive in their jet-black limousine, saw Bertie unpack for them. Later, after dinner, they could see the rich fucks' silhouettes slow-dancing on the mezzanine. Slow-dancing. On their mezzanine. *Who the fuck slow-dances anymore?*

Will and Rose shared their bed that night with an emerging nation of bed bugs, who didn't like to share.

They woke just after 2am, both with the same thought: *maybe it was time to call Tony and get rid of The Stantons forever?*

CHAPTER 14 BAIT-AND-SWITCH

Zack called Will the day before their planned meeting to make sure they'd received the map and co-ordinates, and also to check what plate they were bringing.

"We're not bringing a plate," Will said. "Also, Rose said you should probably stop using regular mail. It might be incriminating." Nearby, Rose chewed carrot, looked over. "And she said we should keep our communications to a minimum."

"Or not at all," Rose called through an orange mouthful. There was an uneasy silence. Zack sighed.

"You're really not bringing a plate?" he asked.

"No."

"Mom's gonna be real pissed. Maybe we should have the meeting somewhere else."

Will was deeply confused. "The meeting was going to be at your mom's place?"

"It's my place too," he said. "She lives upstairs. And she likes people to bring a plate when they come over, even if they're just passing through her living area to get to mine."

"I thought we agreed on an underground location. Remote, ideally with concrete."

"I live in the basement. It has concrete walls. And it's very remote."

Will made a face at Rose, who mouthed "hang up."

"I don't think it's a good idea to meet at your house," Will said.

Rose nodded, face straining: "fucking hang up."

"Well, if you're not bringing a plate, it's not even an option anymore," Zack replied, sulking.

"Why don't we just do it on Zoom?" Gareth suggested. He was sitting next to Zack at a table in the basement, drawing stick figures on white paper. Zack glanced at him, annoyed by the interruption.

"We're not doing a Zoom call. We have storyboards. How are we supposed to show storyboards on a Zoom call?"

"I can hold them up in front of the screen."

Will was listening to the whole exchange: *Storyboards?* He was desperate to get off the call, and Rose was threatening him with a fork. "A Zoom call sounds perfect," he said.

Zack groaned, realized he was outnumbered. "Fine, a Zoom call, no plate. Worst meeting ever."

The Zoom call was scheduled for midday the next day. Thankfully, the WiFi signal from the Stantons was ridiculously strong and Will and Rose were able to connect from their lopsided deck. Zack left them in a "waiting room" for two minutes. When he finally let them join, he was in the basement of his mom's house. Trash was spread across a table in front of him: assorted bits of week-old food, paper, and empty chip packets.

"Hey there!" Zack wrapped his hands in latex gloves. "As you can see, we've been doing some serious prep-work here." *Prep-work?*

"Where are you again?" Will asked, confused. Rose was still pissed about the waiting room.

"I call it 'The Killing Arena,'" he said. "No-one's ever actually been killed here but it's where we do all the planning for the kills."

Gareth's head appeared, blocking the screen.

"It's also the room where he eats onion rings and watches Hulu," he added.

Zack nudged him out of the way, irritated. "Go and get the storyboards ready." Gareth groaned, sauntered off.

Zack repositioned the laptop, his face centered and filling the frame. "Right, let's get this party started." Offscreen, the basement door opened, light spilled down the stairs behind him. Zack's mom appeared, called out with an irritating voice:

"What are you idiots doing down there?" she yelled. Zack sighed, did his best to hide the humiliation.

"We're in a meeting, Mom." She waited on the top step for a moment, then yelled again:

"Are you talking to those fuckers who refused to bring a plate?"

"Yes, it's them."

"Tell them I'm starving up here. Starving!"

"I'll tell them." She left, slammed the door harder than necessary. Zack returned to Will and Rose, whose faces were drained of blood. "My mom said—"

"—We heard," Rose interrupted. "Let's get this over with so you can go and make her some soup before she dies."

Zack liked the idea. "OK, back to the plan." He referred to the trash on the table in front of him. "We've made some serious progress here."

Rose squinted, as confused as Will. "What is all that? Is that trash?" she asked, repulsed.

"Yes! It's trash. We did a dawn raid this morning," Zack said, delighted with himself. It wasn't quite a "raid" and it definitely wasn't at "dawn," more like two idiots grabbing garbage bags from a lawn in the mid-afternoon.

"Whose trash?" Will asked.

"It's from Ned and Beth's house."

"You're killing The Twins first?" Rose interjected, more hopeful than she'd been since hitting the deer.

"Of course," Zack quipped. "Why wouldn't we kill them first? They're twins, everyone hates twins." Finally, Rose felt like they were all on the same page.

"Go on, we're listening," she said.

Zack took a breath, dug a food-smeared piece of paper from a neat pile he'd made earlier. "Well, the good news is we know everything we need to know to make the kill happen, including, wait for it…" They waited. "They're planning a birthday party for The Twins."

Rose sighed, looked at Will: *OK, maybe her excitement was a little premature.* She leaned into the microphone.

"We know," she said. "On Saturday. We got the invitation. We get all the invitations, even though we never go."

"We already shredded it," Will added, just to be clear.

Zack seemed pissed that his big revelation had been spoiled. But he had more: "But what you didn't know is there's going to be a clown at this party."

Rose groaned. "Yeah, we knew that. It was on the invitation. It's called 'The Twins' Clown Party.'"

Zack tensed like a heckled comedian. Time for something big. "Yes, but what you didn't know is the clown's cellphone number!" He held out the crumpled piece of paper, filling the screen. "We have it!" OK, Will and Rose didn't have that. *Why would they?* Before Rose could speak, Will interjected.

"Why do you need the clown's cellphone number?"

Zack was ready for, and excited by, the question. He wet his rubbery lips, almost made the tongue-clicking sound that had cost a midwife her job. "So we can call him up, lure him to a private location… and replace him with Gareth before the party.

It's called a bait-and-switch." Neither Will nor Rose knew exactly what a bait-and-switch was, but it definitely wasn't one of those.

"Or you could just call it a kidnapping," Rose added.

Gareth was suddenly in the frame, alerted by the mention of his name (even though it had happened ten seconds earlier). "OK, timeout," he said, addressing Zack. "What's this bait-and-switch thing? I don't know anything about clowning."

Zack gently nudged him out of view, dismissive. "You're an intern. You'll learn." He returned to Will and Rose, walked out of frame as he continued: "Right, let's press on. The plan's all here."

Will and Rose couldn't see a fucking thing. "We can't see a fucking thing," Rose said.

"Gareth! They can't see a fucking thing!" Zack called from a distance. There was some fumbling, the screen pivoted, turned left, right, resettled on Zack, in front of a concrete wall. Next to him, stuck to the wall, were a series of badly-drawn storyboards. "I've storyboarded the whole thing," he said, gleeful. There were stick-figure drawings on each of the sheets. Rose looked closer, incredulous.

"Storyboards? Why?" she asked.

"So you can see how everything's going to unfold."

"We don't need to see how it unfolds. Can't you just text us when they're dead?" Will nodded, agreeing with Rose. She continued: "Just write 'they're dead' in a text. In caps, with an exclamation point. Or use a fucking emoji if you want to."

"An emoji would be fun," Will added, imagining one with blood everywhere, possibly with the severed heads of two smiling children amongst the blood.

Zack paused, clearly not enjoying their negativity. "You will definitely get that text. And an emoji. But we should go through all the fun stuff first," he said, returning to the storyboards. Ever since he was a boy, Zack had fantasized about doing a TED talk. This presentation was part of that fantasy—and no-one was going to cut it short.

"We're going after The Twins with what I call the 'Exploding Anthrax Balloon,'" he continued, oblivious to their thinning patience. He referred to the first of the boards, a childlike, colored-in title scrawled across it: "EXPLODING ANTHRAX BALLOON!"

"First, we kidnap the clown, also known as 'Mr. Happy,'" he said. There was a drawing of Mr. Happy being pulled into a van, frowning. A huge yellow daffodil was left behind, crushed. "Gareth replaces Mr. Happy." The new Mr. Happy, supposedly Gareth in costume, stood at a front door, smiling. "He entertains the kiddies with animal balloons." Mr. Happy made animals out of balloons. Nearby, Gareth—the live human version—frowned.

"Animal balloons? How do I even do that?" he said.

Zack ignored him, carried on. "At the end, Gareth separates The Twins for a special private birthday balloon show," he said, his voice building in intensity. On the second row of storyboards, The Twins were seated on chairs. Mr. Happy loomed over them with an enlarged balloon, "ANTHRAX" written on its side. "The balloon pops, exposing both children to a lethal dose of anthrax." The drawings took a macabre turn: the balloon popped, The Twins clasped at their throats, parents screamed. An ambulance arrived, paramedics did C.P.R. Zack finished with: "They'll be dead in five minutes."

Gareth was horrified. "Won't the anthrax kill everyone in the vicinity? Including me?" he asked.

Zack quietly chuckled, dismissive, realized he hadn't thought of that. "You'll be fine. Just don't inhale it or get it on your hands." He approached the camera, filling the frame with his head to deliberately obscure Gareth. Will and Rose watched, faces blank. They couldn't care less how he did it, they were just desperate to get off the call.

"OK, sounds like a plan," Will said.

"We'll wait for the text," Rose added.

Zack beamed like it was a success, waved at the camera like a bad informercial host. "Right-o! Bye now!" And he was gone.

Will closed the laptop. Rose turned to him. "You didn't mention they were deadset morons," she said.

"They were more normal in the bar," Will replied, sheepish, knowing they actually weren't.

"More normal? They're not even close to normal! Why did you hire them?"

Will struggled for a good answer, then went with: "No-one else wants to kill children. They're all we've got." Rose sighed, knew he was right. They both looked off, bothered. Will tried to end the moment on a positive note: "Maybe they'll surprise us," he said. She glared at him. Neither of them believed that.

They both feared another night of fetal-position sleep, maybe another "deer" drive. Nearby, Ralph yipped: *he feared the same.*

But then, just as they gathered their meal cushions and were about to stream a documentary about fentanyl, the "dinner-party" invitation came.

CHAPTER 15 <u>**A NEW NORMAL?**</u>

Soon after the Zoom with Zack, Will received a call from Bertie: The Stantons had returned to Europe and the house was theirs again.

They were back where they belonged within the hour. Bertie got high immediately and gave them their mail, which he had stored in a separate box when it arrived.

They had some wine on the mezzanine and went through it: some bills, magazines they subscribed to, occasional photos/ updates from their exiled friends. Rose had become familiar with the over-sized blue envelopes from Beth, which normally included a mundane, glitter-infested invitation to a birthday party or, as she put it, "the anniversary of her womb being empty." As she tore it open, she thought it was probably a reminder of the clown party in two weeks and chuckled to herself: *if only the bitch knew what was coming.* But the blue envelope on this particular day had nothing to do with that. Will noticed the stunned look on her face.

"What is it?" he asked.

"It's from Ned and Beth," she said, handing it over. Will took it, and read, expecting news of more breeding, or The Twins' latest scholastic triumphs—but it was neither of those.

Crisp, silver-embossed lettering adorned bone-white card: "You're Invited To..." Then, two lines down, in cursive and caps: "...*A DINNER PARTY!*" *A fucking what?* Will had to read it again. Twice.

"What the fuck?" Will said aloud. Rose echoed his words with her eyes. They were the ones who hosted dinner parties. *Who the fuck did these fuckers think they were?* Before Will could get it to the shredder, Rose intervened:

"It says 'No Children Allowed.'" She pointed to that actual line at the bottom of the invitation, underlined. They shared a look, incredulous.

"They're punking us," Will said.

"What if they're not?"

A dinner party with no children, where children were specifically not allowed to attend, stated in writing on the actual fucking invitation? They couldn't believe they'd never thought of it. It was genius. Their shock soon gave way to suspicion: why, after all this time, had Ned and Beth decided to have a child-free event? Maybe they'd learned from Will and Rose's silent disdain, their "unfriending" on social media, their complete non-responsiveness to anything they sent? Maybe all their self-absorbed friends had realized the error of their ways and really missed them after all?

"Or maybe it's just a scam to get us there," Rose said as she finished the bottle. "At which point they'll say 'Oh, we were just kidding' and they'll all laugh while their children wreak havoc around us. We'll be trapped." Will shared her concern, and called out for Bertie to bring more wine.

"If that happens, we can just leave," he said. "I'll keep the car running when we go inside." It was a good plan.

That night, they stared at the same spot on the ceiling, thought the same thoughts: if the "no children" approach worked at Ned and Beth's house, it could work at theirs. It would be the beginning of a new normal, eventually the unspoken rule. Before long, it wouldn't be just "no children allowed," it'd be "no mention of children at any point during the evening." For five to six hours every week, everyone would pretend their conversation-killing offspring didn't exist. They would laugh and eat and drink and dance, discuss politics and work and everything in the world that annoyed them. No-one would ever cover their glass or request water or leave early or say they were "tired." *It would be like old times.*

Hope simmered gently, like an egg boiling. Rose and Will spent over two hours staring at the damn ceiling, eventually realized there was water damage (and woke Bertie to tell him). But the questions they had both raised in their minds were profound: if this worked, maybe they didn't need to kill anyone after all? Maybe they didn't need to hire the morons with their storyboards? Maybe their lives could return to normal?

Eventually, excited by the possibilities, they made glorious love. Will was on top so Rose kept looking at the ceiling, thinking about appetizers (and how long it would take Bertie to fix the water damage).

In the morning, Will texted Zack. "Let's put a hold on things," he wrote. Zack replied with an angry, confused emoji.

◆　　　◆　　　◆

In many countries, false or misleading advertising is punishable by death or dismemberment. If you say it's "halal meat" in Cairo and you're fucking lying, they'll cut your limbs off and laugh while you bleed out in the town square. If you tell an Amazonian tribe it's human flesh nuggets and it's really just chicken, you're not likely to get back to your canoe alive.

The invitation from Ned and Beth was, at its core, an advertisement. They advertised an event with specific details, Will and Rose accepted, they bought in to what was being offered.

When the night arrived a week later, they showered, dressed up, chose a medium-priced wine to take, said goodbye to Ralph and Bertie, and got in the car. All in good faith, based on "the advertisement."

At first, it appeared to be everything they had been prom- ised. From the car, which Will left running, they saw adult sil- houettes through cheap curtains on the second floor. Their friends were drinking and chatting. *Ah, a dinner party!* Not as fancy as theirs, but still… a dinner party! The memories flooded back like expensive mimosas.

Ned and Beth didn't have a fake mansion like theirs, but that didn't matter. This was a trial run, a beta version of some- thing much bigger. It didn't matter if the food was second-rate, if the glasses weren't crystal and/or polished. It didn't even matter that there wouldn't be a "Bertie" to serve them. On this night, in this moment, they would happily serve themselves (although pouring their own drinks was going to be humiliating).

They walked up the short driveway, held hands to calm their nerves. They were the second-last to arrive, which wasn't ideal—they had planned, and expected, to be the last. *But, what- ever, this was a trial run,* they thought.

Ned and Beth greeted them at the door with exaggerated smiles and fake kisses, pretended they hadn't ignored them, or their banal cards, for years. *Oh, so busy. Been dying to catch up. Accidentally blocked you on social media, which "we hardly ever check." Loved getting your letters and photos and cards!* All that crap. It went on for five agonizing minutes.

Ned eventually took their coats, Beth forced them to take a "foyer selfie," and Will suddenly "remembered" he'd left the car running and went to turn it off. Rose thought it was way too early to make that call and gave him a look as he left. She was right—it was definitely way too early.

When he returned, Beth guided them upstairs to the be- ginnings of the party: Jack and Kathleen were there, nursing drinks, midway through an argument. They exchanged pleasantries ("you look great!," "it's been so long!"), Beth arrived with a tray of hors d'oeuvres ("Oh, she's carrying them around herself," Rose whispered to Will, "How adorable"), and they eventually took their places at the dinner table, which had been set for eight. Everything was going as planned. Not a child in sight, hardly a single mention of them, except a brief reminder about The Twins' upcoming party. Will and Rose shared a look when it came up, blissfully aware of how close those evil little fucks were to dodging a bullet (or, more accurately, a lethal dose of anthrax).

The main course was served (Beth, again, clumsy), Jack even asked Will to tell one of his classic jokes. He obliged, did one about ugly babies and excrement. Everyone laughed. It felt like old times, just cheaper and a bit "white-trashier."

Dessert was almost ready to be served when everything changed. It began with Brett and Melissa's arrival, one hour and fifteen minutes after the advertised starting time and forty-five minutes after it was kinda OK to be late.

Everyone stopped talking and listened while Ned and Beth answered the front door, greeting them with an exaggerated "Welcome!"

Will and Rose could hear everything from their side of the dinner table: girly squeals, air-kisses, men slapping each other's backs, the usual greetings between unhinged adults. And then, the unthinkable: the sound Will and Rose had feared. To call it "the pitter-patter of little feet" running up the stairs was far too cute—it was a monstrous rumbling. Two sets of shoes, three. Then, the piercing squeal of a baby. *Yep, they'd brought the whole fucking family.* If Ned and Beth had been able to afford a chandelier, its crystals would have trembled violently. Rose and Will met eyes: *oh my fuck.*

Within twenty minutes, the advertised "rules" had been totally abandoned. Children in pajamas weaved between seats, under the table, over furniture. Conversation suddenly became a running commentary of their idiotic deeds ("oh, he's dismantling the air-conditioning unit, isn't he getting strong?"). Before long, The Twins had wandered out of their bedrooms, woken by the ruckus. They joined in and quickly escalated the chaos, which was their main purpose in life. Will and Rose worked hard to contain their rage, but they could not: when a rampant four-year-old fetus toppled Rose's wine, she unleashed:

"We thought the invitation said no children." Her words cut across the room like an Antarctic breeze, silencing everyone. The children stopped gnawing at random objects they didn't own. All eyes descended on her. Rose looked to Will for back-up.

"It did say 'No Children Allowed,'" he added, drawing the eyes to him.

Suddenly, Melissa burst into laughter. Beth and Kathleen followed. There was a snort amongst it all. Even the baby chuckled. *What was so fucking funny?*

"Do you know how hard it is to get a decent babysitter these days?" Melissa said, her laugh morphing into a carefree sigh. Kathleen nodded in agreement, eyeballed Jack, who nodded too, and said something lame like "Yeah, it's real tough." Will shot daggers at him. *Really, Jack?*

"Our two girls are only here to say goodnight," Beth said, defensive, perhaps remembering that she wrote and printed the fucking invitation. She spotted The Twins at the window, tearing at the drapes. "Say goodnight, girls!" They ignored her. More glasses spilled, grubby hands pulled at the tablecloth, carpet and dress shoes were smeared.

When coffee was served, a nerf ball bounced off Will's forehead. Ned noticed and chuckled, then saw Will's reaction (fury, with a side of deep hatred) and pretended to be a host who finally cared about the comfort and wellbeing of his guests.

"No throwing stuff!" Ned said, then went back to his plate. "Five minutes and it's bedtime!" But it was never going to be bedtime. Not ever. There was only one way to put these monsters to sleep.

Will and Rose left shortly after, saying they had to go feed Bertie and douse themselves in gasoline. No-one was really listening, they were all too busy watching the children upend furniture. They found their own coats, took the unopened bottle of wine they'd brought, and showed themselves out.

The drive home was quiet and morose. They stared ahead, glum and broken. As they neared the turnpike, Will took out his phone. She knew what he was thinking of doing, and liked it.

"Are you going to text him?" she asked.

"Yes."

She smiled, her mood brightened.

He typed a message to Zack: "About that 'hold,' I was just kidding." He sent it, they waited.

Zack replied almost immediately: a thumbs-up emoji, followed by a laughing face.

It was back on.

CHAPTER 16 **MR. HAPPY**

Lionel Edgar White never imagined he would grow up to be a clown. He was the child of deaf parents, who also happened to be assholes, so he was often referred to as a "CODAWAAA," the acronym for "Child Of Deaf Adults Who Are Also Assholes."

From an early age, Lionel had to translate and communicate on behalf of his mother and father, a power which he often used to his own advantage. At parent-teacher interviews, he'd translate "fuck-up" to "fully-engaged," and "loathed by everyone" to "eye-fucked by everyone." His parents were lazy and useless at lipreading so they never realized he was fucking with them. They also didn't seem to mind that his teacher said "eye-fucked" when discussing their seven-year-old son.

He failed high school and got a job as a freelance deaf-signer, working for celebrities, senators, and business people whose job it was to make lots of speeches in public. He once appeared on TV next to the governor to provide details of an approaching hurricane and thought it'd be funny to sign "you will all die" instead of "you will all be fine." People panicked, there were some suicides. Lionel told his parents about it after the storm had passed and they all laughed, knowing he wouldn't get in trouble because deaf people don't often phone up to complain when the signing is wrong (and, if they do, no-one listens).

His career came to an end soon after that when he signed the "N" word for a black rapper, not knowing he wasn't actually supposed to sign the entire word. He received lots of offensive (non-white) "hand" emojis on social media and no-one ever hired him again.

He went downhill for a while after that, getting drunk often and signing obscenities at homeless people on his way home, especially couples who were making out in cardboard boxes. Everything in the world annoyed him, all the people having fun and enjoying themselves. One day, he was checking the mail (he'd ordered deaf porn for his parents) and he noticed a balloon tied to the neighbors' letterbox. *Ugh*, he thought. *A fucking party*. He grabbed the balloon and tried to pop it in his hands but it was made of a thick, pop-resistant material: the harder he tried, the more it refused to pop. He twisted it and mangled it and poked his fingers deep into it, but it did not pop. By the time he'd given up, the balloon had lost its shape completely and resembled a deformed baby elephant that had been wounded by poachers. The neighbor, a troubled man who loved nature documentaries and Russian dolls, saw what he'd done and came out of his house in two layers of wildlife pajamas.

"That's fantastic," he said, referring to the elephant balloon. "Can you come and do that at the party?" Lionel had nothing else to do that day (the porn hadn't arrived) so he agreed and the neighbor paid him a hundred bucks. Adults who attended the party were impressed and he quickly built a reputation. He learnt how to shape more animals (by watching ZooTube videos and sneaking into random birthday parties), made a business card, and even created a website. At a party for rich brats, he was approached by a talent agent who represented dwarves, strippers, and sock-puppeteers. He told Lionel he could double his earnings if he agreed to dress up as either a "transvestite hooker" or a "clown" while he made the balloons. He chose "transvestite hooker" but he was not impressive in either fishnet tights or stilettos and he horrified many young children (and their parents). So, reluctantly, and with his agent's help, he switched to "clown" and created a whole new alter ego that belied his deep hatred of the world and everyone in it.

He became "Mr. Happy."

◆　　◆　　◆

On the day of The Twins' birthday party, Mr. Happy had a busy schedule. He didn't usually take more than two bookings on the same day (he liked to start getting wasted early) but Zack had insisted, saying he'd pay double if he dropped by his nephew's bar mitzvah to make a balloon in the shape of a circumcised penis. He thought it was an odd request but he'd had stranger ones—mostly in the form of genitalia and/or bestiality—and he liked money. So, he got in his Mr. Happy van, which featured a cartoon likeness of him on the side (a leaner, less repulsive version of him), and headed to the location. On the way, he thought he'd catch up on some phone calls:

"I need that bill paid, you fucking fuck," he said as he drove. "Do you think I just turn up and do tricks for free? I'm not a cheap fucking hooker." He was waiting at traffic lights during this exchange, window down so everyone in the neighboring cars (including young children) could see and hear him. It's worth noting that he was in full clown makeup at this point.

"Fine, whatever, cunt," he continued. "Put your mom on." He listened as the eight-year-old girl on the other end of the line struggled to find the words. Finally, she said her mom was out. "Oh. She's not home? Well, tell her to call me. Or pay the fucking bill! Bitch can choose." He hung up with his huge gloved hand.

When he arrived at the location, he was surprised to see it was neither a house nor a function center, which is where most bar mitzvahs were held. It was an abandoned warehouse. A faded sign out front read: "Murphy's Screws & Bolts." He checked

Zack's message on his phone, re-checked the GPS. He was in the right place. "What the fuck sort of bar mitzvah is this?" he asked himself aloud, which he did often. He tried to call Zack but there was no answer (Zack was waiting inside, his phone on silent). Eventually, he got out, took a sip of "water" from his hip flask and headed inside.

The rusty front door was ajar. He pushed it open, its creak echoing. Light spilled, revealing a cavernous, empty space with a dirt floor. Definitely no bar mitzvah here. His clown face tensed, confused. "Anyone here?" he called out.

Zack and Gareth were waiting behind him in the shadows. Mr. Happy heard their shoes in the dirt as they approached. He turned, Zack tasered him. His red nose lit up like Rudolph's and he hit the floor with a dull thud.

Will and Rose had a full night of celebrations planned for "The Twins' End Day" (or "TWED" as they asked Bertie to write on the cake). They erected a whiteboard in the living area to keep track of the timeline: the party was due to start at 2pm and Mr. Happy/Gareth was scheduled to arrive and begin his show at 3pm—so it was likely the anthrax would be circulating in the little shits' lungs before 4pm.

If all went well, and Zack and Gareth didn't screw things up, they would be popping expensive champagne by 5pm at the latest, after which they would eat a fatted calf (Bertie had already slaughtered it) and dance to eighties music until the wee hours. Bertie set up a large countdown clock in the kitchen and borrowed a police scanner from one of his felon friends so they could hear when the frantic call went out about "two children dying."

In the meantime, all they could do was wait. It was excruciating, and Bertie's countdown, though well-intentioned, made it worse. Will tried to fill the time by listening to death metal, cutting his toenails and looking at grisly photos of poison victims ("botulinum does that?"). Rose was more constructive: she changed her profile pic on Facebook to the color "eburnean," which helped end female genital mutilation in an obscure Middle-Eastern country. She received a message from an activist immediately after making the change: "Your brave actions—changing your profile pic from a small, annoying-looking dog to the color eburnean—just saved the lives of thousands of young girls, who can now grow up, get married, and be subservient to their powerful husbands until they die. Also, click on the link below to update your internet banking password." Rose felt good about herself for several minutes, then Will's laptop rang: incoming Skype. *Yeah, Zack.*

"Really?" Rose asked as it rang. "We're Skyping now? Didn't we agree on a text?" Will shrugged, checked the clock as he answered it. It was 2.35pm, far too early for the deaths to have occurred. He asked anyway:

"Are they dead already?"

"No, but we have the van," Zack said as he drove, weaving between traffic. His computer was balanced on the dash, wobbling often. "Just wanted to call you guys with an update." He gave them a detailed rundown of the "bait-and-switch," told them the clown had cried "happy tears" as they stripped him naked and left him tied up on the dirt floor. He said a "huge plastic daffodil" had been crushed in the struggle, meaning everything was going exactly according to the storyboards.

Behind Zack, Will and Rose could see Gareth changing into the clown outfit. He was deeply uncomfortable, tangled up in laces and oversized pants. "These shoes are too big," he whined, almost toppling over. Zack half-turned.

"They're meant to be big. They're clown shoes."

Rose and Will glanced at each other, asking the same questions with their eyes: *how much longer and what happened to the fucking text?*

Zack returned to them, and the road. "I've fixed a camera to the front of the clown costume so you'll be able to watch the whole thing," he told them. "It's a clown-cam!" He chuckled. *Oh dear.*

"I'm no good in front of crowds," Gareth mumbled, "I lose control of bodily functions."

Zack grimaced at the thought. Will and Rose did the same. "They're children. They're too young to judge you," he replied, not convinced. "And if you piss yourself, those pants will hold onto anything. Get the makeup on!" The van took a sharp turn, the WiFi dropped out. *Thank God*, Rose thought.

When Zack finally called them back, he had already parked the van in front of Ned and Beth's suburban home. Two balloons were tied to the letterbox which, he noted, was a very handy way of locating children to be killed. Thankfully, Will and Rose now had a split-screen to view the whole thing: Zack, in the driver's seat, and the clown-cam, located on the third button of Gareth's suit, which showed the blurred back of Zack's fat head. Gareth appeared behind Zack, like a carnival worker on meth. The red paint around his eyes and lips was smeared and uneven.

"What the fuck happened?" Zack asked. "You're going to frighten the children."

"I couldn't keep the brush still," Gareth replied. "You were driving all over the place."

Zack straightened Gareth's red wig, tried to tidy some of the lines. "Hopefully they'll be looking at the animal balloons and not your face," he quipped, glancing back at the camera. Gareth attached a bulbous red nose, still clearly nervous. "Remember... giraffe, polar bear, camel," Zack reminded him. He pulled out a handful of airless balloons, tucked them into Gareth's jacket pockets. "...then the "special balloon" for The Twins. This one." He held up one of the balloons: "SPECIAL ONE" was written across it in black marker. Gareth inhaled, ready. *Actually, he wasn't ready at all.*

"Does the camel have one hump or two?" he asked, clueless.

"Just give it a head and something resembling a body."

Zack slid the special balloon into the inside pocket of his jacket. "And make sure you get the hell out of there when the balloon explodes. I don't have the budget to train another intern." Gareth gave him a look, terrified. Rose and Will shared the same look. "Get going, we'll be watching," Zack said as he pushed him through the van door.

Gareth stumbled out in his big shoes, found his footing and headed towards the house.

◆   ◆   ◆

Ned and Beth lived in a very ordinary dwelling. The backyard was quaint, a little small, no pool. It was perfect for a lower-to-middle-class birthday party of this size, pretty and suburban, the kind of place you'd see in one of those "faith-based" movies.

Streamers and balloons hung from trees, and there was a hand-painted sign draped across the back porch: "HAPPY BIRTHDAY TAMARA AND TANYA." Yep, the fuckers called them Tamara and Tanya, almost-identical names that would confuse people for the rest of their lives, which thankfully wouldn't be much longer. Will and Rose watched from the clown-cam as Gareth found a place to perform, occasionally cleared phlegm from his throat. *Really?*

It occurred to them while they were watching that they were doing a favor for thousands of people: teachers, receptionists, waiters, employees at Starbucks, anyone who would ever have to clarify which fucking twin they were. Imagine how many spoken words they were going to save people from uttering? Probably millions, which would equate to thousands of minutes over the course of two lifetimes. No more "Are you Tamara or Tanya?" just: "Oh, those twins are dead." Soon, no-one would ever need to mention them again.

A wall of grubby children applauded as Gareth stepped into the center of the yard. He coughed, awkward: the sound rattled Will's laptop speakers. Behind the seated children, Will and Rose could see familiar faces: Brett and Melissa, Kathleen and the baby. Ned and Jack nursed beers at the back, almost as disinterested as them.

Gareth finally spoke: "Hello kiddies! I'm Mr. Happy!" He raised gloved hands, which obscured the clown-cam view.

Zack interrupted, trying to be helpful: "You're doing fine, Gareth. Everything's fine. Pretend they're all naked and they want you to succeed." *Naked?* It wasn't helpful.

Gareth pressed on: "I've got a fantastic show for you all today!"

Rose stood up, stretched her legs. "Why the fuck are we watching this? How hard is a text?" she said as she paced. Will nodded in agreement, they both kept watching. It was like waiting for a twenty-car pile-up to happen—they couldn't look away.

Gareth pulled a balloon from his pocket. *Here we go*, everyone thought. The Twins were front and center amongst the children, their repugnant red hair arranged in matching pigtails. They weren't impressed by Gareth. The lesser evil one rolled her eyes.

"First up, a polar bear!" Gareth said. The children clapped a little, not convinced. All eyes descended on the balloon as he puffed air into it. Saliva sprayed over the lens and some of the children in the front row. It was messy as fuck, like amateur flute night.

"It's the giraffe first!" Zack shouted into the mic. Gareth wasn't listening. He struggled to get air into the balloon. It squeaked and squelched and finally escaped his smeared lips, flittered away like a stoned moth. There was a low murmur among the adults, someone (Kathleen) said "shit" through a sneeze. Ned and Jack looked at each other, desperate to go hang in his mancave.

"I've seen drug addicts more entertaining than this clown. Where did you find him?" Jack asked.

"Beth organized it. I wanted The Mermaid," Ned replied.

"There was a Mermaid? What does she do?"

"Nothing. She just sits on a paper mâché rock and wags her big fish tail, which has candy in it."

"There's candy in her fish tail?"

"Yep."

"How do they get it out?"

"She wags it, the candy falls out." Jack looked off, intrigued, picturing it. Ned continued: "But if all the candy doesn't come out, the kids can whack it with a stick. Like a piñata."

"They whack it with a stick? What kind of stick?"

"A special magic stick from the ocean. She brings it."

Jack moved on to more important specifics. "Is her top half naked?"

"No, but her tits hang out. According to the photo on the website."

"I think I might book her for Bubba's first birthday," Jack added. "Can you send me the link?" Ned nodded, dug out his phone between swigs of beer. It only took him two clicks.

"Done," he said. "Please invite me." Kathleen looked over, shooshed them.

Back on "stage," Gareth was on his fifth balloon. Zack eye-balled the screen. "You're losing them, Gareth!"

Gareth tried again, tied off a half-filled balloon, started to bend it into shape. He had no idea what he was doing: it popped with a violent bang. The children gasped, becoming frightened. Gareth froze, bumbling, searching for something to say. "OK. That was the polar bear," he said, "And that's how fast they're disappearing... because of the melting ice caps."

Dead silence. The children had no idea what he was talking about. Down the back, Jack's voice traveled: "He's useless and he's political." Beth looked at Ned, horrified. Rose groaned. Zack screamed into the mic, punched keys for no apparent reason.

"Move on to the camel!"

Gareth paused, tried to compose himself. "OK, now the camel!"

Jack shifted his weight, his voice traveling even further: "I bet the camel's a Syrian refugee." Gareth heard him, pretended he didn't. He hunched over, tried to twist the balloon into a neck. *It held!* Maybe he was getting the hang of this. He turned it over, plastic squeaking and bending, but gradually forming the shape of something. Zack, Will and Rose, the children, the adults, even The Twins—all of them were on the edge of their seats as he tied it up, raised it in front of him.

"Voila!" he said, with a smug, unhinged grin.

It took less than two seconds for the adults to decipher the shape of what he'd made, probably longer for the (male) children. It was a giant cock, uncircumcised, with testicles. Beth shrieked, Ned coughed, Kathleen snorted, then covered her baby's eyes (they were closed anyway). Before Gareth realized what he'd done, his artwork popped gloriously. A buildup of his saliva sprayed from the tip.

Beth quickly intervened, stood in front of him and the floppy balloon-cock-foreskin he was clutching. "OK, time for intermission! Cookies and cake! Everybody inside!" The oblivious children screamed with delight, hurried off. Beth turned to Gareth, furious, ready to gouge his eyes out. He straightened, apologetic.

"It was supposed to be a camel," he said. She wasn't impressed.

"You've got ten minutes to sort yourself out or I'm replacing you with Jack and his ukulele," she said. "And, if that happens, I won't be paying you a brass fucking razoo." She stormed off. Gareth had no idea what a brass razoo was, or what its exchange rate was in comparison with the US dollar, but he figured things were not going well. He took a breath, consulted Zack with a whisper:

"What do I do now?"

"Go to the restroom, you moron," Zack replied. "We'll regroup there."

Will and Rose looked at each other, the smell of slow-roasting calf drifting in from the kitchen.

"Is this as fucked as it seems?" Rose asked.

Will nodded: *yep, it most definitely is.*

CHAPTER 17 GARETH

Gareth had never been a very confident person. He was the youngest of six children and his parents constantly reminded him that they had tried several times to abort him ("without success, obviously," they'd say). They even nicknamed him "Forceps," which was later shortened to just "Ceps" in high school.

"It wasn't the doctor's fault," his mother would say about the failed attempts on his fetal life, "You've just got a very slippery head." His father, who fancied himself a comedian, often pulled him aside at family gatherings and told him:

"There's still time (to abort you)."

Gareth spent the majority of his young life in his bedroom under the stairs, mostly because he enjoyed his own company and the door was frequently locked (from the outside). His sister gave him an old set of crayons and he began drawing whatever came to mind, which tended to be mostly dark and disturbing content (there were no lights or windows in his room). One of his teachers saw his work and helped him get a part-time job with the company that made Rorschach Inkblot tests, which are those weird pictures that psychiatrists show their patients to check if they're batshit crazy or not. He drew six hundred different versions of two rabbits fucking and no-one ever guessed it correctly.

Before enrolling in community college, Gareth spent a short period of time as an intern at Pixar: one of their executives had seen his work in therapy (*yeah, the rabbits fucking*) and thought he'd be a great fit for the company's new "dark animation" slate.

To see if he had any talent, he was given a budget to create a "cruel and deeply unsettling" short animation of his own choosing. The result, "Decomposing Mary," was about a group of plush toys who come to life when their owner, an obese woman with significant co-morbidities, dies of an acute cardiac embolism on the toilet. Unable to escape or feed themselves, the toys decide to eat her decomposing body, but she is so diseased that they end up suffering ataxic paraparesis and choking on their own vomit.

The work was not well-received by management: one executive said it was illogical that plush toys would need to eat, another said the toys spent way too much time talking and singing, and not enough time "eating the human flesh." Gareth was not asked to continue with the company. His movie was burned and shredded.

The main restroom in Ned and Beth's house was occupied—and there was a long queue of grotesque little kids waiting outside, many of whom had already half-pissed themselves—so Gareth went to the other restroom near the laundry.

It was a very cramped space, just a toilet and basin, and he was sweating profusely, so he removed the outer layers of his clown costume (including his big red shoes) and unclipped the clown-cam from his jacket.

He closed the door and spoke directly into the camera. "OK, I'm in the restroom. What's the plan?" he asked. Zack's voice spilled through his earbuds:

"The plan is for you to get your fucking shit together! What the fuck are you doing?"

"I told you I wasn't good in front of crowds," he said, catching his reflection in the mirror: his makeup was significantly more smeared and horrific, almost post-apocalyptic.

"The crowd isn't the problem, Gareth. You're the problem. You're always the problem. How hard is it to turn a balloon into an animal? Any fucking animal!"

"It's pretty hard," Gareth replied, pitiful.

"I'm starting to think you may not be cut out for this kind of work."

Rose and Will watched, deeply troubled, muted so no-one could hear their groans of displeasure. "Is he only starting to realize that now?" Rose asked.

Gareth was confused. "Do you mean I'm not cut out for clowning or killing?"

"Neither. You're not cut out for anything! Now I understand why your parents tried to abort you."

"You know about that?"

"Of course I know about that. I'm Facebook friends with your dad. He posts funny memes about it all the time."

Gareth pouted: his dad still hadn't accepted his Friend Request. "Funny memes? Like what?"

"I don't remember. There are too many. But it's always a photo of you with forceps." Zack shifted in his seat, ready to get back to the business at hand. "OK, forget the animals," he said. "Go back and do the 'special balloon' for The Twins. It doesn't matter if you fuck it up and it explodes, that's the whole point."

"Got it," Gareth replied, reaching into his pocket for the balloons—but they were in his jacket outside. Before he could open the door, Beth knocked.

"Mr. Happy, are you OK?" she asked.

Zack heard her. "Tell her you're fine, everything's fine," he said.

"I'm fine, all good. Ready for part two," Gareth called back to her.

"I have a glass of water for you," she added.

"Oh, that'd be great," he replied, opening the door.

"Don't open the door!" Zack shouted, too late (Will and Rose shouted the exact same words).

Suffice to say, Beth was mortified—and it had nothing to do with Gareth's hairless, pigeon-chested body. She looked at his face like a forensic investigator studying a severed head.

"You can't go back out there like that," she said.

"I'll be fine, I just need a little touch-up," he replied, taking the water. "I have a whole other set. They're gonna love it."

"Nope, not happening." She stood firm in the doorway. Gareth persisted.

"Seriously, I'll be OK—"

But she closed the door, locked it from outside. "I really don't want the children to see you again. They'll be afraid of clowns their whole lives."

Gareth tried the handle, called back: "It's OK, really. Really! I won't scare them!" He looked into the clown-cam, addressed Zack. "What now?"

Zack didn't seem concerned. "She'll be back. She promised them a clown show and twins always get what they want on their birthday, even if it's an incompetent clown who frightens the fuck out of everybody." Gareth wasn't convinced. Beth's voice spilled from the hallway, interrupting them:

"You're gonna be the clown," Beth said. *Who?*

Zack leaned closer to his laptop, trying to hear. "What did she say?" Gareth pressed his ear to the door, listening. Outside, Ned stood opposite Beth, confused:

"Me?"

"Yeah, you," Beth said. "You're the new Mr. Happy. It's either that or we get Jack up there with his ukulele and you know how that usually ends up, especially after he's had twelve beers."

Ned quietened, knew she had a point about Jack—he'd had more than twelve. She pressed: "They're expecting a clown out there. Do you know how vicious the school moms get when you fuck up a party? We'll both be Twitter-shamed before the cask wine is finished." Ned swallowed, which was something he did after chewing food and/or when he knew Beth was going to force him to do something he really didn't want to do.

"Fine. But I don't know anything about making animals out of balloons," he said.

"You can't be worse than that idiot." She pointed towards the closed bathroom door.

Gareth spoke to Zack in a raised whisper: "Are you hearing this?"

"She's bluffing," Zack replied, smug. "He can't do a clown act without clowning materials. And all the clowning materials are in your jacket."

Gareth's eyes widened. *Oh, the clowning materials.*

Will watched with bemusement, started clearing spam from his email account. Rose returned from the kitchen with a glass of wine. It was after midday so, *whatever.* She caught the tail-end of Zack's comment. "What are clowning materials?" she asked.

"Balloons, firecrackers, extra noses. Stuff for the clown show," Will responded, like he'd googled it. On the screen, Gareth was conspicuously silent.

Zack asked the obvious: "You have your jacket, right?".

Gareth made a face, indicating "No, I fucking don't."

"It's in the hallway," he said, sheepish. "I didn't want to bring anthrax into a confined space because, you know, it's anthrax."

Outside, Beth confirmed the worst: "His clown stuff is all here," she said to Ned. "Balloons and shit. You practice, I'll get some makeup for your face." Her footsteps trailed off, Ned rifled through pockets, balloons squelched. *They were not good sounds.*

Zack bristled. "He's got your fucking clown bag?"

Gareth didn't answer. Will buried his face in his hands, Rose went for the bottle.

Ned took the "stage" about twenty minutes later, clown nose and wig attached (Gareth had left them in the hallway too). His makeup was a mess of Beth's mascara and cheap lipstick. He started his routine with:

"Hey there little kids! I'm Mr. Happy's younger brother! Are you ready for some fun!!?" No-one cheered, The Twins knew it was their lame dad. Gareth stood on the toilet seat, pointed the clown-cam lens through the window so Zack, Will, and Rose could see everything.

At the back, on his fifteenth beer, Jack quietly chuckled, and mumbled, "This is completely fucked."

Of course, Ned hadn't practiced with the balloons so he was significantly worse than Gareth at shaping them into anything. He popped them in quick succession, inevitably reaching the one marked "Special Balloon." *Uh-oh.*

"Isn't that...?" Rose began to ask, then saw the look on Will's face. *Yep, it was.*

The events that unfolded from that point on would have been perfectly suited to Pixar's "dark animation" slate.

Ned puckered up and blew into the balloon. Gareth watched from the restroom window, didn't think to call out "No!" or "You may die if you suck on that!"

The anthrax flooded into Ned's lungs. His eyes rolled back. He stiffened, clutched his chest. Everyone thought it was part of the act, some people clapped. At least two of the adults filmed with their smartphones (it went viral). Jack, hammered at this point, provided comic relief: "This beats a shitty camel balloon!"

It was at this moment that Zack politely encouraged Gareth to "get the fuck out of there by whatever means possible!" Gareth obliged, broke open the tiny metal latch on the restroom door and scurried across the back lawn. No-one really noticed him, mostly because they had gathered around Ned's spasming body. Beth tried C.P.R., which was the second catastrophic mistake of the afternoon (the third, if you count Gareth's performance). The anthrax drifted to her lungs as well and she was soon part of the act.

Will and Rose stared at the screen, dumbfounded. "I don't think any of this was on those fucking storyboards," Rose said. Will closed the laptop and they went to play Yahtzee and get high with Bertie.

Zack and Gareth fled the scene, Zack told Gareth he was "a fucking idiot" and they returned to his mom's basement to "debrief" and think of a new plan. Later, Zack messaged Will with a sad-face emoji: "Didn't go as planned but at least we know the anthrax works." Will shattered the phone soon after with a meat tenderizer.

People were still filming when the paramedics arrived, Jack was scouring the fridge for another beer and the children had moved onto "hide-and-seek." Not even The Twins seemed to care that their parents were fighting for their lives.

Will and Rose were right: *they were fucking evil.* And, even worse, they were *still fucking alive.*

CHAPTER 18 FAKE NEWS AND A FUNERAL

The first reporter on the scene was Ezekiel Tranter, a freelance journalist and videographer who had heard the words "clown" and "anthrax" on the police scanner in his car.

He was filming a burning building at the time, but the people inside were no longer screaming so it was kinda boring. He packed up his camera gear and headed to Ned and Beth's house, passing Mr. Happy's van on his way there. He made a mental note of the two men in the front seats: they were arguing and seemed odd, especially Gareth.

Ezekiel hadn't always wanted to be a reporter. From a young age, his goal in life had been to work as a stenographer in the Ninth District Court of Appeals: he liked legal dramas on TV (*Ally McBeal*) and he had the perfect tiny hands for typing on those little stenographer machines (or "steno machines," as they're known by those in the biz).

Sadly, Ezekiel was not suited for such a career. It wasn't the speed of his typing or his ability to listen to every detail—it was "the voices" in his head. *Yeah, you read that right:* he heard voices. It wasn't normally a problem for him: at home, they were mostly kind, elderly female voices who asked him how his day had been, helped him cook ("easy on the vinegar"), and told him he "looked hot" when he was getting ready to go out (he didn't, the voices were pathological liars). But sometimes, particularly at work, the darker (straight-white-male) voices would surface: they were often mean and cruel, but they also offered helpful advice and reminded him to do things he would normally forget to do (i.e., "pick up the dry cleaning, you useless prick").

Ezekiel's "voices" problem came to a head during a high-profile Family Court trial in the late 2000s: a divorced couple were fighting to avoid custody of their six-year-old (who was an asshole) and the wife was testifying about how much physical and mental anguish she would suffer if she had to take the child home with her (to her fifteen-room mansion). Near the end of the wife's testimony, the judge became distracted by an "objectum-sexual" porn video on his phone (which involved a middle-aged woman fucking a steel bridge). He asked Ezekiel to read back the last eight minutes of her testimony, which he did, not realizing the voices in his head were mixed in with the wife's words.

"The child causes me mental and physical anguish, he tortures my baby Shih Tzu," Ezekiel read, "And… fucking kill them all, they deserve to die and rot in fucking hell, especially the shit-for-brains judge who watches people fuck inanimate objects on his phone during the trial and jerks off under his robe. Also, get milk. Handsome prick."

The judge called a mistrial and was later demoted to the lower courts. Ezekiel was briefly infamous, people made funny memes about him, and a courtroom sketch of him sold at Sotheby's for six figures (a billionaire with schizophrenia bought it).

The New York Times employed him soon after to cover trials, impressed by the "color" he added to his "reporting." But he didn't last long: one of the lazier, more cynical voices ("Russell") told him to stay home and make up fictional trials to report on, which he did. The People vs. Honey Badger, Pop Tart vs. Burnt

Toast, Inc., and The United States Postal Service vs. MailChimp were all tried and adjudicated in Ezekiel's imagination (and his pajamas). His ruse finally came unstuck with P.E.T.A vs. Pepe's Pizza, which—according to his front page report—was "the first-ever damages case brought by a subway rat against a fast food restaurant for undercooked pizza." Ezekiel was exposed by a rodent expert, who said the type of rat he'd described in his article (a "ceratogaulus") was actually a horned gopher from prehistoric times that was allergic to cheese.

◆   ◆   ◆

Ezekiel sold his footage of the "anthrax clown tragedy" to fifteen local TV news stations, and one syndicated cable talk show.

Will and Rose were still high—and playing their eighteenth game of Yahtzee with Bertie—when they saw it on their local news bulletin: Ned and Beth's covered bodies being wheeled into a Medical Examiner's van. People were crying; Jack was in the background with a fresh beer. A chyron read: "Upper-To-Middle-Class Couple Poisoned At Clown Party." *Upper-To-Middle-Class? Really? Bit generous*, Rose thought. They briefly discussed what chyron the news station would use if they ever followed through with their suicide plan. "Wealthy Hot Couple Fall To Their Deaths?" Or maybe "Pug Decapitates Self, Owners Follow?"

Thankfully, the chaotic events of the day didn't lead back to either of them, nor to Zack and Gareth. The real Mr. Happy, who woke up naked in his van a few hours after the deaths, was arrested when he got back to his office. Yeah, weird: *he had an actual office.* Most clowns work out of their garages.

Detectives on the case didn't believe his story about being kidnapped: they had the recording of his phone call with the eight-year-old girl, which was enough to prove he had a deep and unhinged hatred of children and their parents. At sentencing, the judge said Mr. Happy's actions had caused irreparable damage to clowns and balloon-shapers everywhere.

◆   ◆   ◆

People grieve in different ways. When a person dies in the Lakshadsheep Islands, the widowed partner traditionally mourns them for a year by wearing the exact same (unwashed) clothes they died in. They must also eat the last meal they ate every single day (for lunch and dinner), even if it poisoned them or they choked to death on it.

It works out well for most people: Franny Highsmith had to dress in her husband's lumberjack outfit and eat hamburgers for a year, Danny Truant wore his wife's pantsuit (luckily she hated dresses) and ate avocado toast, and Doris McCarthur donned a bloody surgical gown and consumed vending machine snacks for twelve months (which ended up giving her terminal bowel cancer). But the tradition proved highly problematic for Curtis Flavell, whose wife suffered a fentanyl overdose soon after sucking his brother's cock. She was found naked and an autopsy revealed she had swallowed (which counted as "a meal," according to the Lakshadsheep Islands' constitutional definition). Curtis fled the islands after the funeral and became an off-Tibetan monk, which is when you become a Tibetan monk but you're nowhere near Tibet.

◆   ◆   ◆

Will and Rose grieved Ned and Beth for several hours on the morning after their deaths.

They asked Bertie to dress in his full-black livery and serve them only black coffee (they normally had cream). After breakfast, Rose read a collection of Beth's most profound tweets (including "just found out spaghetti grows on vines #mindblown") and they lit a bonfire in the backyard, burning a photo collage of them (every single photo that existed of Ned and Beth in their house), along with all the burner phones they'd been using to communicate with Zack.

But the consequences of what had happened didn't fully resonate until after lunch (black sausage, black olives). The Twins were not only still alive, they realized, but they could now use their parents' untimely deaths to get ahead in life. College applications, job interviews, dating hot people who were way out of their league. They quietly imagined the fawning, sympathetic leverage the repugnant little girls would have for the rest of their lives. "Oh, your parents were poisoned by an insane clown? You poor thing, let's fuck," or "I'm so sorry to hear your mom and dad died of anthrax poisoning. Sign here for a full scholarship." The whole idea of it depressed them for days.

Ned and Beth's funeral was held on a Friday afternoon. Rose bought a new black dress (she kept the tags on) and Will skipped breakfast and lunch, saying he wanted to save his appetite for the wake "dinner spread." Ned's mom was a master spread-maker (his 30th was a literal feast) so he was expecting to gorge himself silly. Her Chinese dumplings were the bomb.

The church service went predictably, at first. Framed photos of Ned and Beth rested on matching coffins. Tears streamed from a sea of mourners, including Brett, Melissa, and their fidgety brood of four; Kathleen, Jack (whose tears were actually laughing tears because he was watching "Funny Or Die" videos on his phone), and their baby (whose tears had nothing to do with grieving). The Twins were sitting in the front row in matching outfits, already planning which college they'd attend.

A hungover priest with leftover food in his beard mistakenly read the notes from his previous funeral: "There is no greater loss than when our friends and loved ones leave us in the prime of their lives, even if they're homosexuals and God hates them." There was some awkward coughing, and a statue of Jesus started weeping, but he kept going.

"Dwayne was a loving husband to Todd. Sure, they were unrepentant sinners, but there's no evidence the lightning bolt that struck and killed him came from the Holy Father. It was just a coincidence and he died doing what he loved most, which was gardening in a category three storm. He actually loved sodomy more than gardening in storms but, if he'd been doing that when he died, he probably wouldn't have died because he would've been inside, giving Todd, and God, the finger. So, it's all very ironic and tragic, which is why we turn to the Lord in these confusing times."

The organ player, a sixty-year-old woman with cyan hair, took it upon herself to interrupt, playing a very loud hymn about animal sacrifice to drown out his voice. By the time the music was over, an altar boy had quietly rearranged the priest's notes and he resumed his monologue.

"Beth was a devoted mother and fundraiser," he read, "and Ned, a talented app designer whose most meaningful contribution to the world was helping homeless people find love. Tinder for Bin-People, he called it." There were some chuckles, a few people googled it. At least half the congregation wanted to hear more about Dwayne and Todd. The guy running the slide show, who was easily confused and also hungover (from doing mezcal shots with the priest the night before), was still projecting photos of them (their wedding, holding hands on horseback, a naked, genitals-blurred-out shot of them on the gay cruise where they met).

Will and Rose were seated down the back, enjoying the rambling priest and the hilarious photo mix-up, and ready to make a quick exit—so they could get the best parking spot at the meal/wake. Rose wasn't happy with the heels she'd picked, the church WiFi was rubbish, and she was still pissed about how useless Zack and Gareth had been. She didn't bother lowering her voice during the second hymn, which was about a perverted shepherd who coveted (and later fucked) several ewes from his neighbor's flock of sheep.

According to the Latin lyrics, God considered it "a serious but totally-understandable misstep" (not technically "a sin") and forgave him, gifting him a whole new flock of rams and a peach orchard to "get his mind back to the way God kinda likes it."

"I told you they were morons," Rose said, referring to Zack and Gareth. "How hard is it to kill two idiot twins?" An elderly mourner in front of them, Beth's second cousin twice removed, turned and shooshed her. Rose made a face: *what's your problem, bitch?*

Thankfully, after a few more dull speeches, including a gay hip-hop poem by a random teenager (a friend of Dwayne's), it was time to get the hell out of there (Rose's words, which traveled). More depressing organ music played and the coffins floated down the steps on the shoulders of pallbearers (Jack and Brett were among them, no-one asked Will). They waited at the end of the pew for the right moment to escape, knowing there'd be a bottleneck.

But Will was distracted by the unthinkable: Zack. *Yeah, fucking Zack.* He was standing in the second-to-last row, wearing a shit-eating grin and the suit he'd worn to prom in the eighties (*no, he didn't have a date and no-one danced with him*).

CHAPTER 19 **THINGS GET UGLY**

Zack grabbed Will's arm as he headed for the exit, pulled him behind a pylon.

"What are you doing here?" Will asked.

Zack eyeballed him, spoke in a ridiculous raised whisper. "You haven't returned any of my Skype calls. We need to talk."

Will looked around for Rose, but she'd been sucked into the gushing current of mourners and was drifting helplessly through the arched doorway.

"You idiots killed the wrong people," Will told Zack. "They were our dinner-party friends. They laughed at my jokes. We needed them."

"Yeah. Sorry about that. I suspended Gareth. Without pay."

"He's an intern. You don't pay him." Will shifted his weight, ready to leave. Zack blocked his path.

"Forget Gareth, forget the past, I've got a whole new plan," Zack said. "I can have those Twins dead before canapes are served at the wake." *Canapes? They weren't doing canapes, were they?* Nearby, a nun straightening bibles looked over.

"We can't talk here," Zack added, searching for a quieter place. "There!" He pointed. *Where?* "The confessional booth!" *Really?*

Ignoring all common sense but desperate for Zack to stop bothering him and leave, Will agreed—quietly hoping he could still get to the wake before everyone got their grubby hands all over the buffet. "Fine," Will said. "But I'm sitting in the priest's compartment."

The priest's velvet-backed chair was significantly more comfortable than it looked from the other side of the mesh window. No wonder Father O'Malley had nodded off when Will was apologizing for masturbating and calling his dad a "cocksucker" at age twelve.

Not long after he sat and got comfortable, the tiny wooden door to his left slid open: Zack. "Now, where were we?" he asked.

"You were about to tell me about your new plan and I was about to fire you," Will said.

Zack laughed like it was a joke. "That's funny. Do you wanna hear the plan or not?"

Will sighed. "Fine, what exactly do you have in mind?"

Zack leaned close to the ornate metal screen dividing them, lowered his voice. "It's called 'Bomb-Inside-The-Piñata'" he said, delighted with himself.

"I don't understand." Will replied.

"It's a bomb. Inside a piñata."

"I understand that part. But how do you get a piñata inside a wake?"

Zack looked off like he hadn't thought of that, quickly improvised. "You and Rose take it in. As a gift. I've got it in the trunk of my car."

"We can't take a piñata into a wake. It's completely inappropriate."

"A piñata's never inappropriate. Everybody loves a piñata. Besides, it's shaped like a skull so you can say it's a spiritual thing to protect your dead friends' souls. They do it all the time in South American countries."

Will looked at him, incredulous, thought about giving him ten Hail Marys and telling him to go fuck himself (like Father O'Malley had done). Before he could, the door to his right slid open. *An actual confession?* Fuck. OK, no. It was Gareth. He peered in with a toothy smile.

"Hey." *Hey?* Will turned to Zack.

"What's he doing here? I thought he was suspended."

"It was a 24-hour suspension," Zack replied, glancing briefly at Gareth, who was still grinning. Will's patience had thinned to the bone, and his stomach rumbled. The dumplings were probably piping hot by now, he thought.

"Listen, there's no need to kill The Twins anymore," he told Zack. "Their parents are dead so the entire reason for killing them is moot."

Gareth piped up: "Mute as in the button on the remote that makes everything silent?"

"No," Will rose from the chair, ready to leave. "Moot as in 'having little or no practical relevance,' kinda like you." Gareth still didn't get it.

"Wait!" Zack pressed his face against the mesh divider, panicked. "Think of Gareth's future. He needs the credit points." Will rolled his eyes: *yeah, whatever.* He reached for the door handle. "Also, we have a great plan to eliminate the baby," Zack added. Will turned the handle: *still, whatever.* "And we've kept all our messages and communications in case we get arrested and need to incriminate you and Rose to save ourselves." *Oh.* Will stiffened, backed away from the door.

"Really? You're threatening me now?"

"Definitely not, I wouldn't do that," Zack replied. "We're friends."

"We're not friends."

"We're colleagues. And we'd probably become friends if we ever had to share the same prison cell, which would only happen if we suddenly stopped being colleagues."

Will sighed, realized the little toad had him in a corner. He sat back down, pissed. All he could think about was Beth's second-cousin-twice-removed gorging on his dumplings.

"Fine. I won't fire you just yet. But we want the baby dead in two days."

Zack grinned, delighted, already visualizing storyboards. "You got it," he said, glancing at Gareth. "We're back on. Let's go!" He slid the little door shut and scurried off, his footsteps trailing. Gareth followed.

Will exhaled, exhausted, grabbed a handful of mints from the priest's special nook and rose again from the chair—but Zack's door slid open. He turned, dismissive, irritated. "What the fuck now?" But it wasn't Zack. An old woman was there, on her knees, head lowered.

"Forgive me Father, for I have sinned," she began. *Oh.* Will tried to intervene.

"No, no—" But she kept going.

"...it's been two weeks since my last confession..."

"I'm not—" Yep, still going like she couldn't see or hear Will.

"...and I've committed one sin..." *One sin? Is that all?* Will sat back in the chair, intrigued, did his best "holy" voice:

"Just one? What did you do?"

She paused, searched for the best way to say it. "I tried to drown the grandchildren again." *Again?* Suddenly Will really liked this old woman. He wanted to hear everything. The buffet, the dumplings, could wait.

"Tell me more," he said, settling in the chair. "I need to know every little detail before I can forgive you."

◆   ◆   ◆

There was only one dumpling left when Will and Rose finally arrived at the wake. Before Will could get to it—*yeah, you guessed it,* Beth's cousin snapped it up. She may have been twice removed but she wasn't too far removed from the fucking food platters.

Will and Rose had to settle for icing-free cake and non-alcoholic champagne, a complete "non-sequitur" meal. They stood in a quiet corner, hoping to avoid Jackleen, and Brett and Melissa. Outside, a bunch of violent children were smashing multiple piñatas (all shaped like skulls).

Rose chewed slowly, still gobsmacked by the confessional booth meeting, which Will had told her about in the car.

"She tried to drown her own grandchildren?" she asked.

"Twice. And she beat one of them with a two-by-four."

"A two-by-four? That's fantastic." Rose added, smiling. "Did you give her penance?"

"No. I said God owed her ten Hail Marys and three Our Fathers."

They both looked off, chewed and sipped, thought about the impact a two-by-four would have on youthful skin. A child brushed past them, grubby and directionless. Rose grimaced, re-membered the other part of the confessional meeting.

"I can't believe you're giving those fuckers another chance," she said. "They're incompetent."

"We don't have any other choice. And he threatened to snitch on us. Besides, they've shown they're capable of killing, which is a positive." Rose looked at him, not convinced.

In the distance, The Twins were surrounded by relatives, enjoying their newfound attention. Some mourners were even doing selfies with them (hashtag-their-parents-just-died).

"Well, there's no point killing The Twins now," she said, clearly disappointed. "Their deaths are moot."

"That's what I told them," Will replied. "They're doing the ten-month-old next." On cue, probably woken by the mention of its existence, Jackleen's baby started crying somewhere. Will and Rose shared a look, mischievous.

"This time we're not doing Skype or Zoom or stupid fucking storyboards," she said. "Just 'THEY'RE DEAD' in caps in a text. Did you tell him that?"

"I'll tell him."

Rose spat out her last piece of cake, on the move. "Let's get out of here before more children touch my dress. I have to return it tomorrow." They dumped their paper plates and plastic cups on the edge of a sofa, headed for the door—but a thin man in a suit blocked their exit. His name was Ray Malouf and he was about to ruin their lives even more.

"Oh, hello. You must be Mr. and Mrs. Calhoun?" he said, extending a bony, cake-smeared hand to shake. He was pushing fifty, balding, beady eyes behind thick-rimmed glasses. They both ran their eyes over him, judgmental. He was dressed in a cheap suit, looked like an air marshal for a third-world-country airline whose planes crashed often.

"Who wants to know?" Rose asked back.

"I'm Ray Malouf. I'm Ned and Beth's lawyer," he replied. Will eventually shook his hand, mostly because it was just hanging there like a limp dick. Someone had to shake it. Ray kept talking, oblivious to their confused, what-the-fuck-do-you-want-with-us faces: "I was going to call you this week to set up a time to meet. So we can get all the paperwork finalized."

OK, they were really confused now. Maybe he had mistaken them for another attractive and classy-looking couple? "Paperwork?" Rose asked.

"The guardianship documents," he said. *The fucking what?*

"The what?" Will asked.

"Ned and Beth didn't discuss it with you?" He seemed surprised by their confusion. *No, they didn't fucking discuss anything with them because they refused to take their calls.*

"Oh, maybe it was meant to be a surprise," he continued. *A surprise?* He mistook their expressions for delight. It was not "delight." It was "horror," deep, guttural, primal-scream horror. And Ray just kept twisting the knife. "They listed you as legal guardians of The Twins. In case, well, you know... they died. Which kinda happened."

"Legal guardians?" Will asked. "Why would they list us?"

"They obviously thought you'd make wonderful parents," Ray said, beginning to have doubts of his own. *Wonderful parents?* Rose stepped in:

"We'd make horrible parents," she replied. Ray grinned, chuckled, thought she was joking. She made it clear she wasn't. "It's a lovely gesture and we're flattered and all that but we're not interested."

Will nodded furiously. "It's a pass. Thanks, though." They fake-smiled and tried to get past him—but he wasn't letting them go that easily.

"You can't pass. Technically, they're yours now," he said. "Looks like you have an instant family!" The fucker grinned like a sadist who had them tied up by their genitalia. Their teeth ground in unison. The Twins, in their house, at their breakfast table, touching things, breathing the same air as them? *No fucking way.*

Will looked Ray in the eyes, tried to be reasonable. "I'm sure there are plenty of couples out there who really want children. And The Twins should stay with family. Don't they have other family?"

"They're staying with their aunt at the moment but that's temporary," he said. "The thing is, she's got dementia. She can't even remember her own name. And, to be honest, I don't think she likes The Twins."

Rose couldn't contain herself any longer. "We don't like them either! No-one does. They're shit Twins!" As usual, her words traveled across the room. Mourners turned, The Twins glared. Will lowered his voice, continued to be as reasonable as he could.

"What about a state-run facility? They could meet other orphans," he said.

Rose loved the idea, joined in. "Yes. Other orphans! To share stories about all their dead and/or missing parents."

"And if their lives turn out to be shit, they'll always be able to blame it on 'growing up in the orphanage.' It's the best excuse ever for never reaching your full potential. Or any potential!"

Ray didn't share their enthusiasm. "Nope, that's not possible," he said. "The only way to stop the guardianship transfer now would be an annulment, which is highly unusual."

"An annulment?" Will asked, hopeful. Rose dug out her phone, started googling it.

"Can we do that online?" she asked, searching.

"No, you have to apply to the court and it'll take at least thirty days," he said, moving closer to them so no-one else could hear. "But think of the impact it'll have on The Twins. They've just lost their parents in a violent attack caused by a clown. They need stability, love, people who want to take care of them."

Will and Rose looked at him, quietly processing his words.

"We have to wait thirty days?" Will asked.

"And there's definitely not an app for this?" Rose returned to her phone, searching. It was a "yes" to the first question and a "no" to the second but Ray didn't know whether to nod or shake his head. Instead, he just dug out a business card from his jacket pocket.

"Here's my card. Have your lawyer call me so we can make the arrangements for the drop-off." Neither of them took the card so he left it on the sofa next to their abandoned plates, gave them a smug little wave as he left. "Bye, then," he said, slithering away like an inland taipan (world's most venomous snake).

They stared into space, their heads spinning. *How could a simple thing like killing a bunch of children end up so utterly fucked?*

CHAPTER 20 **WEIRD, BUT FUN**

Ray Malouf had dreamed about helping people when he was growing up in the suburbs of Minnesota.

While other boys his age were shoplifting, sniffing glue, and just generally sucking the life out of their communities, Ray was plotting a life of painful "do-gooderness," which was the actual word he used on his website (Rose googled him when she got home). Something deep within him was off-balance, Rose thought. No-one cared that much about doing good. Will agreed.

Ray became a public defender as soon as he finished law school, representing people who desperately needed his help. He fought for better pre-trial conditions for his clients, championed inmate uniform reform (forcing a color change from "orange" to "tangerine"), and frequently posted on social media about all the good things he was doing, normally with a selfie and some random quote about "being good and shit." He famously fought for more diversity in police lineups (popularizing the hashtag #lineupssowhite), which ultimately backfired when his (white) client Jonah Doey, suspected of first-degree murder, was easily identified next to three black women, a transgender teenager, an

Asian man in a wheelchair, and a Native American in full head-dress. On the way to the electric chair, Doey said he was proud to have been part of a movement that made it possible for people of all races, genders, and sexual orientations to be falsely identified and put to death for crimes they didn't commit.

Despite his devotion to helping people and "doing good for others," Ray eventually realized he wanted more money so he could "do more good for himself." He joined a private legal firm and represented celebrities and sports stars, helping them nego-tiate contracts and avoid lawsuits from people they'd assaulted or consensually groped.

His client Bobby McTiernan, a professional basketballer, was widely regarded as the first person to publicly announce he was retiring to "spend more time with his family." Ray advised him to say the line, even though he knew McTiernan loathed his family (his wife was "an influencer" and his children were morons) and just wanted to play golf and drink himself to death, which he eventually did. The headline on his obituary read: "Family man and former sports star chokes on own vomit." His golf buddy, who also died that day and was a significantly more valuable person to society, got a much smaller obituary: "Single man with no sporting talent died too."

After representing a NASCAR driver who drove himself into a concrete wall (and, subsequently, an induced coma), Ray realized he had a special connection with clients who were un-conscious and/or couldn't communicate. He transitioned into estate law, drafting wills and testaments, and fighting for the rights of dead people who couldn't argue with him or question his fees.

He met Ned while he was representing a nonagenarian billionaire, whose pacemaker had exploded after receiving an electric shock (by phone) from his nineteen-year-old wife (who loved him for who he was, not his ridiculous wealth). Ned's com-pany was cleared of any culpability, using the "we make the gun, we're not responsible for firing it" defense. The teenage widow was jailed, and Ned and Ray became besties.

◆   ◆   ◆

Rose had an uncle ("Ron") who studied law and did wills for hookers. Apparently, it was a growing niche market because hookers had lots of spare cash and they died sooner than most people. Surprisingly, they left most of their money to "pet shop owners" and their "pimps' moms."

She texted Uncle Ron on the drive home from the wake, told him they had a "serious fucking emergency involving the guardianship of two evil twins" (her exact words). He had no experience whatsoever in guardianship law but replied anyway: "first, two evil twins is a redundant phrase: you can't have one or three or even four twins," he wrote.

She replied: "whatever, fuckwit, just answer the question about the guardianship." This went back and forth for some time, during which he explained what redundant phrases were and she told him about Ray and the two children they were being forced to look after. Finally, he gave his expert legal opinion: "you're basically fucked." He was right.

They told Bertie all about it when they got home, asked him to make dumplings and chocolate cake (with triple-icing) to lift their spirits. Bertie often came up with brilliant ideas when he was sober and/or baking: he suggested they take a whole lot of compromising photos, maybe even film a weird sex tape, and send them anonymously to Ray. He said it would make him realize how totally unfit they were to be the parents of anyone, let alone two young girls with their whole lives ahead of them.

Will and Rose both thought it was a great idea and spent the rest of the night doing the photos. Bertie used his smartphone and gave them some basic direction: hand there, leg higher, tongue out, whip harder. They even got Ralph involved, but that got weird real quick. It was all pretty repulsive, but they were desperate.

When it was done, Will told Bertie to put on a hoodie and go print all the photos at a Kinko's (a different one to the dossier fucker), then send them to Ray in an unmarked package from a post box outside the city. Bertie followed the plan to a T (which actually means "tittle," in case you're wondering. If you don't know what "tittle" is, look it up or move on, *no-one cares*).

◆   ◆   ◆

Will got the call from Ray Malouf two days later. He wasn't sure how he'd got their number, but both he and Rose were excited to hear from him: they knew he'd have received "the package" by now and he was probably ringing to say he had made other plans for The Twins (perhaps an orphanage, like they'd suggested).

He started with "Hey, it's Ray Malouf." Will put him on loudspeaker so Rose could hear too. "We met at the wake, I was the handsome lawyer in the suit," he continued, chuckling. Rose looked at Will. They had the same thought: *Hurry the fuck up and give us the good news.*

"Yeah, we remember you," Will replied. "What's up?" He made a face at Rose. Ray paused like he was searching for the right words. Then, abruptly:

"Got your package. Weird, but fun. Thanks for that," he said. *Weird, but fun?!* Will pretended to be confused, which he kinda was.

"What package?" he asked.

"The package you sent."

"We didn't send a package."

"It had your names and return address on it." Will stiffened, Rose did too. *Fucking Bertie!*

"Oh, that package," Rose intervened, trying to mop up. "Glad it arrived safely." Ray then rambled on about some legal documents they had to sign, said the drop-off of the children would "happen within the week," and mentioned something about painting the bedrooms so The Twins would feel "at home." He suggested lime or chartreuse, which were their favorite colors. *Fuck that*, they both thought, quietly wondering what color would make them want to run away and become sex workers (it was cerise, they later discovered, although amaranth made children want to strangle other children).

Will was about to hang up when Ray delivered the most disturbing line of the call: "My wife really liked what you sent too. She wants you to come over for dinner some time."

Mother-fuck. They were now instant parents *and* swingers.

◆   ◆   ◆

"Arrival Day," or "4/11" as Will and Rose came to remember it, occurred on a Friday. The Stantons had returned from The Bahamas two days early so Will told Ray to have The Twins "dropped off" at their real house, the shit one across the street. It was actually for the best, anyway: when The Stantons left and their mansion became available again, they could just leave The Twins to fend for themselves or get Bertie to drop off emergency food supplies, which meant they'd hardly ever need to see them.

Bertie painted the upstairs bedroom in amaranth, which matched the blood stains on the carpet, and they bought cerise sheets for the beds, hoping the combination of colors would cause The Twins to run away and strangle each other while giving head-jobs to old men in dark alleys behind IKEA.

The movers arrived after midday and unloaded boxes, carried them up the steps while Will and Rose watched, disheveled and hungover from a restless night. Ray arrived in his regular vomit-suit, chirpy as fucking usual.

"What a great day to start a new family!" he said. They both glared at him, filled with a dread they didn't try to hide. *Weird, but fun?*

"How many more boxes?" Rose asked.

"Not many," he replied. "The other truck has all the toys."

"Another truck?" Rose was pissed, Will was discreetly self-harming with a butter knife. Ray didn't seem to notice or care about their distress. He handed Rose a freshly-printed document.

"Aunt Magda made this list of things they like," he said. Rose took it, reluctant, glanced at it: dot points flowed down the page, and onto the second and third pages.

"For a woman with dementia, she sure remembers a lot," Rose said, reading from the list. "Comb hair before bedtime? Yeah, right." Will snatched the list from her, scanned the page.

"What do all these asterisks mean?" Will asked Ray.

"They're the daily activities," Ray replied. "Two asterisks means hourly." Will checked again, incredulous.

"Who the fuck eats cupcakes every day?"

A second truck arrived (with toys), followed by a minivan, which was driven by an angry woman whose only joy in life was getting children out of her van. The Twins both gave her the finger and tumbled out, scurried up the front steps like they belonged. They brushed past Will and Rose, didn't say "hello" or "thanks for looking after us even though you despise our very existence and tried to have us killed." They just bolted inside to begin pulling things from walls and spreading saliva on surfaces.

Ray watched them go, glanced up at the house. "For some reason, I thought you lived in the really expensive mansion across the street," he said, gesturing at The Stantons' house. "But this is much more homely. Kids grow up to be better people when they have next to nothing."

Rose shot daggers at him; Will was still reading from the list.

"What are butterfly kisses?" he asked.

CHAPTER 21 **LIVING WITH EVIL**

As soon as Ray and the removalists had left, Will and Rose barricaded themselves in the master bedroom and stayed there for several hours.

They gathered up some of The Twins' clothing—the little monsters had tossed their sweaters and scarves on the floor as they rampaged through the house—and tried to teach Ralph to growl at their scent. But his growls were laughable and The Twins' odor made him retch. They wheeled him out of the room.

Bertie had to make quail burgers for The Stantons so he couldn't come to cook dinner or make sure The Twins were locked in their assigned bedroom. Will and Rose tossed a coin: he lost the first (so he'd have to cook) and she lost the second (so she'd have to lure them to their bedroom and lock them in).

Will reheated nuggets (of course) and left them on the kitchen table, which eventually drew them out of the shadows. They ate like the disgusting little runts they were, pausing only to breathe, slurp soda, and dip their chicken in barbecue sauce, which Will had laced with paracetamol (Rose's idea).

Before they'd finished, Rose appeared with a cheesy smile (and a taser behind her back, which Bertie had lent them), telling them it was "time for bed!" She actually thought it would be that easy. They rolled their eyes at her, mumbled the five-year-old equivalent of "yeah, right, whatever, bitch" (which is actually "yeah, right, whatever, bitch.") Will was gently amused and left, pleased his job for the night was done. As he took the stairs, he listened for the sound of the taser. He even waited on the landing, but no taser. Maybe "time for bed" was actually gonna work?

It was two hours before Rose returned to the master bedroom, exhausted. She locked the door, leaned against it.

"They're asleep now, thank fuck," she said. Will was sitting up in bed, in pajamas, laptop open. Clearly, he'd been enjoying his "alone" time. "That paracetamol did fuck all."

"Did you use the taser?" he asked, not looking up.

"Of course I used the taser. Multiple times. They laughed like I was tickling them. They're taser-resistant, like fucking vampires."

He paused, not convinced vampires were taser-resistant. But he continued anyway: "So how did you get them into bed?"

She sighed, kicked off her shoes. "I used that Rohypnol Bertie gave me. Put it in their hot milk."

"You put Rohypnol in their milk?"

She nodded.

"How much?"

"Bertie said one teaspoon, so I used five." She grinned, mischievous, sat on her side of the bed. "We're gonna need more of it tomorrow though. I used the whole bottle."

"Did you comb their hair before they slipped out of consciousness?" He grinned, thought he was funny. She glared at him, made it clear he wasn't.

"Actually, they kinda look cute when they're unconscious," she said, immediately regretting her words. He made a face: *cute?* Her eyes drifted to his laptop, open on a grisly crime scene photo, blood everywhere.

"What are you doing?" she asked, curious, a little disturbed.

"Researching," he replied, eager to elaborate. "I searched for 'accidental child deaths' and got two million hits." He referred to the screen, continued: "Some woman left her baby in a hot car all day and she got off with a fine." She looked, intrigued. It was *The National Enquirer* website. The headline read: "Some Woman Left Her Baby In A Hot Car All Day And She Got Off With A Fine." He turned to her. "When do you go shopping?"

"I do all my shopping online," she replied.

"Well, there must be somewhere you can go and accidentally leave them in the car for a very long period of time. Like, eight hours or more. In the hot sun."

She looked off, thought about it. "Maybe the salon."

"For eight hours?"

"It's possible."

Will gave her a look, incredulous. "OK, book an appointment."

She paused, thought about it some more. "There's a three-month waiting period." He sighed, checked her hair (*it's that good?*). Her face replied: *Yeah, look closer, you have no idea.* "Also, they have an underground carpark," she added. "No direct sun so the car will take much longer to heat up. Probably twelve hours before it's life-threatening." He sighed some more. They both looked off, minds at work. Eventually, she said what they were both thinking:

"If those morons succeed with the baby, maybe we can give them another chance with The Twins."

A week had passed since Zack's promise to eliminate the baby "within two days." Will and Rose were growing anxious, and mildly pissed. No texts or emails had arrived. They checked news updates, the obituary column in the newspaper, even Jackleen's Facebook page, which was full of "adorable baby snaps."

There were no poems or quotes about sudden loss, no selfies with a tiny coffin, no candlelit vigils near their house. Will even thought about calling Jack and casually asking "how things were going." If he paused and said "not too bad," they'd know Zack and Gareth had succeeded. But if he didn't, and the baby was still alive, he'd probably invite them over for "a viewing" of the fleshy pink creature, which would be worse than a live-stream of an old man's upper endoscopy. He decided not to risk it.

Rose was particularly agitated by the delay: the mini egg rolls she had ordered for the planned dinner party with Ned and Beth would not last much longer in the fridge—and she refused to ask Bertie to transfer them to the freezer. *Fuck defrosting.*

She came across a news story about an Alexa that had "encouraged" a child to perform a "lethal viral challenge" on himself—*maybe that could work?* She interrupted Will while he was on the toilet, eager to hear his thoughts. He was quiet for a moment: she wasn't sure if he was thinking or completing a bowel movement (she couldn't see him, thank God: they were not an open-door bathroom couple).

Finally, he spoke through the closed door: "So, we give Jackleen an Alexa as a gift and we hack into the Alexa so it tells the baby to drink toxic detergent?" he asked.

"Exactly. I already found a website that helps you do the hacking," she added. "You just type in what you want it to say and it says it. Later, when the baby's gone, we can use it to 'recommend' they both get out more, perhaps go to a dinner party with upper-class friends to overcome their loss." He groaned, but that was definitely part of a bowel-movement.

"It's interesting," he said, which is what he always said when he wasn't entirely convinced. "Is the baby old enough to understand what Alexa says?"

Rose looked off, realized she hadn't thought of that. "It's ten months old. Can a ten-month-old understand words?"

"I don't know. We should buy an Alexa so we can ask her." They were interrupted by a heavy knock at the door. Rose looked from the second-floor window, expecting to see Bertie with a Rohypnol top-up. But it wasn't him. Her face paled.

"It's that fucking munchkin man and his sidekick," she said. Will flushed, came out of the bathroom without washing his hands. He looked for himself: *yep, it was Zack and Gareth, grinning like stoned Mormons who wanted cookies.*

"Holy fuck," he said. "What the fuck are they doing here?"

"How did they find out where we lived?" Suddenly, Rose had a sepia-toned flashback of their Zoom call with Zack. Her mood brightened.

"Remember he said they'd drop by after the killing to celebrate?" Will looked at her, remembering (in black-and-white). "And we said 'fuck no, don't do that.'"

"Yeah, I remember. Something about high-fives and mimosas?" They both looked at Zack and Gareth again, hopeful, searching for a mimosa bottle. Gareth had a large bag.

"Do you think...?" Rose wondered aloud.

"Maybe...?" Will pondered, even louder.

They bolted down the stairs, two steps at a time. Rose didn't even bother with a robe, her transparent nightgown flapping open in the cold air. They opened the front door, eager-as-fuck, like their Amazon psychic had arrived with a delivery and/or prediction.

"Is it done?" Rose blurted before either of them could speak.

"Is what done?" Zack asked, genuinely clueless.

"The baby. Is it dead?"

"No. But we have the next best thing."

"It's in a coma?"

"Storyboards!" He half-turned to Gareth, gestured to the bag he was holding. "We brought them over so we could show you what we're planning. It's pretty awesome." Gareth shrugged: *not that awesome.*

Will looked past them: Zack's beaten-up car, an eighties-model Volvo, was parked in the driveway. "You came here to show us storyboards?" he asked, incredulous. "How did you know where we lived?"

"Gareth put a tracker on your car when we met at that Piña Colada bar," Zack replied. "Don't take it personally, we do it to all our clients."

"Although the tracker actually took us over there." Gareth pointed towards The Stantons' place. "Which is where your car seems to be parked a lot."

"We go there for dinner parties," Rose added.

"Every night?"

"Every other night. We leave the car when we're drunk."

"You didn't talk to them, did you?" Will asked, mildly panicked.

"No, the butler told us you lived here," Zack replied. "He's very strange."

Rose sighed, exasperated. "Great. Now that you're all up-to-date with our social lives, what the fuck happened to the text?"

"What text?"

"You said you were going to text us when it was done," Will said. "You know, in the church? The confessional, remember?"

He remembered. "Oh, yeah, sorry. I have a real problem with telling the truth in those booths. I think it's a form of childhood trauma. I once told a priest—"

"—It was your idea to go in there!"

Zack thought about it. "It was?"

"Yes." A car passed, headlights cutting across their faces (and through Rose's nightgown). Her patience had thinned.

"Anyway, how about we go back to the original plan, which involves you leaving our house right away, going and killing the baby, and then sending us a text when it's done? OK?" She smiled one of those exaggerated, unhinged smiles, which would be enough to make most people leave immediately. But not Zack.

He stepped forward. "It'll only take twenty minutes to show you the boards," he said. *Fuck.* They both knew he was never going to leave. Rose groaned, wandered off to find alcohol.

Will begrudgingly widened the door. "Get inside. Fast."

◆   ◆   ◆

Zack and Gareth set up the storyboard presentation in Will's home office, which was one of the empty rooms on the east side of the house (where most of the deaths had occurred). Gareth brought little stands for the boards so it was all very professional, like a grunge art exhibition with bad lighting.

Will sat behind a blood-stained desk (yeah, they'd kept some furniture from the massacre), Rose paced with a bottle of wine and a baseball bat ("it helped her think," she said).

"It's called 'A-Dingo-Ate-My-Baby'," Zack began. *A what-ate-what?* Sure enough, "A-DINGO-ATE-MY-BABY!" was written across the first of the boards, in caps and with the exclamation point included. Ralph watched from a cushion in the corner: he barked for no apparent reason.

Rose stopped pacing. "I've got something better. How about 'High-Powered-Rifle-Plan?' Pop. Pop. Pop. It's done," she said. Will nodded, agreeing.

Zack didn't like it when his clients suggested names for his kills. "That sounds great," he replied, condescending-as-fuck. "Maybe we can use that on the next kill." Next kill? *Yeah, right.* He carried on, unperturbed. After the title card, there was a crude drawing of a mangy dingo in a cage. "First, we order a dingo in a cage," he said.

"You can order a dingo in a cage?" Will asked, genuinely curious.

"We already did," Gareth added, proud of himself. "Din-goes-In-Cages-Dot-Com. It arrived this afternoon."

Zack paused, distracted, lowered his voice to Gareth. "You didn't feed it, did you?"

Gareth tensed. "No. Was I supposed to?"

"Fuck no. We need it to be hungry."

Zack returned to Will and Rose, moved to the next board: the dingo leapt out of an open cage. "Second, we put the cage inside the house and let the dingo loose. It eats the baby," he said. The next drawing showed the dingo at a crib, teeth bared, about to eat a screaming baby. "We did several boards with the actual eating but they were not pleasant visuals." Gareth nodded, agreeing. "And that's the plan." Zack checked his watch, pleased with himself. "See, it only took eleven minutes."

Rose looked at the remaining boards: a drawing of Jack and Kathleen sobbing, holding each other, a police car arriving, a shocked policeman's face, a tiny body being wheeled away on a gurney, two policemen sobbing, holding each other, the moon. *Fuck!* "So, it's basically three storyboards for the actual kill and another seventeen for the aftermath?" she said. "Everyone's crying and holding each other. It's like a fucking Lifetime movie."

"What's the moon got to do with anything?" Will asked, confused.

Zack looked, unsettled by all the criticism. "OK, it's not structurally perfect," he replied, "The moon should probably be earlier to set the tone." He glanced at Gareth. "Move the moon to before the police car arrives."

"It doesn't matter where the fucking moon is!" Rose interrupted. "We get it." There was a moment of awkward silence. Zack pouted, Rose finished the bottle, Gareth hovered near the "moon" storyboard, not sure what to do with himself. Eventually:

"So am I moving it or not?"

Will and Rose replied at the same time: "No!!!"

"We'll move it for the digital version," Zack told him, softer. He turned to Will and Rose, pretended this was all going well. "Right, any other questions or comments?"

"I have one," Rose said, swaying a little.

"If it's about the moon—"

"—It's not about the moon. It's about slide four, where the dingo eats the baby." Everyone looked. "Won't it eat Jack and Kathleen too? It's a feral animal that's been set loose in a house."

Zack was ready for the question. "No. It only eats babies," he said. "That smell of babies that women love… this dingo hates it. Viciously. It's been trained for that specific purpose."

Rose nodded: it was the best thing he'd said all night. "I hate that smell too."

"Great. We're all set then," Zack said, gesturing for Gareth to start packing up.

"When is all this happening?" Will asked, standing.

"Tomorrow night. We'll drop by afterwards to debrief and celebrate!"

"No!!!" *Yep, Will and Rose again.*

"A text is fine," Will said, softer.

"Two words, separated by a comma: 'Baby, Gone.'" Rose added, less softly. "And don't come here again. Ever!"

Zack grinned like she was kidding. "OK, got it," he said, on the verge of winking. "We'll do the mimosas on Zoom."

CHAPTER 22 **DINGO + BABY**

Jack and Kathleen lived in a three-bedroom house on the expensive side of town.

It cost significantly more than they could afford but they had found clever ways to supplement their income. The most lucrative of these was an innovative "product placement" program, which Kathleen had signed up for in its beta phase (she had no idea what "beta phase" meant, but she got a free lipstick holder).

For a hundred bucks a week, a random person known as a "placer" would secretly enter their house (with a key, normally left in an agreed location) and substitute products they'd bought at the supermarket with "alternative brands." The idea was that the householder (in this case, Jack and Kathleen) would be forced to use the new product until they went shopping again, during which time there was a "sixty-two-point-two percent chance" they'd learn to like it and buy it again. Coffee, shampoo, cereal, toilet paper, you name it. Sometimes Jack and Kathleen didn't even notice the product had been replaced (i.e., condoms, sugar), and often they'd deliberately leave almost-empty boxes in the pantry in the hope that they'd be replaced with full ones. It was a win-win for everyone, although being a "placer" had its dangers. Many had been mistakenly shot by homeowners or mauled by dogs in the middle of the night, which was when they usually made their "drops." A teenage "placer" had walked in on Jack and Kathleen having sex in the shower one time: he said he was replacing "lube," even though he was holding "corn pops." Jack beat the shit out of him, which led to a two-week suspension (for Jack, and a negotiated settlement for the teenage perv).

◆　　◆　　◆

Jack's suspension had ended when Zack and Gareth arrived at their house on the last Sunday in August, the day after their storyboard presentation. They knew the location of the key to the back door, thanks to a very basic hack of Kathleen's emails (she used the password "hackme").

Zack parked his Volvo across the street just after midnight, oblivious to all the porch-cams. He punched out the headlights, looked across at the house. "That's the one. Number twenty-four," he said, referring to his smartphone. Gareth swallowed, nervous. Before he could speak, Zack continued: "Right, off you go."

"Me?"

"No, Celine Dion. Who just happens to be sitting in the back with the dingo on her lap." Gareth almost turned to look. The dingo watched from its cage in the back seat. It could already sense it was not working with quality humans.

"I'm doing this on my own?" Gareth asked.

"You won't be on your own. I'll be right here, watching everything on the dingo-cam." Zack turned, looked at the cage. The dingo, frothing, pissed, pressed its snout against the wire door. There was a tiny lens on its collar. "See, right there on its collar." He turned back to the dash, punched keys on his laptop. The image from the dingo-cam appeared: the backs of their heads through wire. Gareth sighed, glanced at the house.

"OK, but I get extra credit if I pull this off," he said.

"Fine, that'll make up for all the credit you lost at the clown party." They shared a look, a mini stare-off that Gareth was never going to win. He relented.

"What do I have to do again?" he asked.

Zack rolled his eyes, impatient, like this was the third time he'd explained it. "Take the dingo around back, find the key under the third rock, let him inside through the back door, and get out of there as fast as you can. Just like the storyboards you drew."

"And what are you gonna do?"

Zack resented the question, answered anyway: "I'm gonna sit here and watch the dingo-cam. With the clients. And then I'm going to drive us to the safe house."

"We have a safe house?"

"My mom's house. It's what we're calling it from now on."

The dingo growled, impatient. Zack leaned into Gareth's space. "It's extraordinarily difficult for you to fuck this up, no matter how hard you try. It's the dingo's game to lose and he can't lose."

◆   ◆   ◆

Jack and Kathleen were still awake. They were sitting next to each other in bed, laptops open. She was photoshopping his head onto a meme (something about "fuckwit husbands"), he was reading an article on "hater.com."

"There's a couple here who got divorced, then renewed their divorce a year later just so all their friends and family could remember how much they hated each other," he said. "They had a party and speeches and everything."

Kathleen glanced at his screen. "We should do that," she said. He glanced at hers.

"Really? Another meme?"

"The last one got four-hundred likes."

"The one of me being fucked by a pig got four-hundred likes?"

"No, the one where your head is a volleyball being fucked by a Tom Hanks deepfake." He remembered. They were interrupted by the sound of a baby crying. They both mumbled "fuck" under their breaths.

"It's your turn," she said.

"No, it definitely isn't," he replied. "And these are new pajamas. He always throws up on me after midnight."

She returned to her computer, dismissive. "I have to get this done."

"It's a meme. What's the rush?"

"Wives who hate their husbands need my memes first thing in the morning. They're like protein shakes for the soul."

He sighed, realized she wasn't going to give in. "We really need one of those au pairs."

"Or you could just grow a pair and be the father you always wanted to be." He groaned, closed his laptop. She looked off like she'd just thought of a new meme. "I just thought of a new meme."

"Is it me getting out of bed to be a caring father?"

"No, it's you sucking a dummy, which turns out to be a massive pair of balls." She got back to work immediately. He trudged off.

Will was flossing when he received the text from Zack. The glow of a new message excited him: its content did not. He called to Rose in the bedroom: "I just got a text from Zack."

She was in bed, checking her phone too. "I got the same text. It's a fucking Zoom link."

"He mentioned celebrating on Zoom, remember? With mimosas." Will hovered in the doorway, hopeful. She wasn't convinced.

"Fine, you open it." He did. She waited. Zack appeared on Will's phone, his fat head filling the entire frame.

"Hey!" Zack waved. "Is Rose joining us?"

"No," Will replied, glancing briefly at Rose. "Is it over?"

"It's 'in progress.'" He leaned towards his laptop, shared the dingo-cam screen. "I'm sharing the dingo-cam so you can watch."

"The what?" Rose asked. Will held his phone closer, squinted: it was dark and unsteady, impossible to see anything.

"There's a camera attached to the dingo?" Will asked Zack.

"There sure is. So you'll be able to see everything!"

Rose called out: "We're not watching a dingo eat a baby."

Zack heard her. "It's OK," he replied. "You can look away if you want. I'll do a running commentary."

She groaned, mumbled something about "fucking little munchkin troll."

"Hang the fuck up," she told Will. "Now!"

He hesitated, pretended the connection was failing. "I think I'm losing you," he said.

"I can hear Rose telling you to hang up," Zack said.

"No, I'm losing you, you're cutting out." Will hung up. Rose glared at him: *idiot*.

"We're not Zooming again with that fucker until he delivers proof of death."

◆   ◆   ◆

Gareth found the key under the third rock, opened the back door, slid the cage inside, unhooked the latch on the cage door and fled before the dingo knew it was free to roam.

It only took a moment for the animal to edge forward, nudge the wire door ajar and take in the far-off smell of baby flesh through its enlarged nostrils. It headed for the stairs.

Zack watched, delighted. "You go, girl," he said (it was a male dingo).

Upstairs, Jack stood over the crib with the baby, made stupid "coo-coo" sounds he'd learnt on Youtube, not realizing his words actually translated to babies as "fucking go back to sleep you little cunt or I'll gouge your eyes out." The baby listened, made gurgling sounds back to him that translated as "you wait, fucker, I'm gonna be up all night just to fuck with you and the bitch. I'm not even tired." The conversation went back and forth for several minutes until Jack started "ga-gaaing" (which was like using the "N" word for white babies), at which point the baby gave him the finger and projectile-vomited over his new pajamas. "Take that, motherfucker," it said (or "gaga-woo-woo-blugh").

◆   ◆   ◆

Trevor Simmons became a Product Placement Officer (or "placer") soon after getting out of jail. He had done time for a string of home invasions so the transition came naturally to him: he still got to break-and-enter people's homes, he just left more goods than he took.

He had been assigned to Jack and Kathleen's house after their suspension and, due to Jack's violent shower attack on the previous "placer," was authorized to carry a weapon onto the premises and use it to lawfully defend himself if necessary ("placers" had a very good union).

As luck would have it, Trevor arrived at the house just as Gareth was leaving, neither seeing the other. Zack, however, saw him pull up in his pickup truck, load his Walther P38 pistol and carry a box of groceries around back. "Who the fuck is that?" he wondered aloud. Gareth got in the passenger seat, oblivious. "Do you know who the fuck that was?" Zack asked him.

"Who?"

"Some guy just went around the back with groceries and a weapon." Gareth looked, clueless.

The dingo reached the first floor, turned into the hallway. Jack was leaving the baby's room, his pajamas covered in vomit.

The animal saw him and ducked into the shadows, its movement catching his eye. He turned, looked—nothing. But he could hear its raspy breath.

Kathleen had finished her meme and was trying to sleep when Jack returned to the bedroom. He headed straight for the wardrobe, rummaged through boxes. She peeled back her face mask, irritated, turned on the lamp. "What are you doing?" He pulled a shoebox from the top shelf, sat on the edge of the bed. She saw the vomit all over his pajamas, cringed. "Oh. He vomited on you again."

He grunted, pulled a snub-nosed revolver from the box. "You're overreacting a little, don't you think? It's only vomit."

He turned to look at her, confused, realized what she meant. "I'm not going to shoot the baby," he said, loading the clip. "There's a raccoon inside." She sat up, alert, significantly more concerned than when she thought he was going to shoot their baby.

"A raccoon? Inside? How do you know?"

"Because I heard it breathing. It's in the hallway."

She tensed, looked through the open doorway. "How the hell did a raccoon get inside?"

"I don't know. One of those perverts who replace our groceries probably left the door open on his way out."

She thought about it, remembered. "I hope they replaced that shitty oatmeal. Can you check?" He glared at her: *really?* "On your way to the trash can with the dead racoon." He sighed, headed for the door. She called after him: "Watch where you shoot. I don't want blood all over my feature wall."

Zack and Gareth were glued to the dingo-cam as the animal approached the crib, its nose pressing between the bars. "Here we go," Zack whispered, rubbing his hands together like it was bottom of the ninth. The baby wriggled, restless, unaware.

Jack headed along the hallway, tentative, on edge, gun raised. He looked into the shadows where he'd heard "the raccoon," but couldn't see it. He switched on the light, which spilled into the nursery—the dingo flinched, distracted. It raised its snout, nostril hairs straightening, taking in the vomit on Jack's pajamas like a sea breeze. *The smell of baby.*

"Uh-oh," Gareth said. Zack tensed.

Jack didn't see the dingo as he entered the nursery—it waited behind the door, pounced from behind, jaws latching onto the back of his neck. He stumbled forward, flailing, grabbing at it. Growls and man-curses overlapped. "Mother-fuck-fuck-get-the-fuck-off-me," he shouted, trying to get a clean shot with the revolver.

Trevor was replacing an oatmeal box when he heard the commotion upstairs. He reached instinctively for his pistol, eager for a violent confrontation (he missed jail). Kathleen heard the ruckus too and leapt out of bed, ripped off her sleep mask on her way out the door.

Jack staggered into the hallway, clawed at the dingo as it teared into his neck. In the chaos of it all, his gun went off twice: the first shattered a plastic tortoise over the baby's crib, the second hit Trevor in the chest as he rounded the banister at the top of the stairs. Trevor's pistol fired back as he dropped to the floor, hitting Kathleen in the forehead as she ran from the opposite direction. Blood and brain matter sprayed across her favorite feature wall. It was a spectacularly-coincidental series of misfires and deaths, culminating in the puncture of Jack's jugular vein. His scream was muted, the house fell silent.

And then the baby cried, wide awake, spilling cheerful gurgles that translated as "I'm still fucking here, motherfuckers."

Zack and Gareth stared blankly at the screen. "I don't think the dingo ate the baby," Gareth said. Zach gave him a look: *ya don't think?*

The dingo fed on Jack for the better part of ten minutes (his flesh was surprisingly tasty after marinating in scotch and bourbon for 20-plus years). When the animal's belly was full, it climbed over the bodies of Kathleen and Trevor and headed out the back door, which had been conveniently left open. As it scurried across the yard, disappearing into the night, the video feed from the dingo-cam cut out.

Zach sighed, buried his face in his hands. "That did not go as storyboarded."

CHAPTER 23 HERE WE GO AGAIN

Rose was the first to see the morning news.

The sound was muted but the vision (courtesy of Ezekiel Tranter) could not have been clearer: police and paramedics outside Jackleen's house, a chyron that ruined her overcooked eggs: "Three dead in 'Product Placement' massacre." *Three?* She immediately ran upstairs and woke Will.

"The bearded moron killed all three of them," she said. He stirred, groggy.

There were no texts from Zack on Will's phone but he had sent an email: the subject heading read "Baby Kill Update #1." Will opened it before he'd had coffee, which was ill-advised.

"Hey guys!" Zack wrote. "Was going to drop by for a debrief after the kill (attempt!) but thought you might be sleeping." *Yeah, he actually put "attempt" in parentheses, and added the exclamation point.* "So, I know the dingo-cam was a bit challenging to watch (Rose!) and you guys had some internet issues, so I thought I'd let you know how it all went down," he continued. "Everything was going so well!"

Rose sat next to Will on the bed, started reading too. "What's with all the fucking exclamation points?" she asked. He shrugged. They both continued.

"This is not another 'blame-the-intern' email. On the contrary, Gareth did an exceptional job of getting the dingo inside the house. He gets an A-plus from me for that. To be honest, and you know that's how I roll, things only got out of hand when Jack pulled out his gun. Who knew he had a gun?!" Will sighed, full of dread.

Rose gave up on the email, left the room to give Ralph his lower back massage. "I can't fucking read this shit anymore," she said on her way out the door. "Tell me what happened later, when I'm drunk or unconscious."

Will kept reading. "Anyway, I'm sure you've seen the news by now so I won't put all the gory details here. I wouldn't want to incriminate us all! (insert emoji here—which he did not). Let me finish with some good news." Will leaned forward, eager, actually believing there was (good news). "The dingo got away, which is positive for two reasons. First, he's free to live his life, perhaps hook up with a stray Bullmastiff and start a family of bloodthirsty little mongrels (so cute!). And, second, there's nothing to link any of us to the killings. They're already blaming it on an ex-felon called Trevor and 'his vicious dog,' which fled the scene and ran home." Zack finished with several smiley-face emojis and a sentence that completely disintegrated Will's mood: "And don't worry about the baby—we'll get rid of that little fucker at the big finale!" *Wait, what?* The baby was alive? And what the fuck was the big finale?

Will stood, called out to Rose: "They didn't kill the baby." Something downstairs shattered into a million pieces.

◆   ◆   ◆

Jackleen's funeral was a significant disappointment. The fuckwit responsible for the arrangements—Kathleen's mom, Wendy, who was a nutcase by day—bought matching fucking coffins.

Matching! They even lowered them into side-by-side graves at the exact same time. *Oh, please.*

"Jack would have been seriously pissed," Will said to Rose. They were standing at a distance from the proceedings, next to the tree where people who weren't supposed to be at funerals stood (there was actually a sign on the tree that said: "Stand Here If You're Not Supposed To Be At The Funeral And/Or Are Discreetly Watching The Funeral Because You Think The Murderer Is In Attendance").

"About being mauled to death by a dingo?" Rose asked, too cold to talk.

"No, about the matching coffins and side-by-side graves," Will replied. "He would've wanted to be buried as far away from her as possible, with funerals at the same time so their friends would have to choose. And the eulogies would be filled with all the spiteful things they ever said to each other."

"I like that. We should do that."

Will gave her a look, continued: "I can already hear Jack rolling in his grave."

"He's not in the grave yet." The crane lowering the coffins suddenly stalled, hydraulics screeching. The coffins dangled, swayed by a breeze. The priest coughed, quietly searched through his little book to see if there was a prayer for "awkward burial moments."

"If I die," Rose began, quickly interrupted by Will—

"—if?" She made a face, not appreciating the interruption, kept going:

"*When* I die, I want the gravediggers to deliberately drop my coffin so my decomposing corpse spills out onto the grass."

"Why would you want that?"

"Because no-one will ever forget that. It'll be seared into a hundred subconsciouses."

"You think a hundred people are coming to your funeral?" he asked, not convinced.

"OK, two hundred."

The guy operating the crane called "graveside assistance," which arrived within the hour to tell him the engine was fried and they'd have to tow it to the nearest crane repair workshop. He said it would probably take a couple of weeks to fix, which concerned the crane operator: the bodies would probably decompose by then, he said, and the open graves would fill with water if it rained.

They asked the priest for a solution: he suggested singing a hymn about a sheep who committed suicide by jumping off a cliff (to test his shepherd's faith). He told them the particularly-depressing lyrics normally helped solve these kinds of problems, so everyone agreed and sang along.

Afterwards, when nothing had changed, a dyslexic eight-year-old boy (one of Kathleen's second cousins), said they should just cut the coffins from the wires attached to the crane and lower them into the graves by hand. The priest lit a match and asked the Holy Spirit if it was a good idea and she said yes, which pleased everyone (they were all very hungry). The mother of the boy who came up with the solution was extremely proud of how clever he was, not knowing he would grow up to design and manufacture home office chairs for an alt-right-wing extremist group and The Taliban.

The wake, also organized by Wendy, was similarly problematic. Will quietly regarded her "wake buffet" as an insult to buffets everywhere, including prison buffets, which only served gruel, beans, and razor blades. Wendy's "attempted" spread of food and alcohol featured soggy cake, stiff bread, and lukewarm craft beer that tasted like it had been bottled by teenage millionaires who never washed their hands. Wendy even put a sign on the keg that said it was "Jack's favorite," although she provided no evidence to back that up. When Will questioned her about it in the kitchen, she started sobbing uncontrollably, which meant she was just making shit up.

Will and Rose hovered in the corner of the living room with paper plates and plastic cups, doing their best to look "despondent and broken." They were close to tears at one point, courtesy of undercooked prawns, which helped their "general grieving appearance." People saw them and thought they were really sensitive and loving people who missed Jack and Kathleen terribly. Some gently patted their shoulders and forearms as they passed, offering indistinct mumblings of support. An old guy refilled their glasses with more of Jack's "favorite" beer and said "you'll get through this." Will looked at the beer in his cup and thought "I'm not so sure, old-geezer-in-wheelchair."

"How long do we have to stay?" Rose asked.

Will checked his watch. "Long enough for people to think we had nothing to do with their deaths. Maybe ten more minutes?"

She wasn't pleased with that. "It makes no difference how long we stay," she said. "Murderers always show up to their victims' funerals."

"OK, sorry, I forgot you were a true-crime expert," he said, emptying his beer into a fake pot plant. "We should leave immediately so you can get home and browse the internet for clues to obscure, forgotten crimes that no-one cares about anymore."

She groaned, rolled one eye, emptied her beer into the same plant. "Speaking of which, did you get rid of the SIM cards?" she asked. "With all the incriminating texts and links about dingoes and killing babies?" Her voice traveled, as it usually did. Will often wished her voice would travel interstate for a while, to North Dakota or Connecticut, or perhaps take a gap year to a foreign country (Iran) where women's voices were locked up for a very long period of time, sometimes forever. But it never did.

"Yes," Will replied, "I destroyed all digital communications about 'dingoes' and 'killing babies' because I'm not fucking stupid." Nearby, chewing cake through oversized dentures, a crusty old bag who'd once served tea and installed wiretaps for the C.I.A. overheard their conversation. Rose saw her gawking at them and thought about doing the "neck-slitting motion" that serial killers do to their victims in court—but the old woman was already very close to death and had probably only turned up to get ideas for her own wake.

"Let's leave before I threaten someone's life," she said. Will agreed. But, as they dumped their unfinished plates and plastic cups and turned for the exit, the little weasel of a man they'd hoped to never see again turned up, again. *Yep, Ray-fucking-Malouf was back.* He balanced cake and non-alcoholic punch, blocking their path.

"Oh, hello there," he said, grinning like it was a coincidence. "I was hoping to run into you two." They glared at him, fearing the worst. "I have great news." *Yeah, the worst.*

Rose said what Will was about to say: "You've got to be fucking kidding."

◆   ◆   ◆

The baby arrived two days later with smug-as-fuck Ray and a truckload of clutter: toys that rattled and buzzed and squeaked, a collection of color-coded (and probably unsterilized) dummies, and boxes of disposable (thank God) diapers for Bertie to administer. No drugs or sedatives, which was disappointing.

Will and Rose decided to put the baby's crib (and all its belongings) in the basement to drown out any late-night whining. The realtor told them a college student had been tortured to death down there, which made it an ideal location: if his/her ghost was still hanging around, it might terrify the baby into silence or drive it into a state of madness, which would allow them to have it committed to a mental institution for babies.

Rose googled "mental institution for babies" and discovered it was not possible to forcibly commit anyone under two years old to a state psychiatric facility, even if they had rabies and/or had murdered someone. Otherwise, the internet said, "two out of three mothers in the country would be dropping their newborns off." She sighed, her mood spoiled.

The baby woke them just after 2am on the first night: so much for drowning out the noise. Rose told Will to go check, he mumbled "fuck off," she dragged him out of bed by his feet. On the way to the basement, she checked the age restrictions on a bottle of Rohypnol. *Five years and above, fuck. All these rules.*

They arrived and stood over the crib, watched the baby wail for no apparent reason, probably upset about all the first world problems it would have to deal with in the next twenty years (*"Oh, the WiFi signal in my spacepod is soooo weak!"*).

"What are we supposed to do with it?" Will asked.

"One of us needs to pick it up." Rose looked at him, expecting him to do it.

"Call Bertie, he'll do it."

"I already did. He's washing Mrs. Stanton's panties."

"At this hour?"

"I think it's a euphemism."

"For what?"

"I didn't ask. I really don't want to know."

Will bristled, looked around the room. Old tins, bits of wood, a rusted mattress coated in cobwebs. "I thought there was supposed to be a ghost down here."

"There is." Rose turned full-circle, searching. "But it was a college student as a human so it probably sleeps until midday."

"Great. Why couldn't a nurse have been tortured to death down here?"

"Or a barista. They get up real early and they ramble a lot."

The baby suddenly stopped crying. They both leaned into the crib, delighted. The house had never been so quiet. And then, unexpectedly, thunderous footsteps from above: The Twins were awake. Furniture shifted, objects hit the floor with multiple thuds. The baby stirred, resumed its loathing of the world.

"How are they awake?" Will asked Rose. "Did you give them their 'sleeping medicine?'"

"Of course I did," Rose replied, insulted by the question. "But I think their immune systems are adapting. If I increase the dose, it might be traceable." They both looked off as the noise from above and below pummeled their ears, searching for a solution that wouldn't involve lengthy prison time.

"We've only got two options," Will said, meeting Rose's eyes.

She nodded like she knew exactly what he was thinking. "Pillow suffocation or drowning. They're the only methods we can disguise as accidents."

"That's not what I was thinking."

"Poison can be traced."

"Nup, not poisoning."

"Spontaneous combustion?"

"No."

Rose sighed, impatient. "OK, just tell me what the options are."

"We either to learn to live with them or we give those morons one more chance."

Rose scoffed, incredulous. *Shit options.* "Are you fucking serious?"

"Yes."

"You want to give those fucktards another chance?"

Will nodded, which meant "yes, for the second time."

"There's a pillow right there," she said, pointing at a moldy pillow on the floor.

"You're the one who said you didn't want to get your hands dirty. Remember the whole 'I'll-put-out-the-trash-but-I'm-not-emptying-it-into-the-truck' metaphor?"

Rose grumbled and folded her arms, which was her physical representation of "I fucking hate it when you use my own words against me."

Will headed up the stairs, voice trailing: "I'll call him."

She watched him go, exasperated. Her eyes settled on the baby, whose scream had morphed into a fuck-you giggle. "See what you've made us do now," she said.

CHAPTER 24 **BURN BABY BURN**

In a sunless room on the seventh floor in the east wing of the West Moreton Community Hospital, a wall of life-sustaining medical devices were attached to the charred, disfigured, unconscious body of Frank The Chicken King. *Yep, the motherfucker had survived.*

His wife (and Will's mother) Francine Thampy-Calhoun, an angry woman with brush-resistant hair and a resting face that frightened terrorists, waited at his bedside. Sitting next to her was their troubled daughter Petal, a twentysomething former airline hostess who was twice voted "Most Unhinged" at high school (the teachers voted).

The doctors told Francine and Petal that Frank was unlikely to survive the night and, if he did, he would probably be "very thirsty" and "extremely pissed." But they hung around anyway, hoping he'd wake one final time to say his goodbyes and give them the passwords to everything.

They were both at the vending machine, fighting over the last packet of trail mix (even though they'd never walked a trail ever), when Frank's eyes snapped open. He was awake. And, yeah, thirsty and extremely pissed. "Is anyone here?" he called out, eyes darting between the empty chairs at his bedside. "Hello? Anyone?"

Francine and Petal sauntered in about ten minutes later, neither with trail mix (they didn't have enough change). They realized he was conscious and rushed over. "Frank? Honey?" Francine said, grabbing his skin-grafted hand. "You're awake!?"

"I've been awake for ten minutes," he said, hoarse. "Where the hell have you been?"

"We went to the chapel," she said. Petal hovered, still pissed about the trail mix.

"You were praying for me to wake up?" he asked, surprised.

"Fuck no," Petal interjected. "We needed change for the vending machine. But some guy praying for his dead infant son told us to go fuck ourselves." Frank sighed, looked for the button he could press to slip back into a coma. There wasn't one.

"Is there anything we can get you, dear?" Francine asked.

"Yes," he replied, suddenly alert. "I want those two little pricks dead." They both knew exactly who he meant.

"Can I be the one to end Tony?" Petal asked, frothing. She really hated Tony.

"No-one's 'ending' anyone," Francine said. "He's your brother."

"Half-brother," she mumbled, soft enough so Frank couldn't hear.

"What?" Frank asked.

"Nothing."

He looked at Petal, clearly the apple of his eye. "Of course you can end Tony, sweetheart. We're gonna teach both of those bastards a lesson."

◆   ◆   ◆

Ezekiel Tranter had written enough fake news stories in his career to know when something wasn't quite right. He'd been the first on the scene at both the "Mr. Happy Anthrax Murders" and the "Product Placement Massacre/Dog Attack," two stories he couldn't have spun himself without a straight face (and plenty of mezcal).

The Mr. Happy case had massive gaps in logic—there was no motive for the clown to want Ned and Beth dead, no evidence he had ever bought or even googled "anthrax," and security camera footage that showed two men driving away from an abandoned factory in Mr. Happy's van, the same men Ezekiel had seen on his way to the crime scene.

The deaths at Jackleen's house were similarly suspicious, highlighted by a single piece of damning evidence: bite marks. The deep lacerations on Jack's neck and torso did not match the jaw size of Trevor's Pomeranian, who had been blamed for the crime and was awaiting lethal injection on "doggie death row."

Ezekiel despised Pomeranians, and most small-to-medium dogs, but he loathed injustice more. Even though he knew he had very little credibility when it came to telling the truth, he was determined to find out who was responsible. He turned the south-west corner of his studio apartment into an "investigation wall," filling three whiteboards with evidence from the two cases: photos of the victims and suspects, coroner's reports, crime scene photos he'd hacked from the police database, cool-looking DNA diagrams, and post-it notes reminding him to shower.

But the most startling piece of evidence he found was not on any of his boards, nor in newspapers or TV news bulletins: it was on Facebook, clear as day and ignored by everyone. The two sets of victims—Ned and Beth, and Jack and Kathleen—had been friends.

◆   ◆   ◆

Will bought a new burner phone and messaged Zack from his bullet-riddled-brown armchair in the living room. "Call me ASAP," he wrote. Zack was in a forest when the message arrived: he phoned Will immediately.

"Will! Bro! I was just about to text you," he said. *Bro?* Behind Zack, Gareth piled dirt into a shallow grave: an Akubra hat, and the stiff fingers of a pale corpse, poked out.

"Why were you going to call me?" Will asked.

"To talk about the big finale."

"What's the big finale?"

"It's when we end everybody. The four other kids, the Twins, the ten-month old. Everybody!"

"Why would we ever trust you again?"

Zack leaned against his shovel, softened his voice. "You sound stressed, Will. Is everything OK?"

"No, it's fucking not," he replied. "Four of our closest friends are dead and we're stuck with their shit kids, including two malignant twins and a pink baby that screams and shits everywhere. It's like The Shining-meets-the-fucking-Parent-Trap."

"I hear you, Will, I really do. Parenting's hard work. It's kinda flattering though."

"Flattering?"

"And ironic."

"Ironic? How?"

"Well, your friends picked you to look after their kids even though you were trying to kill their kids. It's flattering and ironic." Will sighed, wished he hadn't texted after all. Gareth hit a tree root with his shovel, cursed.

"Where are you, anyway?" Will asked.

"We're getting rid of the Australian," Zack replied, glancing at Gareth.

"What Australian?"

"The one who ran 'dingoes.com.' We didn't want him to start blabbing—and that dingo he sold us was useless."

Rose arrived with two pillows, saw Will on the phone.

"Anyway, we had a family meeting and decided we're going to give you one more chance," Will told him, glancing at Rose. She rolled her eyes, thought about calling out to Zack ("don't fuck up again you fucking moron," or something).

"That's the best decision you've made since ordering those spicy piña coladas," Zack said. "And I've already got some pretty rad ideas to get it all done."

"No more storyboards or stupid names. Just clean, simple kills." Will added. "And, remember, we now live in the same house as The Twins and the baby—so don't send in any wild animals or anthrax balloons."

"Tell him to use a long-range rifle," Rose called out, impatient. "We'll organize a picnic in the front yard with the kids, blowing bubbles and shit. We'll even put the fetus in its red-fucking-polka-dot pram so it'll be easy to hit."

Will nodded, paraphrased in case Zack didn't hear: "Rose said to use a long-range rifle. We'll have a picnic, bubbles and shit, they'll be sitting ducks."

"Got it, boss. I'll definitely add that to the list of ideas." Zack grinned, quietly ignoring everything he'd said. "Clean and simple, no animals or anthrax, maybe a long-range-rifle-slash-picnic. I'll have a pre-viz done by the weekend." *A pre-what?*

"Whatever. Just text us when you've killed the other four and we'll get the picnic ready." Will hung up, Rose sighed.

"If those idiots screw up again," she said on her way out of the room, "you're sending Tony after them with bread crumbs and a flame thrower."

◆   ◆   ◆

Tony hadn't heard from his half-sister Petal for more than seven years. He hated the cunt as much as she hated him: their last "in-person" meeting had ended with death threats, shattered headlights, and a mutual vow to "see each other in hell." So, it was a surprise when he received a text message from her on a Saturday afternoon. The caller I.D. read as you'd expect ("Cunt").

"Hey T," she wrote. "I'm in town. Wanna catch up?" *T? Catch up?* He almost puked. She said she wanted to apologize for sending him the severed pig's head on his thirtieth birthday. "That was very uncool," she wrote. "I wasn't feeling myself and you deserved better." He suspected she was going through the twelve steps to no longer being a cunt, which involved sucking up to all the people she'd fucked over since becoming a cunt (which had started when she was three—Tony still had the scars).

"I'm real busy at work, you know, making people feel safe in the air," she wrote, pretending she was still working as an air hostess (she wasn't, they fired her). "But maybe we could have a coffee at the airport. There's a great new pop-up café in Hangar 12." A pop-up café in an airport hangar? Tony knew she was bullshitting but he went anyway, curious to see what kind of stunt the little bitch was gonna pull.

The hangar was empty, of course, except for a hessian bag dangling from a rope at the far end. Blood seeped out, and a note was stapled: "Sorry, not sorry. F.U.T. PeTaL." (*F.U.T. was Fuck U Tony, in case you couldn't work it out*).

Tony chuckled, didn't bother looking inside. "Oh, Petal," he thought, "so predictable."

On his way back to the car, he wondered what kind of animal limb he'd send her in return. She hated tongues, he remembered—perhaps he'd Fedex a fresh one from a rare pangolin, which had "the thickest tongue in the animal kingdom" (he'd googled it once for his son's biology project—up to 16 inches, in case you're wondering).

He hummed as he got back in the car, thinking about where he'd buy a pangolin tongue and quietly imagining the expression on Petal's grotesque little face when she opened the package to find it. He wasn't expecting to see Petal's actual face in the rear-view mirror, grinning like she had a pistol pointed at the back of his skull (which she kinda did).

"Hey T," she said. He gnashed teeth, she cold-cocked him.

◆   ◆   ◆

Tony woke an hour later in an abandoned wing factory, one of many owned by Frank's company. He hung upside down from a rusty chain, his entire body covered in buttermilk and cornmeal. Beneath him, a vat of oil bubbled.

Frank greeted him with a thin, vengeful smile. He leaned on a brass cane, pus and blood oozing between his bandages. "I bet you weren't expecting to see me again," he said through broken phlegm. "Were you, son?"

Tony grunted, wriggled, tried to break his restraints. Nearby, Petal gripped a lever attached to the chain, eager to let her half-brother drop.

"Now?" she asked Frank.

"No, lovely, not yet," he replied. "Tony's gonna do some talking first." He shuffled forward, menacing, cane scraping on concrete. "Tell us where your brother is and you'll only get a gentle basting."

Tony spat, defiant. *No fucking chance.* Francine stepped out of the shadows, much calmer than everyone else. She was wearing an apron and hairnet, which she did instinctively whenever she stepped on a factory floor.

"Anthony. Sweetheart. Tell your father where William is," she said. Tony kicked and squirmed, sprayed saliva and buttermilk.

"Now?" Petal asked again, louder.

"No," Francine replied. "Tony. Please. Your father and I don't want to have to dip you in canola. No-one does."

"I do," Petal shouted. They ignored her.

"We just need a home address, nothing more," Francine continued, her calmness wavering. "So we can drop by and say hello. You wouldn't want to keep a mother from her son, would you?"

Tony swayed on the chain, briefly met her eyes—much creepier upside down. "I haven't seen Will for years," he said. "We had a falling out."

"Over what?"

"Over who hates you more."

She bristled, not amused. Frank hobbled forward, stood next to her. "Petal, dear," he called out, eyeballing Tony.

"Yes, Dad?" she replied, hopeful.

"Now!" She let the chain loose with a delighted squeal.

Tony plummeted, the boiling oil swallowing him up like a frozen fish finger.

CHAPTER 25 MUGAMBA

Will had learnt about parenting from a very young age.

When he was six, his mom (Francine) had given him five dollars a month to sponsor his very own child in Namibia. The money was tax-deductible and she wanted him to learn the value of leaving her alone, which he did when he walked to the post office every month to post the check (it was a two-hour round trip). In return for the money, Will received a cardboard money box and a monthly photo of his sponsor child, whose name was Mugamba.

Mugamba was three years old and he lived with his parents, grandmother, and eight brothers and sisters in a small mud hut near Swakopmund. Will's money helped his family buy a goat and blankets to stay warm at night.

The photos Will received every month featured Mugamba playing with his brothers in the desert, working out in a gym made of sticks and rocks, and milking the goat they had bought. They eventually killed and ate the goat, which fed everybody for three weeks. Will got a photo of the skull and bones.

Mugamba grew up to be a strong and healthy little boy, much fitter than any of his friends. In fact, he got so buff that he was recruited by a child soldier army, which often sent scouts around the country to find new talent. He was the number one draft pick, which made his father proud.

Will's geography teacher, Ms. Pettingill, who also happened to be a social justice warrior, noticed several photos of Mugamba on his desk one day: he was wearing his child soldier uniform, holding a bloody machete, posing with a headless corpse.

"Who's the kid with the machete?" she asked Will.

"It's Mugamba. My sponsor child."

She was horrified and immediately tweeted about it. Afterwards, she organized a meeting with Will's parents. Frank and Francine hated going to meetings at the school.

"Have you seen these?" Ms. Pettingill asked them, laying the photos out in front of them like they were crime scene stills from *CSI: Namibia*. They looked. "Your son said he sends five dollars to this kid every month."

Frank and Francine were understandably upset. "He only sends five dollars?" Frank asked.

"That wouldn't even cover the dry-cleaning bill for his cute little uniform," Francine added.

Will started sending ten dollars after that. Mugamba rose up through the ranks and eventually started his own child army, which he called "Will's Army of Death (or W.A.D.)" He even sent an honorary general's uniform to Will, who wore it to "Careers Day" at school. Ms. Pettingill was not impressed: she ranted about it on TikTok, and got fired.

As teenagers, Will and Mugamba stayed in regular contact. Mugamba would often call from a payphone in Namibia to say "hi," or to remind him that his monthly payment was overdue. If Francine picked up, she'd call out to Will: "It's your machete kid."

"Your mom's a funny white cunt," Mugamba would say when Will came to the phone. They'd laugh and talk about third world problems until the coins ran out. Mugamba said he'd come visit as soon as he got off the "Interpol Terror Watch List" or had enough money to bribe immigration officials. They could drink beers and eat chicken nuggets at "one of those American football games," he said. Will could hardly wait.

◆   ◆   ◆

Will was sprinkling crushed paracetamol on cupcakes when a text arrived from Zack. It was just after midnight. He called out to Rose: "The fuckwit sent a text!" She abandoned Ralph's sponge bath, arrived in the doorway as he was reading it. "Oh, fuck," he said.

"What does it say?" she asked.

"It says 'We're out front.'"

"They're fucking not?" They both hurried to the window, looked out. *Yeah, they fucking were.* The Volvo was parked in the driveway. Zack waved, Gareth unloaded a huge sheet-covered object from the back.

"We need to get a restraining order on these fuckers," Rose said.

"That might be tricky. We hired them to kill our friends' children."

"Do you know how easy it is to get a restraining order? I got one on my mom when I was eight, remember?" He remembered. Zack tooted the horn. *Really?*

Will powered up the taser, Rose grabbed her baseball bat. They stood on the porch steps, ignored Zack's cheerful "Hey guys."

"What the fuck are you doing here?" Will asked.

"Don't worry," Zack said, helping Gareth with "the object." "We didn't bring storyboards. This is a scale model of the kill site."

"What kill site?" Rose asked. "I thought we agreed on 'picnic-slash-rifle?'"

"This is much better," Zack said. They walked the two-by-two meter model up the steps towards them, expecting them to make way.

"You're bringing it inside?" Will asked, not moving.

"We could do it out here but we'll need lights and power. And everyone who passes will probably see it." They hovered on the second-to-last step, Gareth straining under the weight of it. "We only need twenty minutes to take you through it."

Will finally relented, much to Rose's disdain. "Fine, hurry the fuck up." He made way, they shuffled inside. "Put it in the living room," he called after them. "And don't break anything."

Rose glared at Will. "They're out of control. Call fucking Tony. Now."

Will tried, but Tony didn't pick up (of course—he was still deep-frying).

◆   ◆   ◆

Zack's model was an intricate one-to-two-hundred scale version of a mansion on three acres, complete with several outdoor "activities." There was a jumping castle in the front yard, a slippery slide near a huge pool, and a petting zoo on the west lawn.

"We call it 'Camp Death,'" Zack announced, forgetting the whole conversation they'd had about "no more stupid names."

Rose looked over the model, confused, almost recognizing it. "Where is this?"

"It's the Stantons' country manor," Zack quipped. "Bertie said we could use it."

Will and Rose stiffened like they'd been caught naked (and midway through fucking) in the shower. "Bertie said fucking what?" Rose asked.

"When did you talk to Bertie?" Will pressed.

"Well, we originally went over there to ask if we could use the regular mansion but Bertie said The Stantons wouldn't be leaving until summer," Zack replied. "So he suggested the country manor. He even gave us the keys and a complete set of blueprints so we could make the model. I thought he was weird at first but he's actually kinda cool."

"I don't understand," Rose said, "Why would you talk to Bertie without asking us?"

"You guys said 'no calls.'"

"How much did he tell you?" Will asked, still feeling naked.

"Everything," Gareth added, smirking. "He really opens up when you smoke a crack pipe with him." Will and Rose shared a look, horrified.

"Anyway," Zack continued, "Let's get back to the plan." He wet his lips like he was going to talk for a really long time, then pointed at the jumping castle. "This is the 'Inward-Imploding-Jumping-Castle-Of-Death.' It'll implode as soon as a child enters, suffocating them within minutes."

"Will they feel pain?" Rose asked, hopeful.

"Yes. A lot." *OK, he had their full attention.* Zack pushed a button on a control panel: air squeezed out of the castle like a popped balloon. It collapsed and shriveled. Ralph yipped and spun his wheels, presumably imagining a child inside.

Gareth leaned in, delighted. "I came up with the shriveling bit," he said. Zack gave him a look, irritated by the interruption. He continued:

"Then there's the 'Slippery-Slope-To-Certain-Death.'" He pointed to a cardboard slide dipping into a pool. "Water's toxic enough to dissolve a leg of lamb." He pushed another button: little bubbles appeared on the pool surface. Delightful. "And if by some miracle they survive all this, we have a final, irresistible death-trap in store for them," he said. 'The Rabid-Animal-Petting-Zoo.' He directed their eyes to the caged-off petting zoo on the lawn. Inside, there were assorted plastic animals: goat, deer, rabbit, pig. "They've all been injected with a vicious form of rabies from Sudan. And none of them have been fed for a week." Rose picked up the rabbit, Will chose the pig.

"A pig with rabies?" Will asked.

"It's more like a really wild boar," Zack replied.

Rose studied her rabbit, not convinced. "Rabbits and goats are herbivores. They only eat plants."

"Not these ones." He gave her a stupid little wink. She didn't appreciate it, put the rabbit back. "The beauty of this plan is our ability to shift the blame," Zack continued. "The Twins suffocate in the jumping castle? Blame the manufacturer. The baby fries in the toxic pool? Blame the chlorine supplier. The four-year-old gets mauled by a pig in the petting zoo? Blame the animal trainer."

Will and Rose quietly imagined each of those scenarios. "What do you need us to do?" Rose asked, suddenly on board with the plan.

"Gather The Twins and the baby and get your friends' four other brats to the location," Zack replied. "Death will do the rest." Gareth looked at him: *Death will do the rest?*

"If all this works like it's supposed to, maybe Brett and Melissa will stay on for a few days," Rose said, looking at Will. "We could have a brunch."

"If it works, their four children will have died violently," Will reminded her. "I doubt they'll want to hang around for brunch."

She looked off, disappointed. Will noticed, tried to end things on a positive note: "Maybe a cook-out though, the weekend after."

She beamed, started visualizing sides.

CHAPTER 26 **W.W.H.**

Rose's mother, Irene Deidre Thampy, was a triple-A-rated tranche of shit—so it was probably for the best that she had abandoned Rose at a convent before her first birthday.

As a young girl, Irene had told her mother she only had two dreams in life: to make license plates for cars and become the world's first female astronaut. Her mother laughed and kept beating her with a blunt stick. "You have to go to jail to make license plates," she said. "And you'll need to study really hard, and give blowjobs to lots of overweight men at NASA, to become an astronaut."

"What's a blowjob and how do I get into jail?" Irene asked.

It wasn't until high school that Irene rediscovered her passion for "space travel." A visiting businesswoman, who had once worked as a brain surgeon, introduced her to the concept of "fake-it-till-you-make-it," which she had practiced throughout her own various careers. "I may have paralyzed some patients, and killed others, but I gained strength as a woman and realized brain surgery was not for me," she said in her keynote speech to students. "If I'd followed the traditional patriarchal path, years of grueling study and internships, it would've been a complete waste of time for everyone."

Inspired by this philosophy, Irene convinced her boyfriend Daryl to help her board an unmanned NASA rocket ship prior to its launch at Cape Canaveral. She knew if she could just get inside the cabin and pretend to know what she was doing, everyone would support her dream. Neither of them made it past the first layer of electric fencing.

Daryl pled to misdemeanor trespass, Irene went to trial, where she used the "fake-it-till-you-make-it" defense and was jailed for four years. Ironically, they sent her to the only prison in the state that did not make license plates for cars.

Soon after she was released, Irene met a recovering heroin addict who believed in her (revised) dream to make license plates while orbiting the earth. She got pregnant and gave birth during her afternoon shift at a cat café (thankfully, the cats cleaned up the afterbirth).

Their life as parents was joyful for the first few hours. Irene realized that being a mother was the true purpose of her life. But the crying and constant diaper-changing soon became unbearable. Irene's boyfriend returned to his first true love (heroin), and she became bitter and resentful at Rose, buying her a tiny smartphone so she could send her nasty texts ("u ruined everythink, u little cunt!") and cruel memes featuring babies being dropped and burnt in boiling water. She got a response from Rose's crib one night ("hwsghsgshhtt") and realized she'd had enough of all the back-and-forth. Imagine what it would be like when Rose turned one?

The St. Mary's Of The Angels Convent had received so many abandoned babies on its front steps that Mother Superior decided to construct a cushioned, twenty-four-hour dropbox. It took Irene two attempts to successfully leave Rose in the box: she mistakenly left a video starring Lou Diamond Philips the first time, only realizing two hours later when a teenager at Blockbuster called to tell her it was overdue (and asked if she'd left a baby in their returns slot). The nuns were watching the Lou Diamond Philips movie when she arrived, but agreed to switch it with Rose when it was finished.

Irene was much happier after that. She did an "astrology" course (*yeah, not what she thought*) and didn't try to contact Rose again until her eighth birthday. Rose burned the letter she sent, filmed herself urinating on it while it burned (with her tiny smartphone), and uploaded it with a fuck-you emoji to Irene's Facebook page. It got a hundred likes, mostly from felons. Rose filed for a restraining order and Irene never tried to contact her again.

◆   ◆   ◆

Rose made an invitation out of clipart and comic sans to entice Brett and Melissa to the country mansion. "You're Invited to Camp Fun!" it read. As soon as she hit send, Melissa called, breathless.

"Hi Rose!" she said. "Got your email! How are you?!"

Will arrived, noticed the pained grimace on Rose's face. "I'm great. So good to hear from you! We've missed you!" Rose stuck two fingers in her mouth, made a vomiting gesture. She put the call on loudspeaker so Will would have context for all her snide/funny expressions.

"We can't wait to see you!" Melissa said. "I didn't know you had a country mansion!" *All these exclamation points!* It was like a fucking exclamation point party!

"Well, you know how much people love chicken nuggets."

"William's still working in the factory?" Melissa asked, snarky (she always used William's full name when she was trying to be snarky). Will's face hardened. *Working in the factory?* She was a nasty little bitch when she was sober.

"Yep, still working in the factory, which he still owns," Rose quipped, pretending to be chirpy. "He's got four factories now, actually. You should come visit sometime."

"Oh, the kids would love that. Me, not so much. All those innocent little birds' lives lost for profit."

Will bristled, desperate to grab the phone and scream obscenities down it. Rose stayed on topic. "Anyway, can you come? To the camp?"

The invitation finished printing on Melissa's inkjet. She snatched it up, eager. "Yes, of course!" she said. "I already printed the invite for the kids' scrapbook." Yeah, she kept a scrapbook for every useless piece of paper that crossed the children's paths, even drawings they dribbled on and a note she once got under her windscreen wiper when she took them to the mall ("Thanks for parking me in, bitch," it read). Will wondered if she'd put the crime scene photos and their death certificates in the scrapbook too.

"Great!" Rose said. "See you then!" She hung up before Melissa could ask about the strength of the WiFi and whether they needed to bring their own towels.

"This is going to be a very long weekend," Will said.

"Not if they die quickly," Rose replied.

On his way back to the bedroom to Google "idiots with scrapbooks," Will got a message from "Tony." "Hey bro, sorry I haven't replied suuner," it read. Tony was shit at grammar.

"It's OK, Tony. Where r u?" Will replied.

"Just chillin' with wifey." *Wifey?* "Where r u?"

"At home, getting ready to go to the country mansion."

"Country mansion?"

"In Pflugerville, remember? You came one time."

"Oh, yeah, I remember. What's the address again?"

"No idea. Rose navigates."

Tony's reply took a while. Will waited, looked at photos of a Lubbock woman who had four hundred scrapbooks. At least ten of them were filled with newspaper articles about what a fuckwit she was for keeping so many scrapbooks. One of the headlines (from The Beekooka Times) read: "This Lubbock Fuckwit Has 300 Scrapbooks Filled With Useless Shit Like Parking Tickets."

Finally, a message arrived from Tony: "BTW this ain't Tony." Will read it twice, confused, thought he was trying to be funny. Before he could respond, a follow-up: "It's your dad." OK, it definitely wasn't Tony: he would never mention Frank, not even as a joke. "Your brother took a dip in some hot oil, I'll get Petal to send pics."

Will tensed, thought about calling out to Rose. Instead, he wrote back: "What do u want?" The answer was immediate:

"To watch you fry like your brother."

◆   ◆   ◆

There was a time, just before he turned seven, when Will thought his father actually liked him.

"Wanna come to the factory with me?" his dad asked. Frank never took him or Tony anywhere, and he'd always told Francine the factory was off-limits to the children—too many buttons and levers and salmonella puddles to play in. But this day was different. *Maybe he trusted him now?*

"I'll be running the place soon," Frank told him in the car, "And you're the oldest so you'll be my vee-pee of communications." Will had no idea what a "vee-pee of communications" was but, if he got to wear a badge with his name and title on it, that would be the greatest thing ever.

It was a Saturday so the factory-floor was empty, conveyer belts turned off. Frank led him into the special gold elevator for executives, which they took all the way to the top floor. There were two offices there, one for Frank and a much bigger one for Randolph, Will's grandfather and "the boss of everything," which was one of the names Frank called him.

"Your grandpop's getting old," Frank told Will that day, "and he's starting to lose track of how businesses are supposed to run."

"He's not making good nuggets anymore?" Will asked his dad.

"He's making the same nuggets he made fifty years ago," Frank said. "And you have to adapt if you want to survive, son.

There are much better, cheaper ways to make nuggets nowadays. You'll see."

Will was confused and a little saddened: *he loved his grand-pop more than anyone.* While Tony and the other kids were stuffing their faces and running rampant at family gatherings, Will would sit with Randolph and listen to him talk: stories about life and goiters and the rich history of nugget-making. His grandpop would take him to fun places all over his spectacular mansion: the pristine library where no other kids could go, the creepy bell-tower where a butler died, the stables filled with horses and a miniature donkey, the chicken nugget museum, and the gentlemen's smoking room where not even the adults were permitted.

He'd tell Will a story in each place they went, he'd say "fuck" and "shit" and didn't apologize and, when they were ready to move on to another location, he'd hand Will his gold-plated letter opener and tell him to mark that he'd been there. "So I remember you when I come by here again," he said in his most gentle voice. Will etched "W.W.H." ("Will Was Here") into dozens of walls and floorboards and doors and shelves all over Randolph's property. His grandpop made him feel like he belonged somewhere. *Everywhere.*

Will once invited Randolph to attend his "Bring Your Dad, Grandad or Gender Non-Binary Parent To School" day: Frank was busy ("entertaining clients") and Will knew his friends would think he was awesome if Randolph brought a tray of freshly-cooked samples from the factory, which he promised he would.

But Francine intervened: "Your grandfather wears an adult diaper. He'll piss or shit himself and embarrass the entire family." Will was the only one without a parent that day. His friend Diego brought his stepdad Carlos, who was a former member of the Sinaloa cartel. He gave little bags of white powder to all the children, told them to "keep it somewhere safe until you turn eighteen" and threatened to have Mrs. Hallstrom tortured and killed if she said anything. Everyone laughed (except Mrs. Hallstrom). Later, Will saw Carlos handing out more bags to some of the other dads in the hallway. They had a playfight, then Carlos showed them his gun.

◆   ◆   ◆

Frank sat Will in his big leather chair and stood behind him, gave it a gentle swivel. "If you're going to be my vee-pee of communications, you'll need to pass a test," Frank said, clearly up to something.

"A multiple choice test?" Will asked.

"No, much easier than that." Frank slithered to the locked drawer of his mahogany desk, unlocked it with a key. "One of the simplest and most effective forms of communication is a letter between two people." He pulled out a sealed yellow envelope, thick and ominous. "This is a letter from me to your grandpop."

Will looked at it, eager. "It's a big letter," he said.

"Yes, it's a very big letter. With lots of words about how great your grandpop is." Frank leaned against the edge of the desk. "Your job is to get it from me to him as quickly as possible."

Will thought about it, looked towards Randolph's darkened office. "But grandpop's not here today."

"No, he's not. But I need it delivered to his desk today. It's very urgent." Frank met his eyes, hoping the boy would catch on.

"Can I have the key for his office?"

Frank smiled: *good try.* "Grandpop doesn't give that key to anybody. But there might be another way." His eyes drifted, exaggerated, eyeballed the air-conditioning vent above them. Will caught on immediately.

"I could go through the little hole."

"You could definitely go through the little hole." Frank beamed. The boy had inherited his sneaky mind. *This was going to be much easier than he'd imagined.*

The vent between Frank and Randolph's offices was about fifteen meters long, just wide enough for a seven-year-old boy to fit. The grille at either end was easily removed, sometimes requiring a gentle kick. Frank encouraged Will as he slid towards the chequered light at the other end. "Keep going, you're passing the test." When he reached the grille, Frank was at his fatherly best: "You're doing a very good job, son. Now, if you can't open the cover with your hands, kick it with your feet. Not too hard, you're not allowed to break it." Will did exactly as he said. The grille popped open with a slight push.

He'd never seen his grandfather's office before: it was as magnificent as all the places he'd taken him in the mansion. The walls and shelves burst with eccentric items from all over the world, the furniture smelled of grand and exotic places, and there was a grandfather clock with a chicken that clucked on the hour (of course). Will could've stayed there for hours—but his father's voice spilled down the open vent, impatient: "Hurry up, your time's running out."

Will did what he was told to do and put the special letter from Frank into the bottom drawer of Randolph's polished oak desk—that was where he looked first when he arrived each day, Frank told him. He closed the drawer, turned to leave, noticed a photo frame in the center of the desk, the first thing grandpop would see when he arrived each day. It was a photo of the two of them, him and Randolph, arms around each other on the creepy belltower. There were no other photos, just that one.

Frank called out again, agitated: "Time's almost up. You're gonna fail the test."

◆   ◆   ◆

Agents from the F.B.I.'s Child Protection Unit arrived the next afternoon. They'd received an anonymous tip-off that Randolph was buying and selling child pornography through his vast nugget distribution network.

They searched his office, upended furniture, looked in the drawer where Will had left Frank's letter. They didn't find anything. Randolph gave them fresh nuggets and barbecue sauce on their way out; they thanked him and apologized. A competitor probably had it out for him, the lead agent told him.

When Randolph had arrived at seven o'clock that morning, the same time he arrived each day, he sat at his desk with
a Colombian latte and looked at the framed photo of him and
Will. He never usually looked in his bottom drawer, or any of his
drawers—*that was one of Frank's many lies*—but his eyes drifted
there on this particular day, drawn to it by a familiar etching in
the wood: "W.W.H."

Randolph never confronted or questioned Frank about the
incriminating photos he'd arranged for Will to put in his drawer.
He noticed scratches on the grille, played back the security camera footage from a hidden lens in the center of his grandfather
clock. Will asked him later if he got his happy letter from Frank,
he said he had. They never spoke of it again.

Randolph kept Frank at a distance from that point on, hu-
mored him with meaningless errands, pretended he still trusted
him like a son. When he died ten years later, he split his assets
equally between all of his children (except Frank) and the chari-
ties he supported. But he gave the factory, his majority holding
of shares and control of the company, to Will, the one he trusted
most not to lie or cheat or fuck his nuggets up.

Frank almost throttled the executor during the reading of
the will. When security came to drag him out, he frothed and
yelled like a possessed child, told Will he was going to start his
own company and ruin him and Gold Gourmet Nuggets forever.

CHAPTER 27 **PFUGERVILLE**

Will told Rose about the messages from Frank on the drive to the country mansion.

"He fried Tony in canola oil and now he's coming to get you?" she asked.

Will nodded. "Something like that." He handed her his smartphone. "Read the texts for yourself." She took it, scrolled, read. Something bothered her.

"You told him we're going to Pfugerville?" He looked over.

"Yeah, but there are dozens of 'country mansions' in Pfugerville. It'll take him forever to find us." She didn't seem convinced. He tried harder: "Besides, he's probably got Francine and Petal with him. They add weight and stupidity."

Bertie was in the back seat with Ralph; he'd managed to get the weekend off from The Stantons so he could help with "the big finale." The Twins and the baby were traveling separately, in an Uber. Will had requested "the most dangerous and worst-reviewed driver possible" and got Terrance, a registered sex offender who had mounted the curb with two wheels when he turned up. He was on the phone (texting a minor) and wearing a flat jacket, which he used to protect himself from "road rage incidents." Will and Rose were delighted.

"If you have an accident and roll the car, we forgive you," Will told him as Rose loaded the bassinet in the passenger seat, deliberately forgetting to fasten the straps.

"And if you need to stop and do shopping or go to a salon for eight to ten hours, that's OK too," Rose added. "They love sitting in a hot car on their own." The Twins glared at her, one of them gave her the finger.

"See you guys soon!" Rose said, ignoring the finger and locking the front and back doors.

Will did a creepy, slow-motion wave as they drove off, muttered to Rose through pursed lips: "Why didn't we think of this earlier?"

◆　　◆　　◆

Will and Rose were relieved when they arrived at the country mansion: Zack had come through with the promises of his model—the jumping castle, the petting zoo, the pool slide were all there, ready to cause maximum harm.

They pulled up at the front steps next to Zack's Volvo. Rose got a text from Melissa: they'd loaded their four "lovelies" into the minivan, she wrote, and would arrive within the hour. *Lovelies?* "The monsters are on their way," she told Will.

It was finally happening. In the back, Ralph yipped. Bertie opened his flip-phone, started a "countdown to death." The Uber arrived soon after, ruining all the positive vibes: Terrance said it had been a safe drive with "little-to-no road-rage incidents." *Little-to-no?* He refused to elaborate. Will and Rose quietly hoped their luck would improve.

Bertie took the children to their rooms, while Will and Rose visited the "Security Control Room" on the second floor. Zack and Gareth were already there: they'd added additional monitors to the huge wall of black-and-white monitors, showing every camera in every room. There were at least three in each the "death sites," including an underwater camera in the toxic pool, and collar-cams on selected animals (goat, boar, deer) in the petting zoo.

"We are 'go' for launch here," Zack said. Gareth rolled his eyes.

"So how exactly does all this work?" Rose asked.

Zack swiveled his chair, revealed a mini-console on the desk in front of him. "These are the 'Buttons of Death.'" He pointed to a series of buttons, labeled accordingly: "ACTIVATE TOXIC POOL," "IMPLODE CASTLE," "HOT COFFEE."

"What's 'Hot Coffee?'" Will asked, moving closer than Zack appreciated.

"Oh, that's for Bertie to bring us coffees. It goes directly to his phone."

"Why don't you just text him when you want a coffee?"

"Because the button's easier. And there was an extra button on the console—we thought we needed one for the petting zoo but then we realized the animals don't need a button to attack. They'll just automatically attack when a child enters. They're that hungry." He grinned, pleased with himself.

Will and Rose sighed in sync. "OK, got it," Rose said. "What now?"

"Now we wait for the children to go play. When do the rest of them arrive?"

Rose checked her watch: "Thirty minutes."

"OK." Zack looked at Gareth, Rose looked at Will. An awkward silence. "How about we get some coffees?"

"I'll have a latte," Gareth said immediately. Zack pointed his finger at Will, meaning "what coffee do you want?":

"Regular coffee. No cream," he said. Finally, Rose:

"Whatever, I don't care. Lemon tea."

"Got it." Zack leaned forward, hit the "HOT COFFEE" button. It glowed. Nothing else happened. More awkward silence.

"How will he know I want a lemon tea?" Rose asked, eyeballing the button.

"He won't. When he texts, I'll text the order back." A text arrived on Zack's phone. "See?"

Rose sighed, headed for the door. "For fuck's sake." Will followed. Zack started texting, called after them:

"Do you still want the coffees?"

◆　　◆　　◆

Brett was a terrible driver and Melissa was worse at navigating than Mungo Park, which was probably why their one-hour trip turned into a three-hour cross-country ordeal.

In the back, their four children—Toby (6), Chad (5), Ellen (4), and Katy (3)—drifted between various states of chaos. Don't bother remembering their names: they may be dead soon (no spoilers).

"It's odd, don't you think?" Brett asked Melissa, somehow oblivious to the ruckus behind them. Melissa was on her laptop, searching for someone who could paint "abstract cats." They'd started a new business venture that involved "finishing" whatever a person was doing before they died. Car restoration, house extension, movie script, self-help book, even a rock opera. For a fee, they'd give closure to a dead person's loved ones by completing whatever wasn't completed at the time of death (although they wouldn't do criminal and/or weird sex acts).

"I know, it's very odd. Who the fuck paints abstract cats?" Melissa replied. "No wonder he killed himself."

"No, it's odd they invited us. Will and Rose."

Melissa looked up, realized what he was talking about. "They have kids now. They need other kids to play with their kids. It's classic novice-parenting." Toby fired a spitball into his dad's neck, cackled.

"Cut it out back there!" Brett said, pretending they respected his authority. Another spitball stuck briefly to his cheek. He returned to Melissa: "If we die, who are we giving the kids to?"

Melissa looked off, ignored the passing driver yelling obscenities at Brett ("drive faster, you fucking sloth!"). "Definitely not Will and Rose," she said. "What about your parents? They have extra rooms."

He paused, wished he hadn't asked. "Yeah, that's probably not gonna work."

"Why not?"

"The open relationship thing, remember?"

"No. What open relationship thing?"

"They have an open relationship now. So they need the extra rooms for the extra people. When they stay over."

"Your parents are having an open relationship? Aren't they sixty or something?"

"Dad's seventy-two, mom's sixty-eight. I told you all about it at Thanksgiving."

"Thanksgiving? Was I drunk?"

"You were mellow. And you asked me about the creepy guy carving the turkey. And I said 'that's Hubble. He's fucking my mom.'"

"The creepy guy carving the turkey was fucking your mom?" A spitball lodged in Melissa's hair. She didn't notice. "We're never going to your parents' house for Thanksgiving again," she said as her phone chimed: incoming text from Rose. "Jesus, really?"

"What is it?" Brett asked, looking over.

"Rose wants to know where we are," she said, reading. "She ignores us for five years and suddenly she can't live without us."

Will and Rose waited for the minivan at the top of the front steps, flanked either side by The Twins and the baby in a stroller. Bertie was there with Ralph, both dressed in liveries. If you ignored their posture and wretched faces, you'd think they were "Downton Abbey" staff waiting for their masters to arrive.

"I thought you said they'd be here within the hour," Will said.

Rose sighed. "Brett's probably driving. Have you seen him drive?"

Finally, the minivan passed through the front gates. One of The Twins tugged at Will's hand, eager to escape and wreak havoc somewhere. "Stay still and smile," Will told her, squeezing her hand to limit the circulation. "Or I'll burn your hair." She obeyed: *little cunt loved her hair.*

Rose gripped the stroller's handle, its wheels teetering on the edge of the top step. The baby continued to wail like it had actual problems. "You should keep it quiet when they arrive," Will told her. "We have to look like we're happy and in control."

"Fuck off," she replied. "I'm trying not to have an 'Odessa Steps' moment here." Will shrugged, didn't get the reference. If you didn't get it either, you have three options: (1) look up the "Odessa Steps" sequence on Youtube; (2) go to film school; or (3) move on without caring what the reference is. Option one requires internet access and will take two minutes, option two will take three years and will be a complete waste of your parents' money, and option three is free and won't take any time whatsoever.

The minivan pulled up, stalled. Brett was out first, hair clogged with spitballs. "Hey!" Bertie opened the door for Melissa, she didn't move.

"Hi," she said, still checking her laptop: some guy in Winnipeg said he could paint cats with human heads. She asked for a quote.

"Welcome!" Rose said, exaggerated, hand tightening on the stroller. The children tumbled out of the van, ran inside. Brett watched them go. "Don't worry," he said, carefree, knowing full well they were likely to cause significant damage somewhere. "They'll settle down when we give them their iPads."

Melissa kept the laptop open as she got out of the car, which was her way of saying "no-one here's important enough for me to close the lid and have to retype my password in later."

"So good to see you guys!" Will said, working harder than Rose. Brett and Melissa paused at the bottom of the steps, looked up at them.

"Look at you guys," Brett said. "You're like one of those celebrity families on TV."

Will forced a chuckle, gripped The Twin's hand tighter. "Not sure about the celebrity TV bit, but we're definitely a family," he said.

"A very happy family," Rose added, getting caught up in the moment. "And we're even happier when we see other happy families."

Will nudged her: *too much, too early*. "Pace yourself," he whispered.

Above them, on the second floor, Zack and Gareth watched from the window. "I don't understand," Gareth said, studying Brett and Melissa. "We're doing all this so they can have dinner parties with these deadshits?"

"Maybe they're a revelation after appetizers and alcohol," Zach replied, not convinced.

"Have they both got spitballs in their hair?" They looked closer.

Brett headed up the steps like he'd been invited inside (he hadn't). "Let's get this party started," he said, chirpy. "I get the penthouse room!" (there wasn't one).

Melissa followed, somehow punching keys on her laptop. "I'm gonna need the WiFi password asap, and we didn't bring towels," she said, glancing at Rose as she passed. "And tell Bobo to be careful with my suitcases." She gestured towards Bertie, who was still standing next to the minivan. *Bobo?*

Rose and Will shared a look: *we're doing all this to have dinner parties with these deadshits?* Bertie discreetly checked his countdown to death. *Not long now.*

◆   ◆   ◆

Ezekiel added two extra whiteboards to track the social media accounts of Jack and Kathleen, and Ned and Beth. He listed likes and tags and shared photos, eventually realizing that two more sets of friends were common to them both: Brett and Melissa, and Will and Rose.

He was printing a fortune cookie message for his Tinder date when a selfie from Brett appeared on his Facebook feed. Yeah, he printed his own fortune cookie messages (mostly "your fortune is the guy in front of you"), then asked Mr. Chai at Chai's Chinese Restaurant to insert them into his date's cookies (which he did, for a generous Yelp review). It never worked, even when he tried "you will die a horrible death if you don't fuck the hottie sitting opposite."

Brett's selfie was a heavily-filtered side profile of him driving, with the caption: "heading to Camp Fun with the fam!" The hashtags were mostly meaningless, except for "#willandrose."

Ezekiel texted his date, told her he'd be late, then studied the photo more closely: yep, there was a road sign in the background. He zoomed in, sharpened the focus. "Pfugerville."

CHAPTER 28 <u>**THE KIDS ARE NOT ALL RIGHT**</u>

The Stantons' country mansion was one of only five in the town of Pfugerville.

Frank marked them all on a map, which he spread out in the back seat of his bright yellow Hummer. If they stopped and checked each one for only thirty minutes, he calculated, it would take them a maximum of seven hours to locate Will, and another two hours to batter and fry him.

Petal was at the wheel, but only because Frank had lost four fingers and the majority of skin on both hands. Francine sat in the passenger seat, filed her nails. They were in the middle of one of their inane conversations, which happened regularly. "So, if the penny drops, that means I finally understand something I didn't understand. And if I drop the mic, I said something that was pretty damn impressive," Petal said. "So what does it mean if I'm waiting for the other shoe to drop?" Francine thought about it, clueless.

Frank raised his voice from the back: "It means your neighbors are fucking and you're waiting for the woman to orgasm, which is when her shoe drops."

Francine half-turned, tut-tutted him under her breath. "That's not what it means, Petal." Before he could argue back, a sign caught his attention. He checked his map.

"It's the next exit," he said.

◆   ◆   ◆

Petal wasn't Frank's biological daughter, although he didn't know it (if he did, she definitely wouldn't be the "apple of his eye"). Only Petal and Francine knew—and Will too, because he was in the next room when she was conceived.

Every Tuesday afternoon for six months of his fifth year, Francine would take Will with her to see Dale, a greasy cashier she'd met while shopping. Frank was at work, Tony was in child-care and she couldn't leave Will home alone—so she was stuck with him (and he with her).

She'd give him candy and soda and let him watch TV while she played weird games with Dale in his bedroom. She made sounds in there she never made with Frank. Sometimes Will thought she was going to die, which pleased him. But then she'd emerge, buttoning up her blouse and ready for a cigarette. "Let's go," she'd say.

Frank got suspicious of the Tuesday outings, which prompted her to finally talk to Will on the way home. Normally she just sucked on her post-coital cigarette all the way to the house but, on this particular day, she wanted to chat.

"Let's practice what you're going to tell dad," she said. Her makeup was a mess, which she attempted to tidy in the rearview mirror. "'Mommy took me to the library,' that's what you'll tell him," she said. "Go on, say it."

Will pouted, didn't say it. *Fuck her.*

She dug into her handbag, looked for lipstick. "If you don't say it, Frank will get all confused and suspicious." She took her eyes off the road, still searching for the fucking lipstick. The car began to veer left but she continued, unperturbed. "Then he'll get angry and he'll pack his bags and leave. We'll have no money, no food, no nothin'..." She finally found her lipstick, straightened the wheel, returned them to the correct lane. She met Will's eyes in the mirror, deadly serious.

"That little dog of yours will have to be put down. And not by lethal injection. That costs too much. You'll have to bludgeon him to death in the backyard. I'll have to start prostituting myself and you and your brother will be taken by childcare services," she said, barely pausing for breath. The car jerked as one of the tires crossed into the opposite lane. "You'll be placed in a foster home with strange and deformed children, possibly touched inappropriately by your alcoholic foster father..." Cars veered out of their way, honked frantically.

"You'll grow up bitter and cynical and vengeful, wind up selling crystal meth and doing time in prison, sharing a cell with a big brute of a man who wants to sleep in your bunk bed every other night." The car veered even further into the other lane as a truck approached, ominous, bearing down on them. "You'll get paroled with no hope of ever finding gainful employment, have two kids with a crack whore and die alone from a heroin overdose in a back alley somewhere." A thunderous horn caused her to pull erratically at the wheel, narrowly escaping the truck's path—but she didn't stop talking.

"The thing is, William... sometimes it's OK to tell a little lie or do a naughty thing. It can be better for everybody in the long term." She paused, softened her voice. "So... are you gonna say we went to the library or not?"

Will looked at her stupid hair and smudged mascara. He may have only been five, but he already knew he was much smarter than her. "Frank checks the odometer so the library won't do," he said. "I'll say we went to the arcade."

Her lips curled into a proud, motherly smile. In fact, she'd never been prouder of any child ever.

She got pregnant a few weeks after that and they stopped going to see Dale. Frank was none the wiser.

◆   ◆   ◆

After lunch and lots of raspberry cordial, Will and Rose expected the children to flee to the nearest exits (and, ultimately, their deaths). But that's not what happened. They stayed inside. It wasn't cold or wet, neither hot nor humid—in fact, the weather was perfect. And yet, they stayed in-fucking-side.

Zack and Gareth had decorated the entire downstairs area with huge posters of smiling, playful children doing all the activities they wanted them to do: tumbling about in the bouncy castle, plummeting down a slippery slide, cuddling fluffy animals in a petting zoo. Three massive flatscreen TVs played images of the same joy and fun. It was a big, colorful, audiovisual invitation to die. But no-one noticed, or cared.

The children planted themselves in chairs and sofas in the living room, burying their fat little heads in iPads. The Twins sat either side of Toby, transfixed by the game he was playing. Katy, Ellen, and Chad all gawked at tablets of their own. It had the gripping social interaction of a coding room.

Will and Rose huddled at the back, on the verge of panic. "How long are these little shits going to stay like this?" Rose asked.

"I have no idea," Will replied. "I thought the hardest part was going to be retrieving their bodies."

Brett approached, still eating a cupcake from lunch. "I told you they'd settle down when we gave them their iPads," he quipped. "Adorable, aren't they?" Rose cleared phlegm. *Adorable?*

"What time do you think they might go outside and play?" Will asked.

"Outside?" Brett chuckled, looked at Will like he'd said something insane (like "we need them to go outside so they'll die!") "They won't go outside now. Not unless there's a raging fire in here."

Will shared a look with Rose: *worth noting.* She tried to stay upbeat: "We thought they might like all the rides and activities we organized."

"They're not very outdoorsy," Brett replied, talking through a mouthful. "And Melissa doesn't like too much sunlight on their skin."

Melissa arrived, still holding the laptop like it was an extension of her forearm. "What don't I like?" she asked, overhearing.

"Sunlight on the kids' skin."

"Oh, yeah. They're not very outdoorsy anyway. Look at them." Will and Rose couldn't look, not again. Melissa checked her screen, irritated. "Are we in some kind of WiFi blackspot here?" she asked Will. "Because I'm only getting three bars."

"Three bars is about the best you'll get here," Will replied, happy to bring her mood down to his level.

She bristled (job done). "Jesus, Will. You didn't mention that when you invited us."

"Sorry."

Rose saw a tiny window of opportunity, pounced: "It's much better by the pool. You might get four bars. Why don't we all go out there?" *Brilliant.*

Will followed her lead. "Yes. By the pool. The kids could splash around, we could have some Piña Coladas. It'll be like Sandals."

Melissa glared at him like he'd cupped her breast. "I'm working, Will. Do you know how hard it is to find someone to paint abstract cats?"

"No."

"It's fucking hard." She looked at Brett, whose thoughts were elsewhere (another cupcake?) "Tell him how hard it is, Brett." He turned at the sound of his name, clueless.

"Yes, I agree. Whatever she said is right."

Rose pivoted to Melissa, confused. "Is this the thing where you take back people's wedding gifts if they get divorced?"

"No, that was eight years ago." Melissa was pissed she didn't know. "This is the thing where we finish what people were doing when they died."

"Oh, that's sweet."

"And very profitable."

"So, if a serial killer dies while he's making a pants suit out of human flesh, do you finish the pants suit?"

"We don't finish criminal acts."

Will chipped in: "What if a base jumper dies during a jump? Do you finish the jump?"

Melissa sighed, tired of the questions. "The jump finished when he hit the ground."

"Not if he landed in trees."

She groaned, stormed off. "I'm gonna go sit under a router and try to get an extra half-bar." They watched her go, pleased. Brett sauntered back to the kitchen, which pleased them even more.

Rose noticed movement on the other side of the room. "Oh, look." She nudged Will, who looked. "One of them's getting up." Ellen, the four-year-old, stood up from the sofa and headed for the door.

"Here we go," Will whispered. "Once she goes, they'll all follow." They both watched, on tenterhooks. Ellen took a sharp turn near the door, stopped at a power outlet. She plugged in her tablet. Motherfuck! Will and Rose slumped, defeated. *Almost.*

"We need to do something," Rose said. "Now."

Will and Rose arrived at the control room to find Zack and Gareth eating Cheetos and watching the living room on two different screens: nothing was happening on either of them. Zack turned as they entered, chewing. "Why aren't they going outside?" he asked.

Rose sighed, closed the door. "Because they're shitheads and they have iPads," she said. "And they're not 'outdoorsy,' whatever the fuck that means."

"The baby doesn't have an iPad," Gareth added. They all looked at him, incredulous.

"No, he doesn't," Rose replied. "So he'll probably hit the pool soon. Keep an eye on him." Gareth actually looked at the stroller, expecting movement.

Zack swiveled, stated the obvious: "My plan's not gonna work if they never actually leave the house."

"We know." Will folded his arms, Rose did the same. Their eyes drifted across the wall of screens, death sites devoid of children. It was like an abandoned theme park in Chernobyl.

Rose looked at Will. "What about the fire idea?"

Zack turned. "What fire idea?"

"Brett said they won't leave their iPads unless there's a raging fire," Rose explained. They all thought about it.

"Won't they just run outside and keep using their iPads on the front lawn?" Gareth asked, still eyeing the stroller. He was probably right, which was rare.

"But they'll lose the WiFi signal and their batteries will eventually die," Will added.

Rose brightened. "That's it. We cut the power to the router, the living room, and all their bedrooms. No WiFi, no way to charge their repugnant little tablets."

"It's good but it's not enough," Zack said, stroking his chin stubble. "They might play boardgames. Or shit like 'hide-and-seek.'"

"Kids don't play 'hide-and-seek' anymore," Gareth added.

"Normal kids don't. But these kids aren't normal. Look at them." He looked.

Rose suddenly got nostalgic. "When I was in the convent, the nuns told me never to pull on the bishop's velvet robe. They said he didn't believe in underwear and his cock might pop out."

"The nuns said 'his cock might pop out?'" Gareth asked.

Rose ignored the question, continued: "I didn't particularly want to see his cock—the old guy was eighty-five—but the fact that the nuns told me not to do it made me want to do it even more."

"So, did you do it?" Gareth, again. She ignored him.

"My point is, if you tell kids not to do something, they'll want to do it."

Will beamed. "It's brilliant." Zack grinned: *yeah, that'll work.*

Gareth looked at Rose. "Are you seriously not gonna tell us if his cock popped out?"

◆   ◆   ◆

Will and Rose served sugar-heavy pastries and more raspberry cordial for afternoon tea, hoping it would boost the children's energy levels before they cut the power and made "the announcement." Most of the little sloths were too busy on their tablets to care, so Brett had the snack table to himself. Melissa had gone to the rooftop for better WiFi (*good luck,* Will told her).

They waited ten minutes, then texted Bertie to shut off the router. It only took a minute or two before the children realized they were "offline." Toby was the first to panic, uttering four words that terrified everyone: "I don't have internet."

Rose and Will stood at the front of the room like summer camp coordinators (without the whistles and deviant tendencies). "Kiddies! A little announcement!" Rose said in a politely-raised voice. None of the kids looked up: they were too busy restarting their iPads. Brett continued to gorge on pastries, oblivious. Melissa arrived from the roof, flustered and (of course) clutching her laptop.

"What the fuck happened to the WiFi?" she blurted.

Rose ignored her, continued: "Sorry everyone, the internet's down for the weekend. And we have limited power. Apparently a deer hit a pole somewhere." There was an intense groan of disapproval, lots of "fuck yous" and "motherfucker" and "fucking deers suck."

Before their heads stopped spinning, Will delivered the knockout blow: "Also, due to circumstances beyond our control, the jumping castle, slippery slide and petting zoo are off-limits for the whole weekend."

Rose added a chirpy "Sorry!" Then: "But we can play boardgames and hide-and-seek!" More groans, a "fuck hide-and-seek" from the back. The two-year-old said "bitch" through a fake sneeze. Finally, Brett finished eating and caught up with what was happening.

"Wait, what? We can't pet the animals?" he asked, confused.

"No petting," Will replied. "No swimming, no sliding, no jumping. Nothing."

Toby tossed his iPad, pouted. "That's not fair. Why can't we?"

Melissa stood behind him, pretending to be a mother bear. "We drove all this way. Who says they can't use the rides?"

"We had a safety check done," Rose replied. "None of the equipment is safe. People could die. Everyone here could die."

"These kids have a constitutional right to go outside and do whatever they want," Melissa shouted, searching for "constitution" on her laptop before realizing she was still offline.

The kids gathered behind Toby, defiant, with "Children of the Corn" faces. Their shrill, childish voices overlapped:

"Mommy! It's mean!"

"We didn't do anything wrong!"

"They're our rides!"

"I wanna pet the fucking rabbit!" (*that was the three year-old*).

The whining spread like a raging fire. Soon, the room erupted in chaos. Encouraged by Brett and Melissa, the children clawed at the "outdoor-activity" posters like animals, smearing pastries, spraying cordial. They rocked one of the TVs on its stand: the image distorted, cut out. Cables detached. The TV toppled, shattered. It was like a mini-Antifa rally with a dollop of alt-right insurrection.

Rose and Will clasped hands, delighted with themselves. "We did good," Will whispered.

"We did fucking good," Rose added.

"How long do you think it'll take?"

She checked her watch, looked back at the vicious little humans as they swarmed around the second and third TVs. "It'll take an hour or two for the anger to subside, then they'll sulk, weep, and slip into denial before bedtime. By morning, when their tablet batteries are dead, they'll be dying to rebel and go play outside. We won't be able to stop them."

They smiled and looked at each other, thought about high-fiving. But Rose had a better idea: "Let's make love."

They went upstairs (thankfully).

CHAPTER 29 NASTY PIGS

Gertrude Stanton, wife of Arthur Theodore Stanton, had long suffered from a rare combination of two irrational fears: zoophobia, the fear of animals, and phasmophobia, the fear of ghosts. There was no scientific name for her combined fear of "animal ghosts" so her psychiatrist called it phazoomophobia.

When she was eight, she made the front page of *The National Enquirer* under a seven-column headline: "Homework Ate My Cat!" She was pictured, frowning, with her cat's bloodied collar and bell. Randy (the cat) was a two-month-old Toyger-cross who had indeed been killed by her homework, otherwise known as the class mascot Jerry, an endangered green iguana. It had been her task to take him home for the weekend to care for him. Unsurprisingly, the newspaper headline was a little exaggerated: Jerry didn't really "eat" Randy—he severed his carotid artery with a claw, then drank some of his blood—but the sub-editor was planning a career in stand-up comedy and couldn't help herself.

Gertrude felt terribly guilty about the incident, although she was quietly thrilled about appearing on the front page of a trashy tabloid. Her father, a billionaire ship-builder, did not approve and asked his butler to buy and destroy all copies of the newspaper within a fifty-mile radius. Gertrude was suspended from school and the iguana was euthanized, which caused some of her classmates to paint "Lizard-Slayer" on her locker. The nickname stayed with her through to junior high, after which it served her well.

Randy's death weighed on Gertrude's mind for many years: she began to believe that he had returned from the dead to haunt the family mansion. She woke to the sound of his jingling collar, found mysterious puddles of urine in the hallways and felt the touch of his cold nose when she sat at the kitchen table. Although all of these events were explainable, including the urine (her grandfather) and the cold nose (*yep, also her grandfather*), Gertrude's phazoomophobia intensified into adulthood.

When she met and married Arthur, a failed entrepreneur who had peniaphobia (fear of being poor), he convinced her to transfer all of her houses to his name to deter Randy and other unwelcome animal spirits from ever turning up. She agreed and it worked for almost three decades, during which time Arthur amassed an extensive property portfolio. But then, Will, Rose, and Ralph discreetly entered their lives.

At first, Gertrude thought Bertie may have spilled wine— but it wasn't wine. She found paw marks on the inside of the toilet bowl, a hairball under the bed, and a gnawed plastic ball between sofa cushions. She suspected Randy was back and immediately called Carol, a paranormal interventionist she'd met at the salon. Carol was the founder of the #MeBoo movement, which campaigned to expose toxic male ghosts who groped and leered at women without consent.

After Carol examined the mansion, using an array of state-of-the-art detection equipment, dry-ice, and a bent coat-hanger, she gave Gertrude the troubling news: the house was indeed haunted, but it wasn't Randy. It was a two-legged dog and a disturbed married couple, who'd probably lived and died in the house many years earlier. She said the male ghost was white and most likely a misogynist with rape fantasies, although she had no evidence to back that up. For a recurring fee (direct debit), Carol did a special chant and sprayed anti-ghost potion in every room. It smelt exactly like Febreze.

Despite Carol's assurances that the spirits wouldn't return if she had the annual "chant and spray" and her debit card didn't expire, Gertrude decided to limit their visits to the mansion. They only stayed when there were renovations at their other mansions or when they were traveling between mansions on either coast.

The arrangement suited everyone, particularly Bertie, Will, Rose, and Ralph. Often, when he knew The Stantons were coming, Bertie would deliberately *not* clean up Ralph's mess to frighten Gertrude and make them leave sooner than they'd planned.

The stay in November was only supposed to be six days. Gertrude was irritated that Bertie had taken time off for the weekend: his replacement, an Iranian refugee named Rashid, always undercooked quail and had no idea what "turning down the bed" meant (he thought it had something to with the inbuilt speaker system).

On the night before departure, Rashid interrupted their dinner. "There was a phone call earlier," he said, hovering in the doorway. Arthur was horrified and ignored him.

Gertrude sighed, rested her cutlery. "Leave the message by the phone, Rashid."

"It was your neighbor at the country mansion," he continued, not recognizing her cue to fuck off.

"Which country mansion?" she asked, eager to end the conversation as quickly as possible.

Rashid checked the message he'd written. "P-ugg-er-ville."

"It's Pfugerville, Rashid."

"Call him back and tell him no," Arthur interrupted with a mouthful of undercooked bird flesh.

"No?" Rashid asked, confused.

"Whatever he's asking, it's a no. No, he can't use our pool; no, he can't park in front of our driveway; no, he can't land his helicopter on our lawn."

"He said there are animal noises."

Gertrude almost choked on bone. "Animal noises?"

"Coming from your mansion." His words hung in the air like a malevolent odor. Gertrude snatched up her smartphone, searched.

"What are you doing?" Arthur asked.

"Calling Carol." She stood, glanced at Rashid on her way out of the room. "We're taking a trip. Get the driver."

It was just after midnight when Brett woke to the sound of Melissa unzipping suitcase compartments. He turned on the lamp to find her pulling on a neon-green tracksuit, the same one she wore for the first week of every January (or until her "do-more-exercise-and-believe-in-yourself" New Year's resolution ran out of steam).

"What are you doing?" he asked, squinting and confused.

"I'm going out to the petting zoo."

He sat up, suddenly wide awake. "You're doing what?"

"Going to the petting zoo. To see the piglet." She sat on the edge of the bed, slid her feet into sneakers.

"Did you not hear that whole thing about it not being safe? 'Everyone could die,' remember?"

"Nonsense. They were just being dramatic. Rose loves a bit of drama."

"Or she could have been telling the truth. To keep us safe."

Melissa scoffed. "It's a piglet! How life-threatening can a little pig be?"

He thought about it. "Maybe you should wait until tomorrow."

"I've waited thirty years, Brett. Do you know how badly those pigs ruined my childhood?"

"I know." He sighed, ready to hear it all again. "They were real nasty."

"Thousands of hours of therapy, poor life choices, low self-esteem, a loveless marriage. All of it can be directly traced back to those pigs."

"A loveless marriage?"

"Not ours."

"You were married before?"

"No, but my therapist said the third one will be 'loveless.' Because of the pigs."

"The third one?"

"Anyway, none of it matters if I can pet the piglet. Then I can finally be true to myself and move forward with my life. I may not even need the second and third marriages."

"Why didn't you pet one before? They have them at the mall every other Saturday. I could've brought one home, dead or alive."

"Because I wasn't emotionally ready, Brett." She stood, exasperated. "Jesus! I'm the victim here, remember?"

She headed for the door, turned back, dramatic. "Are you coming or not?" *It wasn't a question.* He hesitated; she dangled a figurative carrot he couldn't resist: "There's a miniature pony."

He launched out of bed immediately.

Soon after making love to Will, Rose returned to an article she'd been reading in the winter edition of "Dinner Party" magazine. It was titled "How Soon Is Too Soon To Invite Your Grieving Friends For Dinner?" There was a softly-lit photo of a housewife holding a phone, eyeballing an enormous clock.

Rose called out to Will, who was applying lip balm in the bathroom. "Do you think Brett and Melissa would like peach rice pudding?"

He replied through stiff lips: "Peach what?"

"It's rice pudding with peach elements. It says here it's the perfect appetizer for people who've just lost their grandma."

"Why?"

"I don't know. Maybe it reminds them of their grandma."

"No, I mean why would you serve appetizers to someone who's just lost their grandma?"

"To help them move on. There's an article about it in here."

Will poked his head through the doorway, saw what she was reading. "I thought we weren't having a dinner party until four weeks after their deaths."

"You suggested four. But I think two is still do-able." She turned a page, searching for something she'd read earlier. "Especially if we can convince them to do 'speed grieving.'"

"Speed grieving?"

Before she could elaborate, Will's phone chimed: a message from Zack.

"What is it?" Rose asked.

He read it, confused. "One chocka mocha and a frappuccino with lime." He sighed, speed-dialed Zack—he picked up on the first ring.

"Zack speaking."

"Why are you sending me a coffee order?" Will asked.

"Oh, sorry about that. I must've sent Bertie the urgent message."

"What's the urgent message?"

Zack checked, read from his phone: "Urgent! Come to the control room."

"What's so urgent?" Rose looked over, bothered.

The door to the control room opened behind Zack: Bertie, flustered, clutching his phone.

"Oh, Bertie's here," Zack said, cupping the phone. "It's OK, Bertie, I sent you the wrong message. Could I get a chocka mocha? And Gareth wanted... Gareth?" He turned to look for Gareth—not there.

"Zack? Are you there? What's so urgent!?" Will's voice spilled down the line.

Zack ignored him, returned to Bertie: "Just the chocka mocha for now, maybe with one of those hazelnut cupcakes we had for lunch." Bertie left, Zack uncupped the phone. "Sorry, did you guys want coffees too?"

Rose snatched the phone from Will. "What's so fucking urgent, dickwit man?"

Dickwit man? Zack paused, glanced at the screens.

"It's Brett and Melissa."

CHAPTER 30 **ANIMALS/OUT**

Brett and Melissa tiptoed down the stairs in matching neon tracksuits, crossing multiple screens in the control room.

Zack and Gareth watched, beady-eyed. "See, they left their bedroom," Zack said.

Will and Rose watched from the back of the room, slippers on, bathrobes tightened. "Where are they going?" Rose asked.

"She said she wants to pet the piglet," Gareth responded. "Something about an unresolved childhood trauma."

"Oh fuck, the pigs story." She looked at Will. "Remember that story?"

"Is that the one involving anal rape?" Zack and Gareth turned, eager to hear more.

"No, you're thinking about Brett's miniature pony story. The pigs story is when she was emotionally abused in her uncle's pig pen."

He remembered. "Oh yeah, they fat-shamed her."

Brett and Melissa reached the front door. "It's OK, they're not going anywhere," Zack said, smug. "It's locked."

A moment later, Brett opened the door and they left. Zack stiffened, looked at Gareth. "It *was* locked."

"You told me to unlock it," Gareth said, "so the kids could get out." Rose sighed, Will bristled, Zack pretended he still had everything under control.

"It's OK, the animals in the petting zoo have been specifically trained to only attack children and babies," he added.

"Kinda like the dingo?" Rose quipped.

◆   ◆   ◆

Outside, Brett and Melissa hurried across the lawn, fading smartphone lights cutting through mist.

When they arrived at the petting zoo, Melissa poked her hand through the wire gate, unclicked the latch. She pushed it open: hooves stirred in the dirt.

There were three cameras covering the action, including a deer-cam—which, as you'd expect, was attached to the deer's neck collar. Will and Rose continued to watch from the back of the control room.

"Maybe we should go out there and intervene at some point," Will suggested. "So, you know, they don't die?"

"We need them alive," Rose added. "I've already downloaded recipes."

Zack grunted, dismissive. "Chill, guys. It'll be fine." Will and Rose shared a look: *chill, guys?*

Brett and Melissa hesitated at the open door of the enclosure. The animals were wide awake and hungry: steam drifted from nostrils, mouths clacked, furious eyeballs caught shards of moonlight. Melissa entered first: from the main camera, high up in the corner, she looked like one of those fuckwit tourists you see on the news—the ones who think entering the gorilla enclosure at the zoo will end well.

Brett followed, oblivious to the escalating unease. His phone light found the goat first.

"Oh. A little goat. Hello," he said. It bared jagged teeth, he backed off.

Nearby, Melissa's sneaker sank into excrement. She grimaced, looked down. A floppy-eared rabbit was there. She reached to pet it. "Hey there, Mr. Bunny."

In the control room, Zack was no longer chilled. He spoke like Melissa could hear him: "No, no, don't do that," he said. "It's not a nice bunny."

The rabbit's head snapped back with a violent hiss. It shot red-dagger-eyes at her, ready to pounce. She turned, startled, her light landed on something in the corner. It was out of shot so they couldn't see it on the screens—but her face softened like she'd found what she was looking for.

"Little pig!" she said, moving towards it.

On the other side of the pen, Brett accidentally dropped his phone. Its thin light beam went out. "Shit." He lowered to his knees, searching. His hands fumbled through damp hay, found the furry leg of something, obscured by darkness. "I think I found the miniature pony," he said.

Melissa wasn't listening. She slowed as she approached her "piglet," eyes wide. "Hello little pig." But it wasn't a piglet. Dark, insidious eyes met hers from behind two off-white tusks. "Tusks?" she thought, slightly unnerved. She retreated, uneasy, half-turned to Brett. "Maybe we should come back in the morning, they might be happier."

"I found the pony," he replied. Melissa turned her light in his direction.

"That's not a miniature pony. And you're cupping its balls." His hand was indeed cupped around balls—the hairy testicles of a spotted deer. Like all the other animals here, *not fucking pleased and very fucking hungry.*

Low growls stirred all around. Hooves scratched about in the dirt. Suddenly, the "piglet" charged. The spotted deer widened its jaws. The bunny pounced. Brett and Melissa screamed and ran for the gate—*too late.*

In the control room, the goat-cam cut to static. The two other cameras were clogged by dust and fur and speckled blood.

Zack broke the stunned silence. "Maybe we should try that intervening thing now."

◆   ◆   ◆

The gate of the petting zoo was swinging on its hinge when Will and Rose arrived. Zack and Gareth caught up, exhausted by the walk. Will's flashlight settled on the spotted deer, its mouth stained with blood. Brett and Melissa's mangled bodies were now the center-pieces of two separate feasts.

"Oh, shit," Rose said. "There goes my peach-fucking-rice-pudding."

"Where are the rest of the animals?" Gareth asked, doing a headcount. Will looked at him. They all backed away from the pen.

"How many others were there?"

"I don't remember," he said. "But I'm sure there was a bunny."

"There was definitely a bunny," Zack added. They were interrupted by the sound of movement behind them: they all turned in different directions, nervous as fuck. Zack flinched like he felt a tongue.

"Maybe we should go back inside," Rose suggested. Suddenly, Will's phone rang, shrill. He checked: "Tony" on the caller I.D. He glanced at Rose as he picked up:

"What do you want, Frank?"

Frank had already crossed out two of the marked mansions on his map: only three were left. "Hi there," he said, chirpy. "Petal and your mom say 'hi' too." Petal scowled at him in the rearview, "did not" she mouthed. Francine snored.

"What do you want?" Will asked.

"I thought I'd give you an update on where we are."

"Why would I care where you are?"

"Because we're gonna be seeing each other real soon." Frank referred to the map. "We already checked two mansions, only three to go. The next one could be you."

Will bristled. The others listened in. "We changed plans. We didn't go the country mansion after all. We're at a beach in Venezuela."

Frank chuckled. "You're a terrible liar, Will. Always have been. 'Mom and I went to the arcade!' Yeah, right, whatever. See you soon!" He hung up, pleased with himself.

Will cursed under his breath. Rose didn't need to ask, but Zack did: "Who was that?"

"Frank."

"Who?"

"Frank The Chicken King," Rose added. Gareth's ears pricked up. He turned to them.

"You know Frank The Chicken King?" he asked, beaming, suddenly forgetting they were surrounded by rabid animals.

"He's my father," Will replied. "And he's coming here to kill us all."

"He makes great wings," Gareth continued, oblivious to the "kill us all" bit.

"Us all?" Zack asked, more confused than anybody and not a fan of wings. "Why?"

Will sighed. "It's a long story, I'll do a podcast if we survive."

Rose headed towards the house. "We need to get out of here," she said.

"Running won't work," Will reminded her. "Not with Frank. There's a reason he's the number-one manufacturer of legs and wings in the country: he never gives up." She stopped, abrupt, realized he was right.

"Why does he hate us too?" Gareth pouted. Everyone ignored him.

Rose turned back towards the petting zoo, an idea forming. Will looked where she was looking: he could tell from her face that she was about to come up with something truly disturbing. "Are you thinking what I'm thinking?" he asked her.

"Use the children as human shields?" she replied. It wasn't what Will was thinking—*but it was a fantastic idea.*

"That's not what I was thinking, but it's a pretty cool plan B."

"What were you thinking?"

"Two words: Child. Soldiers." She thought about it for a nanosecond, her lips curling into a smile.

"I love it," she said, immediately turning to Zack. "How many guns do you have?" He was still confused. *Frank who?*

Will got in his face. "How many guns did you bring?"

"Guns?" Zack asked. "We didn't bring guns. They're too messy." On cue, a feral marmot passed with a human hand in its jaws.

Will and Rose looked at each other, quietly searching for a solution. Rose got there first: "You should call him." He met her eyes, *didn't need to ask who.*

◆   ◆   ◆

Will hadn't spoken to Mugamba for more than five years. He'd been sending him the money every month but most of their communication was by text or funny WhatsApp messages (Mugamba sent the craziest and most violent gifs, most of which he filmed himself).

It was midday in Namibia when Will called. Mugamba picked up on the second ring. He had one of those chunky satellite phones he could use anywhere on the continent. "Hey man!" he said, casually. For some reason he spoke in a thick British accent, almost Cockney.

"Hey, it's Will."

"I know, I have caller I.D., man. We get that in Namibia too."

Will chuckled. "Of course you do. How are you?"

"Good. I was just thinking about you." He chewed the remains of something he'd killed.

"Really? Why?"

"My child soldiers just massacred a busload of white UN ambassadors. One of them looked like you." Will paused, not sure if he was kidding. "Fuck it, they all looked like you." He laughed; Will laughed too. *He wasn't kidding.*

"Anyway, what are you doing?" Will asked, eager to shift topic.

"Right now?"

"Yeah."

"I'm showing my child soldiers how to attach decapitated heads to the ends of sticks." Will swallowed. *Please be kidding this time.* "I'm fucking with you, Willy-boy," Mugamba said, chuckling. "I'm actually showing them how to make tea cosies to wear on their heads during winter. So they'll be warm and look like Bob Marley."

"Bob Marley wore a rastacap."

"Not at home."

"OK, well, that's great," Will replied, not about to argue. "Children need warm heads, especially if they're going to be out massacring UN diplomats at night."

"For sure, bro," he said. Behind him, a bunch of children in uniforms sharpened sticks. "Anyway, what's up? You need an extension on your payment?"

"I need your advice."

Mugamba shifted his weight, delighted. "Of course you do. About lovemaking?"

"No, about training child soldiers." There was a pause, the crackle of static. Then, clearer than 5G:

"I thought you'd never ask."

CHAPTER 31 **AN ARMY PREPARES**

Ezekiel did not go home alone after his fortune-cookie Tinder date.

For the first time in three years, a woman agreed to accompany him for consensual sex. Her name was Siobhan and she had lied when she opened her cookie message after dinner. Even though it read "The love of your life is sitting opposite," she told him it was "You have teriyaki chicken in your teeth." He laughed, thought she was cool for lying about it. He also wondered if Mr. Chai had screwed up again and given her the wrong one—so he checked when she went to the restroom and saw that he hadn't. *Phew!*

Siobhan was a pathological liar. She was also a white supremacist who wrote children's books in her spare time. Her most popular title, "Stewie Goes On A Trip," was about a Neo-Nazi sloth (Stewie) who travels (very slowly) to Charlottesville to attend a "Torch Relay Competition." Along the way, he meets a homophobic desert rat and a turtle who's dealing with shell guilt. Together, they learn the value of friendship, kill and eat Ancona (black) chickens and discover it's OK to hate animals who don't look or smell like them. Don't bother trying to get it at your public library—the waiting list is insane.

After a night of frenzied passion, Ezekiel woke to find he was alone in bed. He searched for a note, then thought perhaps Siobhan was going to surprise him with a bacon-and-eggs breakfast-in-bed. But he couldn't hear sizzling and he couldn't smell bacon, and he remembered the only food in his fridge was a half-shriveled lime. When he finally got up and ventured into the living area, he saw Siobhan was sitting at his computer next to the whiteboards.

"What are you doing?" he asked. She didn't turn.

"I noticed you were trying to solve these two double-murders," she said, typing faster than a stenographer on Adderall. "So I thought I'd help out."

He moved closer, looked over her shoulder: dialog boxes opened and closed, raw code flashed across the screen. She was Assange-like. "How?"

"I hacked the bitch's emails."

"Which bitch?"

She paused, checked: "Melissa."

"And?"

"And you were on the right track." She half-turned to the whiteboards, referred to the intertwining red thread between photos of everybody: Will and Rose, Brett and Melissa, Ned and Beth, Jackleen. "Two of the four couples who know each other are dead, and the other two are meeting up in Pfugerville this weekend."

"Which means whichever couple survives is the killer," Ezekiel added.

"Or the killer isn't either of the couples and kills both couples. Either way, if you're gonna win a Pulitzer and we're gonna be a white-power-couple, we need to go to Pfugerville."

Ezekiel grinned, thought she meant "power-couple" that just happened to be white. "Pfugerville's a big town," he said. "How do we know where they are?"

Siobhan turned back to the screen, punched a few more keys—the "Camp Fun" invitation opened. "The bitch's emails." Ezekiel looked.

She stood, on the move. "If you have a car, I'm driving it."

◆   ◆   ◆

Soon after their phone conversation, Mugamba emailed Will a thirty-page e-book titled "How to Form and Train Your Own Child Soldier Army (and Other Fun Activities for Your War-Torn Community)." It had been translated from Swahili and was a bestseller on the Dark Web and Amazon (the river in Brazil, not the online retailer).

Will and Rose followed the instructions in the book as closely as possible, ignoring the chapters "Human Flesh Sandwiches and Other Snacks for Kids," and "Campfire Jokes About Killing Fragile White People."

They set up three separate work stations for the "Training and Weapons-Building" phase: the kitchen was the "Exploding-Weapons Lab," the living room was "Sharp and Pointy Weapons," and the dining room was "Toxins and Bioweapons."

Will drifted between the work stations to keep everything on track, just like he did on one of his finely-tuned, chicken-nugget factory floors. Rose blew a whistle to move each pair of children to the next station: it was like one of her boxercise circuit classes, minus the spandex and self-delusion.

In the kitchen, Bertie poured a gasoline mixture into a row of recycled soda bottles on the counter. Ellen and Katy, wearing goggles and oversized latex gloves, looked on.

"What are these sodas called?" Ellen asked. Will and Rose arrived, helped arrange more bottles.

"They're called 'Molotov Cocktails,'" Will explained.

Bertie handed pieces of white cloth to the girls. "Put these in the tops of the bottles," he said, demonstrating. They mimicked exactly what he did, their little hands perfect for the task.

"Are these like the cocktails our mom drinks all the time?" Ellen asked.

"No, they have less alcohol," Rose replied, giving them more cloths. "How many did she used to drink?"

"Six or seven before dinner."

"Where is our mom?" Katy asked.

"She's in rehab."

"What's rehab?"

"It's a place for people who drink six or seven cocktails before dinner."

"What about Dad?" Ellen asked.

Will and Rose looked at each other, searching for a reason. She had nothing. He tried: "Have you heard of cryogenics?"

"Does it have something to do with his crying problem?"

"What crying problem?"

"Dad cries all the time. At everything. He even cries during porn."

"Your dad lets you watch porn with him?" Rose asked, surprised.

"Only to see the animals," Katy added. An alarm chimed on Rose's phone—*perfect timing*. She blew the whistle, raised her voice so they could hear in the other rooms.

"That's time, everybody! Move to the next work station!"

Will nudged the girls off their stools. "You two are going to the toxins table."

"Do we need face masks?" Ellen asked.

"No, you'll be fine."

In the living room, Toby and Chad made thin wooden darts out of twigs. Rose arrived. "We're moving tables, boys. You're going to the kitchen to make petrol bombs." Chad hurried off, eager; Toby loitered.

"We heard about rehab," he said. "Does that mean we have to call you 'mom' now?"

"Fuck no," Rose replied. "Kitchen. Petrol bombs. Now." He left. She sighed, picked up a box of finished darts.

The Twins (Tamara and Tanya, in case you forgot) were at the final station in the dining room, dipping darts into a saucer of toxic liquid. Rose arrived with the new box, Ellen and Katy rushed in behind her to take their seats.

"We're rotating, you two," she told The Twins. "Didn't you hear the whistle?" Rose blew it again. "Whistle, hear it?"

Tamara groaned, not going anywhere. "Explain it again like I'm a six-year-old," she said.

"You're five."

"Four. But pretend I'm six."

"OK." Rose tilted her head, which meant "OK, fucker." "When you hear the whistle, you move to the next station. For you two, that's the 'sharp and pointy weapons' table." She pointed towards the living room. "That way."

"No, I mean, explain this game we're playing."

Oh, here we go. Rose titled her head back the other way, which meant "Alrighty, cunt." "Well, it's like a video game," she said.

Tamara held up one of the poison darts. "But these are real."

"Yes, but the people you're gonna hit with them aren't real. They're holograms."

"What's a hologram?"

"You're six. You should know."

She made a face, pointed at Tanya, who was still dipping darts. "She's four. Explain it to her." Tanya looked up, clueless but petulant.

"I'm four-and-a-half."

Rose sighed, exasperated. "I'll explain everything at the next station. Let's go, bitches." She left.

The Twins looked at each other: *bitches?* No-one had ever called them that before—they kinda liked it.

◆   ◆   ◆

It was just after nightfall when Frank's Hummer pulled up at the front entrance, fender nudging heavily-padlocked gates. They had been delayed six hours by a minor medical emergency—Francine had choked on a combination of chicken wing-bone and trail mix during a roadhouse stop between mansions. Petal tried to do the Heimlich maneuver, it failed miserably, a trucker intervened with a corkscrew and did a tracheotomy.

The on-call surgeon at the Pfugerville Community Hospital was impressed with the trucker's work, especially his use of a colmated cork (from a bottle of Pétrus) to plug the gaping hole he'd made in Francine's throat.

"How does a trucker afford Pétrus?" he asked the charge nurse after removing the cork. She didn't know so they asked a passing janitor, who said the trucker was probably smuggling fentanyl across the border. They agreed, the nurse alerted Border Patrol and the trucker was arrested. At sentencing, drunk on Pétrus, he said: "Ojalá hubiera dejado que la perra estúpida se ahogara hasta la muerte," which translated as "I wish I'd let the stupid bitch choke to death."

The surgeon recommended Francine not talk for two days and stay overnight for observation. Frank said "yes!" to the no-talking part but "no" to the overnight stay: they had important business to take care of and they needed her, he said. The nurses bandaged her up, Petal gave them free chicken vouchers in exchange for additional opioids, and they were back on the road.

◆　　◆　　◆

The Stantons' country mansion was the last to be crossed off Frank's map. He was out of the car first, and Petal followed. They both noticed the rides, lights still on.

"Oh. They have a bouncy castle," Petal said, wide-eyed. "Looks like they're having a party."

"Not for much longer," Frank said, ominously.

Francine joined them, unsteady, throat bandaged. She noticed the camera above the gate, pointed and grunted. Frank looked, approached the lens. "We're here," he said, slow-waving like a lunatic on Purge Night.

Zack and Gareth watched Frank's bulbous head on a soundless monitor in the control room. "What did he say?" Zack asked.

"I don't know," Gareth replied. "But it wasn't about legs or wings."

Frank turned to Petal. "Get the guns." She made a beeline for the trunk, but Francine blocked her path, tried to speak—it was a hoarse, breathless mess of words.

"You're not supposed to talk, Mom," Petal said. "You'll ruin your vocal cords permanently." *Permanently?* Frank edged forward.

"Let her talk," he said. "She may have a really good idea." Francine spoke again, more raspy nonsense. Petal nodded, seemed to understand. "What did she say?" Frank asked.

"She said 'Can we all agree to aim for the legs?'" Petal replied. "So there's no hard feelings at Thanksgiving dinner."

"You're not supposed to talk, honey," Frank told Francine. "And Will's never coming to Thanksgiving dinner again. *Ever.*"

"Unless he's in a body bag," Petal added, guffawing like an idiot. Frank laughed too. *What a hoot!*

Zack and Gareth watched as Petal and Frank gleefully unloaded weapons from the trunk. "Now might be a good time to tell Will," Gareth said.

◆   ◆   ◆

The Stantons picked up Carol on their way to the country mansion. She was on the phone when their stretch limousine pulled up, did one of those dismissive "I'm-so-busy-all-the-time" waves as she got in.

She sat opposite Gertrude and Arthur, adjusted her hideous tweed coat, and briefly cupped the phone as they took off. "Sorry, I'm just finishing up with a client," she said, returning to the call with the loudest voice possible. "Listen to me, Ferrara. You're the victim here. And it's not OK for him to be giving you cunnilingus while you sleep. It doesn't matter if he's 'between worlds.'"

Arthur was rich enough not to care what he said aloud. "Who's she again?" he asked Gertrude, who was listening intently to Carol's conversation.

"It's Carol, the paranormal expert."

Carol cupped the phone again, correcting her: "Paranormal Therapist," she said. Arthur glared at her, returned to Gertrude.

"And what exactly does she do?"

"She gets rid of animal spirits," Gertrude replied. "That's why she's coming with us to the manor."

Carol abruptly wrapped up the call. "I have to go, Ferrara. Don't go back to sleep, he's probably floating around the room somewhere with his tongue out. We'll Zoom later, I'll do a chant."

She hung up, sighed, mistakenly thought they asked for a recap of her privileged conversation with a patient. "That was Ferrara. She's having problems with the spirit of her dead Anatolian Shepherd."

"She was married to a man from Anatolia who looked after sheep?" Gertrude asked (Gertrude was a moron, in case you forgot).

"No, Gerty, an Anatolian Shepherd is a really big dog."

"The ghost of her dead dog is giving her cunnilingus while she sleeps?" Arthur asked, incredulous.

"It happens all the time, especially with terriers and dachshunds."

Gertrude suddenly had an idea, looked at Arthur: "We should get a really old dog."

He groaned, pressed a button to lower the partition separating them from the driver. "How long to the manor, Jaime?" he asked. The chauffeur glanced at the GPS.

"Two hours and twenty-seven minutes, Mr. Stanton."

Arthur groaned again, closed the partition. Carol waited for complete silence, then leaned forward to ruin it: "So, Gerty, tell me about these animal noises your neighbor's been hearing."

CHAPTER 32 DIE HOLOGRAMS DIE!

Frank, Francine, and Petal headed towards the mansion like soldiers of the apocalypse—actually, that's bullshit, they didn't look anything like soldiers.

Frank could hardly walk from third-degree burns to his tendons, Francine was still high on opioids, and Petal was, well, just a generally clumsy and useless person. But they did have serious weapons that required minimal human skill to be deadly: AR-17s, Walther PK pistols, a machete.

Will and Rose watched their approach from the control room. "Your mom's put on weight since Thanksgiving," Rose said.

He leaned closer to the screen, squinting. "And she's wearing a scarf, which makes her neck look fat," he said. "Why would she wear a scarf?"

Rose looked. "I think it's a bandage."

Zack turned, shifted topic. "Are the children ready?"

"No, but there's always plan B," Will replied.

"What's plan B again?"

"Using them as human shields."

Zack nodded, remembering. "That's a very good plan B."

Gareth swiveled to face them: "If we end up going with that, could we get a couple of children in here?"

Will and Rose looked at each other, made a decision with their eyes. "We'll send the baby," Rose said.

"One baby? There's two of us."

"It's a fat baby. Have you picked it up?" He hadn't.

"And it's in a reinforced stroller," Will added. Gareth seemed OK with that.

Zack distributed walkie-talkies and they dispersed: Rose took Bertie, Ralph, and the four girls to the roof, Will and the two boys went poolside with the baby.

Petal was the first to reach the house. She slipped between trees on the west side, AR-17 clasped and ready. Ahead of her, the bouncy castle wobbled gently, its air pump chugged. She stopped about ten meters from the entrance. Nearby, hooves crunched on twigs. *The deer?* She turned, unsettled, carried on.

At Rose's direction, Tamara launched the first projectile: a fiery Molotov Cocktail landed behind Petal, exploded on the grass. She shrieked, backed up, raised her weapon as another one landed five feet in front of her. She looked up towards the roof, saw the girls peering over the edge. They unloaded more cocktails, raining down on her like mini-asteroids. She dodged, scrambled, shielded her face. One connected with her leather boot: she kicked the flames out, pointed her gun upwards and fired.

The bullets chipped at cement. The children ducked: Rose stood behind them for cover. "Don't worry about the bullets, girls," she yelled over the gunfire. "They're blanks. It's all part of the game." Bertie hurried between the children, handing them bottles and lighting their cloth wicks. "Keep going! Hit the crazy hologram woman!" Rose yelled. They launched them one after another. The Twins giggled with delight: Rose had never seen children so happy. Ralph ran back and forth, yapping with excitement.

Below, Petal headed for the bouncy castle as the cocktails peppered the grass all around. She pivoted, sidestepped, rolled like an overweight green beret and dove through the castle gates, her gun bouncing out of her hands. Gareth's voice crackled through Rose's two-way: "She's inside its walls." Petal scrambled for her gun, her feet sinking beneath her.

In the control room, Zack nudged Gareth. "Hit the implode button!" He did.

Petal grabbed her gun as a loud pop sounded, followed by a rush of squealing air. The walls collapsed in on her, swallowing her up like a marshmallow in hot cocoa. The tip of her gun disappeared inside the shrinking opening, her screams muffled. The girls gathered at the roof edge, clapping with joy. Rose looked on, delighted, almost motherly.

Zack and Gareth did an awkward high-five. "That's how you fucking implode," Zack said.

Tamara (*one of The Twins, in case you forgot*) turned to Rose, beaming. "We were bad bitches, weren't we?"

"You sure were," Rose replied, tempted to smile, perhaps affectionately pat her head—but she resisted. Their moment was broken by the rat-tat-tat of gunfire. *Petal?* Rose and Tamara rushed to the roof's edge: bullets tore through the plastic walls of the castle, puffs of air exploding outwards.

"The hologram's still alive!" Tamara pouted. The walls of the castle quickly flattened around Petal. She straightened, gathered her breath, gripped the gun tighter.

Zack and Gareth's smiles abruptly faded. "Uh-oh," Gareth said. "We didn't plan for that."

Rose turned to Bertie. "Do we have any more cocktails?" His face said no. Ralph grumbled.

Petal puffed her chest, looked up at them, smugly defiant. "You're all gonna die real soon," she shouted.

Tanya, the other Twin, turned to Rose: "What do we do now, boss?"

"We're gonna play a whole new game," Rose replied. "It's called 'Human Shields.' Who wants to go first?" They all put their hands up, squealing "Me! Me! Me!"

Before she could pick somebody (she had her eye on Ellen, who had the most girth), Petal called from below: "I'll let you all live if you tell me where my lowlife brother is."

Rose looked down, flanked by the girls. "No chance—"

"—bitch," Tamara added, folding her arms.

Petal groaned, pointed the gun at them. "OK then, you all die." Her chubby finger caressed the trigger, about to fire—suddenly, out of nowhere, the rabid goat took her out like a rush-hour bus, its jaws latching onto her neck. She flailed, tumbled backwards, the gun—and lots of her blood—spilled everywhere.

Rose and the girls watched, stunned but delighted. Katy, the youngest, giggled first. Everyone joined in, including Rose and Bertie. Ralph yipped, spun his wheels. It was like the closing scene of a really bad sitcom.

Zack and Gareth looked at each other, thought about another high-five. "That's one mean motherfucking goat," Zack said. His two-way interrupted:

"Is anyone there?" Will asked.

"Roger that, we're here." Zack replied.

"We have activity near the pool."

Francine hobbled past the outdoor patio next to the pool, pistol in hand. She paused, distracted by movement in the grass. She turned full-circle, her hoarse breath clouding the night air. Her eyes settled on something near the pool: an odd, ominous shape backlit by the aqua hue of pool lights. *The stroller.* It teetered near the edge, mist smothering its wheels. Her expression softened, confused: *what's a stroller doing out here?*

She approached, heard the ga-ga ramblings of the baby. "It's OK, little one," she whispered, her limited motherly instincts kicking in. She lowered the pistol and leaned in, pulled back the tiny blanket inside to reveal—a walkie-talkie. Baby sounds spilled from its speaker: goo-goo, gee-gaa-goo—then, Will's voice—"Watch out, Mom!"

She straightened, panicked, raised the pistol—too late for incoming darts, both piercing her neck.

Hidden under a row of strategically-placed sun lounges, Toby and Chad reloaded straws with fresh darts. Next to them, Will was holding the baby and a walkie-talkie. "Again," he said. They unleashed more darts, dotting Francine's cheeks like acupuncture pins. She swayed, unsteady, sucked in air. "More!" Will shouted. The boys loaded and fired. Francine grabbed at her throat, wheezing. Her heel caught on a tile and she tumbled, splashed into the pool, her pistol firing into the sky.

Her arms flailed about in the water, toxic liquid coated her, gushing into her mouth and neck wounds. She gulped, sank under, clawed back up, gasped for air. Bubbles formed around her like a chicken fillet in hot oil. Toby and Chad did little fist bumps. The baby smiled at Will, silently defecated: *he didn't smile back.*

Zack and Gareth watched the feed from the underwater camera as Francine boiled in the acidic pool, its water bubbling like a witches' cauldron. They did a high-five without turning-

"That's two-for-two," Zack said. "Time for a latte." He pushed the "Hot Coffee" button.

Rose, Bertie, and the girls watched the pool through the kitchen window. "That's two dead holograms, bitch," Tamara said, tugging at Rose's blouse. "How many more?"

"Only one," Rose said, annoyed by the tugging (it was a new blouse).

Tamara pouted. "But we're having so much fun killing holograms."

"Don't worry. We'll find you more."

Will's voice spilled through Rose's two-way: "We're all clear at the pool, target has dissolved." The boys stood at the edge, looked into the cloudy water. Will tucked the baby back in its stroller, looked towards the house. "Has anyone seen Frank?"

Zack and Gareth checked the screens, searching. "No," Zack said.

"So where is he?"

Suddenly, a deep, ominous voice stirred behind Zack and Gareth: *yep, Frank.* "I'm right here." He stepped out of the shadows, AR-17 in hand, machete tucked in his pants. In all the excitement of Francine's grisly death, they hadn't noticed him enter. He grinned through blistered skin.

Zack and Gareth stood, turned, raised their hands. "Now would be a really good time to be holding that human baby shield," Gareth said.

Frank moved closer, eyed the radio in Zack's hand. "Tell my son I said 'hi.'"

Zack lifted the two-way to speak: "Will, your dad said—"

But Frank didn't let him finish. He unloaded a full clip into Zack's head and torso, coating the monitors in blood. Gareth stiffened, Zack's brain matter dangling from his fringe. His bottom lip trembled. "I'm just the intern," he blubbered.

"I don't care!"

Will and Rose heard the gunfire, and Gareth's end-of-life squeals, on their radios. Both noises stopped abruptly, followed by the sound of approaching footsteps. Frank picked up Zack's blood-speckled two-way, spoke into it with his most theatrically-morbid voice. "If you're listening, son," he said. "I'm coming for you next!"

He shattered the radio on the floor, dramatic. Will and Rose both looked off, quietly calculating how many bullets the children's bodies could deflect.

◆   ◆   ◆

Ezekiel chuckled as he turned pages of "Stewie Takes a Trip." Siobhan, trying hard to drive stick, looked over. "What are you laughing at?" she asked.

"The turtle and the desert mouse just arrived at the dyke bar," he replied.

"Why is that funny?"

"Because it's a Neo-Nazi turtle and a homophobic desert rat surrounded by lesbians and a genderqueer barperson. It's funny."

"It's not meant to be funny." He looked at her, thought she was being funny. She wasn't. "It's supposed to be educational. For children."

"For children? But the sloth's constantly masturbating."

Siobhan sighed, snatched the book off him. "Let's just focus on the story at hand. Our Pulitzer, remember?" *Our Pulitzer?* He swallowed, troubled, suddenly regretting the swipe-right and the fake-fortune-cookie. *Were they traveling too fast for him to jump and roll?* "We're almost there," she said, glancing at the GPS. A passing sign read: "Pfugerville, 30 miles."

Will and Rose gathered the children in the basement, Bertie brought Ralph. They could hear Frank moving between rooms on the floors above them.

"From my calculations, we should be OK with plan B if he has less than two clips," Rose said. "Assuming the clips have no more than twenty rounds and we use Bertie as the final shield." Bertie overheard, approached.

"Use me for what?"

Will had another idea. "There's still time for plan C."

Plan C? Rose turned: "There's a plan C?"

"What's plan C?" Bertie asked, hoping it didn't involve him.

Will lowered his voice: "It's called 'Lock the Children in the Freezer and Flee.'" Neither of them got it. He glanced at the walk-in-freezer under the stairs, continued: "By the time Frank gets through that door and finds a bunch of shit children and a baby that needs a diaper-change, we'll be crossing state lines."

"Oh, I see," Rose replied, finally understanding the plan. "So it's more like 'Run for Our Lives and Let The Children Fend for Themselves.'"

"Exactly."

Bertie immediately started rounding up the children. "Everybody inside the freezer. Hurry up!" The girls looked at him with fuck-you faces, reluctant.

"It's a whole new game!" Rose added, nudging them towards the open door. "And there's ice cream in there too!" They shuffled forward, still reluctant.

Will used the stroller to corral them. "Last one in doesn't get anything!"

Tamara resisted, pulled at Rose's hand. "Are you coming too?" she asked.

"We'll be out here, standing guard," Rose told her. "Don't worry, we won't leave you behind. You're my favorite little bitch now." Tamara smiled and hurried off to the freezer; the others followed her lead. Rose watched, suddenly glum: *it was the first lie she'd ever told that stung a little.*

Will closed the cast-iron door, punched numbers on a keypad—heavy bolts locked into place. He turned to Rose and Bertie. "Let's get the fuck out of here." Ralph wagged his tail.

The Mercedes kicked up leaves as it sped through the main gates. Will gripped the wheel, Rose watched the mansion shrink in the rearview. The sting of her lie had yet to weaken. In the back seat, Ralph was asleep in Bertie's lap, exhausted.

"There's only one thing that bothers me," Rose said.

"What?" Will turned, vague, mind elsewhere.

"Running doesn't work against Frank. He never gives up, you said. That's why he's the leading manufacturer of legs and wings in the south-west."

"You're right, I did say that," he replied. "But he won't come after us. He'll be dead."

"How will he be dead?"

Will grinned, mischievous. "I didn't tell you everything about plan C."

Rose turned to face him, eyes wide and ready for an explanation. "OK. And?"

"Whole place is gonna blow when Frank touches that keypad." She stiffened, her face whitened a little. He didn't notice, carried on: "Mugamba talked me through it. Keypad's wired to a detonator, which ignites the gas tanks in the storeroom. Kaboom!"

"So the children—"

"Kaboom! Everyone!"

"Oh." Rose looked off, clearly bothered. Will noticed, but pretended he didn't.

CHAPTER 33 **THE DEER**

Will and Rose didn't always loathe children. There was a time, long ago, when a child was all they ever wanted. *Seriously.*

Soon after they were married, they got drunk and had the talk most couples have at some point—normally *before* they legally bind themselves to each other forever. Will and Rose were so wrapped up in their perfect, soft-lit, romantic bliss that neither of them ever thought to bring it up. They talked about the house they'd buy, the furniture they wanted, the trips they'd take, the food they'd cook, *the dinner parties they'd have*—but never the children they wanted, or didn't want, to have. Maybe they were afraid of ruining what they had. Or maybe they just assumed they both felt the same way.

It wasn't until two weeks after the wedding that the topic finally came up. They were in their underwear, eating takeout from Mr. Chai's Chinese Restaurant and drinking cheap wine on the floor of their newly-rented apartment. They had unpacked all their clothes and furniture and had a functioning kitchen, but wanted to indulge in the takeout-on-the-floor-in-underwear cliché, which seemed so cool and romantic in the movies (*yeah, they were pathetic back then*).

After two bottles of wine, they gave up on the stupid cliché, got dressed and moved to the table: "Fuck that," Rose said. "The floor is freezing and I need a knife and fork."

When dinner was finished, they opened their fortune cookies at the same time: Will got one of Ezekiel's by mistake ("The guy sitting opposite you is so hot right now"), Rose got "You will die alone and poorly dressed." Her face soured, Will noticed. "What does it say?" he asked.

"It says I'm going to be 'poorly dressed' at some point."

"You?"

"Yes."

Will scoffed, took a gulp of wine. "As if."

"What does yours say?"

He hesitated, read it aloud as a train roared past the window. *Yep, they had that cliché too, but not by choice.* When it had gone, Rose made the crinkled face of someone who hadn't heard a word. "I didn't hear a fucking word, read it again."

He made it up the second time, mostly because he hated repeating himself but also because he wanted to be funny: "It says 'Three of your children will want to be just like you, the fourth will die trying.'"

She stiffened like he'd suggested tantric sex. "Four children?"

He pretended to read it again. "That's what it says." They looked at each other for a moment, waiting for the other to speak, quietly wishing they had a waiter to interrupt them. "These things are written by a stoned teenager jerking off in his bedroom." He scrunched it into a little ball, drank more wine. Rose looked at hers again, specifically "die alone." After a long, uncomfortable pause, she met Will's eyes.

"I only want three."

"Three what?"

"Children."

"You want children?"

"Don't you?" She studied his face, waiting to see if he was going to lie.

"Of course I do." *It wasn't a lie.* "But I was thinking… more like, say, two?"

"Two could work. Let's split the difference."

"That would be two-and-a-half."

"Two kids and a small dog. But I get to choose the dog."

They clinked glasses and got to work immediately (on having a child, back on the floor).

◆　　◆　　◆

Rose thought about designing a flowchart for the first pregnancy, but she and Will fucked so regularly in the first year it didn't seem necessary. It would happen soon enough, they figured. *How hard could it possibly be?*

When nothing had happened after 369 days, she decided to do a flowchart after all. It was meticulous, incorporating her full menstrual schedule, dietary and medicinal strategies, recommended sex positions, and some spiritual techniques like "Gregorian chanting during orgasm" and "bathing in Tannis root." After trying everything, some 245 days later, Rose reached the final branch of her flowchart: "Are you pregnant now?" The answer, in the loneliest and most isolated box on her chart, was "No (fuck)."

The sales assistant at Rosemary's Baby Supplies—which is where she bought the Tannis root and some Satanic gifts to send to the nuns (fuck them)—gave her the details of a cheap-but-effective gynecologist who helped infertile couples get pregnant. His name was Dr. Hedley O. Niztik and his website said he'd go "to hell and back to get you pregnant!" *Yeah, there was a photo of him in a black cape.* Rose made an appointment and they visited his clinic for preliminary tests. Afterwards, he summoned them to his blood-red office to give them a diagnosis. He was wearing the cape.

"It's not good," he said, stroking a black cat on the desk. "You're gonna need some serious intervention if you want to breed."

"Intervention?" Will asked. The doctor passed them glossy brochures from a fresh box under his desk. There was a photo of him on the front, in the cape and holding the cat. A metallic red font read: "Populating The World: Your Options."

"We have three options you can choose from," he said, gesturing for them to start reading the brochure. "Option one is called 'The Beast Comes.'" Rose looked up: *The Beast Comes?* He grinned, mischievous. "Cool name, huh?" She said "no, not at all" with her eyes.

"What does that even mean?" Will asked, not sure he wanted the answer.

"I'm glad you asked." He looked at Rose, deliberate. "Basically, we drug you and strap you to a gurney in one of our private rooms," he said, matter-of-fact, "and then a Satanic 'beast' comes in and fucks you while you're unconscious."

Will and Rose glared at him, stunned. The cat eyeballed them, enjoying how stunned they looked. Finally, Dr. Niztik chuckled.

"I'm kidding," he said. "It's not a Satanic beast. It's a guy called Slobodan from the Baltics. He has great genes and he's extraordinarily virile." He waited long enough for them to bristle, then chuckled some more. Rose shot daggers. "Felicia didn't mention it, did she?"

"Who?" Rose asked, about to clock him.

"Mention what?" Will was deeply confused.

"Felicia. At reception. She was supposed to tell you how funny I am. Just so it wouldn't get awkward when I started cracking a few jokes."

"No, she didn't mention it," Rose replied, impatient. "Why don't you just tell us the actual options without any jokes?"

He sighed, shifted in his chair. The cat wandered off, expecting to be bored. "OK, fine," he said. "There are three options—

that part wasn't a joke. Option one is where we take your sperm and your eggs, whisk them together in a bowl and pop them back in your oven." He couldn't resist a tiny smile. Rose groaned, Will turned pages of the brochure. "Option two is when we take your sperm and your eggs and put them in someone else's oven, and option three is when we take your sperm or someone else's sperm and your eggs or someone else's eggs and put them in your oven or someone else's oven."

They both looked at him, exhausted by the explanation. "So, which option would you recommend for us?" Rose asked.

He glanced at their test results, ran his tongue over teeth. "There's nothing wrong with your sperm or your eggs, and your oven's robust enough to cook seafood pizzas. So I think you just need a little whisking."

Will and Rose shared a look, relieved. "Option one then?" Will asked.

"Correcto. It's the best of all the options because it'll be your biological offspring and your oven, which means you'll never have to question whether its father was a serial killer and you won't have to deal with a meth-addicted teenager carrying your baby."

The intercom buzzed, followed by Felicia's chirpy voice: "Slobodan's here, Dr. Niztik. Which room should I send him to?" He stiffened, pressed the "reply" button with a forced grin: "Thank you, Felicia, very funny." He looked at Will and Rose. "She's funny too." They left immediately.

Rose researched Dr. Niztik as soon as they got home. Despite his inane sense of humor and odd design schtick, his reviews on Yelp were overwhelmingly positive: "The jokes suck but he got us pregnant within a week," "Yeah, the cape is batshit crazy but he turned out to be our superhero," and "Cringeworthy comedian but a great GYN and he's cheaper than an eighty-year-old hooker with the clap."

The procedure only took an afternoon, and Rose was pregnant within two weeks. They indulged in all the clichés that followed: painting the spare room, purchasing random baby toys, and attending breathing classes with lots of other people who thought the world needed more versions of them.

It was during these sessions that Will and Rose stumbled across a new bunch of friends—three couples—who were all in the same trimester. They would loiter in the carpark after class like high school kids at a mall: the women would share stories about stretch marks and cravings; the men would talk sports and lament their lack of sex. On a cold night in August, as the class was entering its final weeks, the loudest of the couples made a suggestion: a dinner party. *And so it began.*

It became a weekly event. The loud couple, Trey and Raya, were spectacular hosts. They attended to every craving, served non-alcoholic cocktails to the women, even played piano and sang showtunes after dessert. It was the life Will and Rose had dreamed of and they never wanted it to end.

Dr. Niztik always wore his cape for their ultrasound appointments. He made the same inappropriate jokes every time, and Rose and Will learned to politely groan. But something changed during their visit in the twenty-eighth week. He lost the stupid grin, didn't joke about the size of the baby's "pecker." He was quiet for an unusually long period of time, his eyes studying the sonogram. Finally, he turned to them.

"There's no heartbeat," he said.

Rose laughed. It was one of those abrupt, high-pitched, don't-be-fucking-ridiculous laughs. She waited for him to say he was kidding—but he didn't. "Is this when you tell us we need Slobodan to come in with tiny defibrillator pads and revive him?" she asked, her voice beginning to tremble. Dr. Niztik didn't chuckle, his stone-cold expression didn't shift.

"I'm sorry," he said.

Will and Rose sat in a park afterwards and watched other people's children play. That night, they drifted to opposite ends of the apartment: Will sobbed in the laundry, Rose cried in the shower. They didn't attend the next dinner party or the three after that. They barely spoke to anyone.

It was a month before they decided to give it another shot. Dr. Niztik was delighted to see them. He didn't wear his cape or make a joke. Their second attempt lasted eighteen weeks, the third only eight. By the fourth, at eleven weeks, Dr. Niztik stopped telling them he was sorry. He just bowed his head and buried his face in his hands. He said he'd help them explore the other options—surrogacy, donated eggs or sperm—but they'd had enough. They were exhausted and bitter and fucking angry at the world. *If children didn't want them, they didn't want children.*

The final dinner party of the year was on a Thursday. None of the couples expected *or wanted* to see them—it had only been three weeks since their last miscarriage. But they turned up anyway, armed with expensive wine and Prozac-assisted smiles, determined to show they were OK and getting on with their lives. *It was a bad idea for everyone.*

All three of the other women were nursing their newborns. Trey and Raya deliberately sat Will and Rose at the far end of the table, away from sounds of suckling and goo-gooing. No-one told jokes or laughed much, people began stories and then stopped them when they realized they were talking about babies. Books they were reading, movies they'd seen, food they'd eaten, work, vacations, home improvements—everything they talked about came back to the same, inescapable *elephant in the womb.*

It didn't even help when Rose tried to ease the tension: "You can talk about your babies, it's OK," she said. "In fact, we'd love to hear how much they're ruining your lives." Everyone laughed. It didn't last.

On the way back from the restroom, Rose overheard Raya and one of the other women in the kitchen. "We can't keep doing this," Raya said, her voice lowered. "I feel really awful for them but it's like a wake when they're here."

The first dinner party of the new year was scheduled for the last Friday in January. Will and Rose weren't sure if they wanted to go, so Raya's email was something of a relief. "We're going to take a little breather from the parties if that's OK with everyone," she wrote. "Bub's teething and Trey's work is pretty intense. Sorry, love you all, catch up soon. XXXOOO."

Will and Rose decided to treat themselves to an expensive dinner that Friday, and drove past Trey and Raya's house on the way home. The lights were all on, the cars were parked. They could see silhouettes through the drapes on the second floor, showtunes blaring. Laughter and goo-gooing. They'd never felt more worthless in their lives.

◆   ◆   ◆

Rose couldn't remember the last time she'd vomited. It was definitely in her teenage years and most likely involved alcohol, probably Blue Curaçao, which had been her go-to drink at parties. So it came as a surprise when she threw up on the jute rug in February. She hadn't been drinking, they hadn't eaten pork or seafood the night before.

It happened again the following day, and the day after that. She did a test and told Will, they hugged but didn't celebrate. *It was way too early for that.*

James Randolph Calhoun was born on a sunny November day. Dr. Niztik wore his cape for the delivery: Will and Rose had specifically requested it. Afterwards, the doctor visited them in the maternity ward with blood-red roses and a tiny, custom-made cape for the baby. They laughed, he told appalling jokes.

Later, Rose wrote a review of him on Yelp: "A crazy, unfunny fucker who wears weird outfits and never, ever gave up on us."

◆   ◆   ◆

The clichés of bringing-up-baby soon took over their lives: endless crying, diapers, sleepless nights, porn (Rose only). Chicken nuggets were no longer the number one priority of Will's life. Rose didn't care that she had no friends and nothing else to do all day but feed and clean a tiny pink human with nothing to contribute to the world. Their new life was exhausting and isolating and utterly fulfilling.

On the eve of James' first birthday, Rose received an actual letter in the mail, which was weird. It was from Raya, who had resorted to pen and paper after being blocked by Rose on social media. "Hey Rosie," she wrote. "I see you're no longer on Facebook and Instagram so I thought I'd write you the old-fashioned way." *Oh, please.* Rose groaned, hovered the letter over a lit flame. "So happy for you guys, hope you got my big bouquet of flowers after the birth" (she'd burnt that bouquet). Will entered as the paper caught alight.

"What are you burning?" he asked. She turned, her movement snuffing the fire.

"A letter from the cunt."

"My mom can write?" Will approached, curious.

"The other cunt. Raya." She tried to get a new flame from the lighter, but it wouldn't catch.

"What did she say?"

"The usual crap. Love you, miss you, so happy for you." Rose kept trying to light it. "She even invited us to a dinner party. Apparently, they've decided to start having them again." They looked at each other, shared the same sense of loathing.

"We should go," Will said, suddenly realizing he'd said it aloud.

"Why would we do that?"

He thought about it. "So we can watch them all grovel and feel guilty." It was tempting, but Rose needed more: guilt and groveling would only last thirty minutes, an hour tops. Will persisted: "Also, James is going to need some friends soon. If we can get their kids over to our place for a playdate—"

"—we can kill them," Rose interrupted, realizing she'd just said that aloud. Will looked at her, mildly concerned. She smiled. "I'm kidding."

He continued: "—we can turn them against their own parents. A comment here, a joke there, a photoshopped photo they 'discover' of their dads fucking hookers."

Oh. Rose tilted her head, intrigued but bothered. "That kind of brainwashing could take years."

"Ten, maybe fifteen. It's slow-burn revenge. By the time they're young adults, they'll loathe their parents as much as we do."

She beamed, giddy, loved the idea. "Slow-burn revenge. It's brilliant." The lighter ignited, a flame danced, ready. She killed it, went upstairs to choose an outfit.

◆   ◆   ◆

It was raining on the way to Trey and Raya's house. Will and Rose argued over what safe word to use when either one of them wanted to leave the party. She proposed "rhododendron."

"How am I supposed to use that in a sentence?" he asked, wiping the fogged windscreen with his jacket sleeve.

"I don't know. Just say 'rhododendrons are pretty flowers. Does anybody else think they're pretty?' Or something like that."

"I'm not saying that. Who says that at a party?"

"Fine, don't say it. Just whisper 'rhododendron' in my fucking ear."

"Or I could just whisper 'let's fucking leave' in your ear."

She sighed, folded her arms. *Ugh.*

The deer in the middle of the road enjoyed the feeling of headlights on her textured fur. It was like a spotlight at the end of a runway and she liked being the center of attention, although she wasn't interested in a career in fashion ("fuck those divas.") Her mother hated the term "deer caught in headlights" and told her never to flinch if she ever saw the lights of an approaching vehicle. "Let the fuckers swerve," she said as she cleaned her antlers. "Humans are panicked, insecure creatures. They will always weaken first if you stand your ground." Her advice had not worked for her younger sister, who had practiced it in the fall with a passing eighteen-wheeler.

But on this night, in this rain, *she wasn't fucking moving.*

Will's mother had told him never to swerve for an animal, not even a duck and her waddle of cute chicks—but he didn't listen to her advice. He panicked and swerved. Rose screamed. She met eyes with the deer as they passed, headed for a steep embankment. The deer watched them, mouthed "Oh!" Her water broke soon after.

The Mercedes rolled three times, rested on its roof. Rose stirred first, still strapped in and covered in blood and shattered glass. She turned, panicked, searching: James wasn't in his car seat. She stumbled out, disoriented, found his little cape first. The rest was a blur, which was probably for the best.

It was a year before Will and Rose ate a meal together. The clink of cutlery punctuated the silence. They chewed, stared into the space beyond each other.

Finally, Will spoke: "Maybe it's time to have a dinner party of our own."

CHAPTER 34 THE END (FOR REAL)

"We need to go back."

Rose looked at Will. He was distracted, his mind elsewhere—so it took a moment for her words to process. "Go back where?" he asked.

"Back to the house."

"Why would we go back to the house?"

She searched for a reason he'd accept. "My recipe book."

"Your recipe book?"

"I forgot it."

"I'll get you a new one." He accelerated.

"It has notations and scribblings in the margins."

"I'll get you—"

"—and my name and contact details are on the front." He stiffened, eased off the accelerator. She continued: "So if it doesn't burn after the explosion, they'll know I was there."

He slammed on the brakes. Rubber burned. Dust stirred. Bertie woke from a nightmare, confused: "The drugs aren't mine!" They ignored him.

"Really?" Will looked at Rose. "Where did you leave it?"

"By the bed. I think." She looked off, not sure, pretended she was (sure): "I'll be in and out within five minutes." He sighed, groaned—and turned the car around.

Bertie was wide awake, but still confused: "We're going back?" Ralph stirred.

◆   ◆   ◆

OK, let's just pause for a moment: to be clear, this is not one of those stories where the protagonists go on and on about how much they hate children, they want the children dead so bad they hire an assassin to attempt to kill the children several times in cruel and twisted ways, and then, seemingly out of nowhere, they end up deciding the little shits aren't so bad after all and rescue them from the clutches of death, after which they all laugh and go home, eat popcorn and watch Netflix together, and live happily ever after. *Awwww, so sweet.* No. Fuck off. *This is not that fucking story.*

◆   ◆   ◆

The mansion was still intact when they returned. Will parked the Mercedes at a distance, closer to the gate than the house. They both searched for signs of Frank.

"I can't see him. Can you see him?" Will asked, squinting.

"No."

"Bertie, can you see—" But he'd gone back to sleep, Ralph too.

Rose unclipped her seatbelt, on the move. "I'll be five minutes, like I said."

"Four-two-three-three," Will said. She paused, confused.

"What's that?"

He shut off the engine, turned to look at her. "The combination for the keypad. At the freezer. It won't explode if you use the code, followed by the hash key."

"Why would I need the—

"—You didn't forget your recipe book. You never forget your recipe book. You carry that thing around like it's the nuclear codes."

She thought about spinning another lie, but didn't. Her face softened, apologetic. He looked towards the house.

"It's one of the little girls isn't it?"

She looked at the house too. "We call each other 'bitches.' She's like a tiny killing machine."

"Please tell me it's not one of The Twins." Rose tensed, made a face—he knew that face. "Fuck me. One of The Twins? Which one?" She tensed again, shrugged. "You don't know? So which one were you gonna save?" She shrugged again. It was starting to get really repetitive. "You're going to save both fucking Twins?"

She nodded. "If one dies, we'll have a backup." She met his eyes, genuine. *Reminder: this is not that fucking story.* Finally, he weakened. *It's not.*

"OK, you've got five minutes," he said. *It's really not.* "And then I'm leaving." *That fucking story.* She got out, he watched her head towards the house. He bit his bottom lip, conflicted, couldn't help himself. "Rose!" he called through the window. She stopped, turned back, listened. "Maybe get that annoying little boy too. The one who made kickass darts. He could fill in for Tony at the factory for a while."

She struggled to hear, called back: "Which one?"

"The one who made—"

The house exploded behind her.

Rose hit the dirt, the windscreen shattered. A smoke cloud mushroomed. No-one could have possibly survived.

See? Not that fucking story.

◆   ◆   ◆

Flames licked at charred bricks as Will and Rose approached the ruins of the house. The four outer walls had been shattered, exposing burnt and crumbling furniture inside. Will looked at Rose, saw her distress.

"At least they died having fun," he said, immediately realizing it was a stupid thing to say. She glared at him.

"They died in a freezer."

"Eating ice cream!"

She sighed, looked off, *more devastated than she ever thought she'd be.*

Smoke cleared. A far wall collapsed, revealing the walk-in freezer—charred around its concrete edges but completely intact. It was half-buried in the burning ruins like a fireproof safe. Rose's face lit up. Will beamed, realized he was beaming and stopped immediately. They rushed over, breathless and giddy.

Frank's bandaged, charred hand was still clinging to the steel door handle. Wires protruded. "He should've stuck to legs and wings," Will said.

Rose untangled the fingers: most of them crumbled into dust. She pulled at the handle. Will helped. They heaved it open: ominous, frosty air gushed out like it was a cryogenic tomb. Inside: darkness, then the children spilled out with mild frostbite and delighted screams, wrapping Rose and Will in stupendous, affectionate hugs.

"The bitch came back!" Tamara yelled, joyful and more irritating than Rose remembered. It was heartwarming, tear-inducing, worthy of a grand, emotional musical crescendo. *Oh, please.*

In the sticky, saccharine excitement of it all, nobody noticed another car arrive—Ezekiel and Siobhan. They coughed through smoke as they approached, capturing everything with their phones. Ezekiel arrived first at the freezer lovefest: he took two hundred photos but it was "Man Hugs Child" that captured the world's attention.

Will was actually grimacing from the smell of the baby's unchanged diaper when frostbitten Chad (the annoying little boy) hugged him—but the still photo of the moment told a different story. It was triumphant, uplifting and emotional (Will's grimace looked like a relieved smile)—and it appeared on the front cover of *Time* and at least two thousand newspapers across the globe, often with a variation of the headline "CHILDLESS WHITE COUPLE RESCUES ORPHANS."

Soon after Ezekiel took that famous photo, Rose noticed him and Siobhan. "Who the fuck are you?" she asked. They froze, lowered their phones. The children eyeballed them, suspicious.

"Are these more holograms we can kill?" Tamara asked.

"We're reporters," Siobhan replied. Ezekiel swallowed, nervous. Will and Rose shared a look: *we're fucked.*

◆   ◆   ◆

Jaime, The Stantons' driver, saw the smoking mansion first and pulled up inside the main gates. He lowered the partition to the back. "I don't think we should go any further," he said. Arthur turned, looked through the windscreen: *What the fuck?*

They all got out of the limousine, stunned. Arthur quietly calculated how much the deductible would affect his net worth. Gertrude's face paled: she flinched, thought she heard hooves.

Carol filmed with her smartphone. "This is definitely the work of animal spirits," she said. "I'm gonna need—"

Jaime saw the approaching goat but didn't honk his horn— he figured he was doing the world a favor. The goat met Carol's spine with deadly force. The ghosts of nearby goats bleated with delight.

◆   ◆   ◆

Ezekiel and Siohan's photos and reporting (they shared a byline) won them a Pulitzer. Their account of events portrayed Will and Rose as selfless heroes: they had risked their own lives to put the children inside a fireproof freezer while thwarting their maniacal attackers. Frank, an unhinged and jealous father, was blamed for everything, including the deaths of Jackleen, Ned and Beth, and Brett and Melissa.

It was the most honest reporting Ezekiel thought he'd ever done—even though it was complete bullshit. Later, after a torchlit wedding in Charlottesville, Siobhan published a series of

"Will & Rose" children's books: "Will & Rose Save The Melting Ice Caps," "Will & Rose Castrate Pedophiles," "Will & Rose Go To A Neo-Nazi Retreat."

In the weeks after the explosion, and thanks largely to Ezekiel and Siobhan's reporting, Will and Rose became global celebrities: they appeared on talk shows, where they said their parental instinct "kicked in" to save the children, that they just "loooved children so much." They signed autographs. There were memes about them. Wherever they went, people carried signs and cutouts of their faces on sticks. They were the toast of the town.

Carol's estate successfully sued The Stantons for eight-ninths of their wealth. It was a landmark ruling: Carol had been on their property when the goat viciously killed her so they were found liable. In court, Gertrude thought she heard Carol's spirit whisper "fuck you" in her ear.

But you're probably wondering what happened to the children. *Oh, the children.* When their media tour had finished, Will and Rose bought the "mezzanine" mansion from Carol's estate—it was a bargain. There, they started a home for orphaned children—people all over the world donated. They had more than 100 little shits in the first year and they taught them everything they needed to know about life—and death.

Mugamba gave classes in weaponry (*yep, he finally got off the terrorist watch list*), Bertie taught biological weapons and poisons, and they hired some ex-cons to do classes in alternative methods of killing. Tony recovered from his burns (and lost testicle) to do workshops in hand-to-hand combat and deep-frying.

By the time the orphans were finished at "The James Randolph Calhoun Home For Children Whose Shit Parents Are Now Dead," they were triple-A assassins, ready to rid the world of self-absorbed breeders everywhere. It was wonderfully self-sustaining and they never ran out of students.

Within a year, Will and Rose were inundated with friend requests. Everyone was desperate to have dinner parties with them. Rose made a new flowchart, and they began a rigorous selection process, which made infertile couples a priority. Soon, they had at least eight new couples—and a waiting list of two hundred in case any of them started to annoy them (or got cancer and/or facial disfigurements). But when the time came to send invitations, Rose hesitated. They had finally begun to enjoy other's company: perhaps trying to kill a bunch of children had brought them closer together. The family they always wanted was themselves. *Really?* Yeah.

They celebrated the anniversary of Frank's death with a private candle-lit dinner on the mezzanine. Bertie made quail burgers. They laughed and relived Petal and Francine's brutal deaths. Will opened a bottle of expensive wine he'd been saving, caressed Rose's thigh as he leaned over to pour—

—and then it happened. The unthinkable.

She covered her glass with her hand.

Will stiffened, horrified. *You've got to be fucking kidding.*

ACKNOWLEDGMENTS

My parents loved having dinner parties.

I remember interrupting them in my pajamas long after bedtime, drawn by the laughter and clink of glasses. I didn't understand what alcohol was, or what it did, but I enjoyed the way everyone behaved when I crept into the living room to see what they were doing: they drank and ate with wild abandon, played vinyl records and sometimes danced (poorly). There was frivolity and affection and a warm glow about everything. I was always sent to bed within minutes of my glorious entrance, left only to wonder what had happened afterwards. As an adult, I discovered I had exited at exactly the right time.

My mother died in 2004, my father is now 91 and thinks I'm a Catholic bishop. It's probably for the best that neither of them will ever get to read this book—especially the bits involving nuns and priests and hymns about suicidal sheep—but they should know that the most joyous parts of their lives, *the parts that mattered most,* inspired me.

It has taken several decades to write this book. During that time, I have met lots of loathsome, inconsiderate and mildly-irritating people (*your three-year-old child needs to recline, really?*) who have shaped my view of the world and enriched my creative cynicism. Those people don't need to be named (I don't know most of their names anyway, *except Ted O'Brien, you fuck*) but they deserve some acknowledgment here; without them, life would be pleasant and unfunny. It's really hard to make fun of a friendly neighbor who pets your cat and says "Hi," but the neighbor who thinks leaf-blowing on a Sunday morning is a good idea—let the fun begin, motherfucker.

Speaking of which (cats, not motherfuckers), no-one has helped me more on this journey than my four non-human housemates: Lupita, Marina, Pipen and Miguelito. They are the finest of comedians: they're funny without knowing it and never laugh at their own jokes. They also remind me to take a break from the computer sometimes, and feed them.

I'd like to thank my oldest friend Simon Condon, who is one of the funniest humans I know; my aunt Pauline Holmes, who has listened to many of my unfunny stories; my brother Peter Noonan, who introduced me to sadistic physical comedy when he bludgeoned me with a pool cue in the eighties; my dear friend and filmmaking colleague Carine Chai, who has endured my silliness for over a decade; and Elsa and Bo Westerberg, who have supported me tirelessly and are living proof that great parenting can produce wonderful children.

Finally, I'd like to acknowledge a bunch of "Aussie blokes" who have been longtime supporters of my comedy work: Brad Harris, Matt "Disco" Harris, Ron Goodman, Shane Barker, Glen "Cocka" Coxall and Chris "Plugger" Barker. If this book is ever quoted at *The House of Juan* on a Saturday night, I will know it was worth writing it.

ABOUT THE AUTHOR

Michael Noonan lives in Monterrey, Mexico with four cats who dislike children more than he does.

As a young boy in Australia, he drew "movies" on his father's computer paper and forced his long-suffering family to endure them (via a cardboard-box viewing machine) on Sunday evenings. His first black comedy, in which his entire (white) family were slaughtered in the woods, got multiple laughs (from his actual family) and made him realize that making jokes about misery and death was kinda cool.

He went to film school and did a Ph.D. about comedy and disability, which would've got him canceled if there had been such a thing back then. He has worked as a university lecturer, accountant, journalist, barman, dishwasher, video store clerk, candy bar assistant and burger-flipper at McDonald's.

He's not very funny in person, so don't approach him (especially in food courts).

www.ingramcontent.com/pod-product-compliance
Lightning Source LLC
Chambersburg PA
CBHW051423170626
46809CB00006B/2300